**At ten p.m. on the night after**

the last day of school, ten-year-old Katy Werling rushed down Emily's driveway in her pajamas and onto the steep moonlit blacktop road. She turned left to trudge up the forest-lined hill, her backpack stuffed with still-clean weekend clothing slung across her back. Two hundred and fifty steps to her own driveway.

"Monique? Here, girl. Come," Katy called happily for the dog, trying hard to ignore the shadow-filled forest and the yawning blackness of the ravine on the far side of the road. Her heart pounded; she could feel it in her head. She pushed a strand of dark hair off her face and behind her ear.

An owl hooted.

"Come on, girl. I'm coming home!" She aimed her voice toward the ravine, where the owl sound had come from. Daddy said raccoons and skunks and possums and all kinds of other critters lived down there. It was the kind of place dogs loved. And Monique would be no different. Katy was certain of that, just as she was certain the black stray she had insisted her family adopt earlier today was the same black dog who had been in her dreams—the one who would save her life.

Down in the ravine, a dog barked.

"Monique? Where are you?" Katy peered at the shadowy trees.

# Kudos for Mary Coley

Coley received a 2015 Delta Kappa Gamma "Oklahoma Creative Women" award in YA fiction, and was named a finalist in the 2015 New Mexico/Arizona book awards for two novels.

~*~

A member of the Oklahoma Writer's Federation, in 2010 Coley received the OWFI award for Best Juvenile Book. She has also placed in many of the organization's annual contests over the past ten years, including short story and novel category wins.

# The Ravine

by

## Mary Coley

*The Black Dog Series, Book One*

**The Ravine**

Cover Art by *Debbie Taylor*

The Wild Rose Press, Inc.
PO Box 708
Adams Basin, NY 14410-0708
Visit us at www.thewildrosepress.com

Publishing History
First Mainstream Mystery Edition, 2016
Print ISBN 978-1-5092-0781-7
Digital ISBN 978-1-5092-0782-4

*The Black Dog Series, Book One*
Published in the United States of America

# Dedication

I dedicate this novel to the world's
furry family members
in honor of the joy, entertainment, and
unconditional love they bring us.

~*~

In remembrance of Rusty, Reggie, Oreo, Levi, Cindy,
Jordan, Gunner, Annie, Oscar, and Lexi,
and in celebration of family members
Trixie, Shiloh, and Penny.

Chapter 1

*Friday*

At ten p.m. on the night after the last day of school, ten-year-old Katy Werling rushed down Emily's driveway in her pajamas and onto the steep moonlit blacktop road. She turned left to trudge up the forest-lined hill, her backpack stuffed with still-clean weekend clothing slung across her back. Two hundred and fifty steps to her own driveway.

"Monique? Here, girl. Come." Katy called happily for the dog, trying hard to ignore the shadow-filled forest and the yawning blackness of the ravine on the far side of the road. Her heart pounded; she could feel it in her head. She pushed a strand of dark hair off her face and behind her ear.

An owl hooted.

"Come on, girl. I'm coming home!" She aimed her voice toward the ravine, where the owl sound had come from. Daddy said raccoons and skunks and possums and all kinds of other critters lived down there. It was the kind of place dogs loved. And Monique would be no different. Katy was certain of that, just as she was certain the black stray she had insisted her family adopt earlier today was the same black dog who had been in her dreams—the one who would save her life.

Down in the ravine, a dog barked.

"Monique? Where are you?" Katy peered at the shadowy trees. Patches of moonlight flickered into the ravine, reflecting off rocks and tree bark. She didn't like to go down there this time of year. The spring rains had fed too many sticker vines and bushes, not to mention all the ticks and mosquitoes. But there was sort of a path. If she found it, she could go down a little ways so that Monique could hear her better and find her way out. "Monique?"

Seconds later, when the dog barked again, Katy was certain the animal was in the ravine. She could see the rocky path; bits of it glowed white in the moonlight. "Monique? Here, girl." Her nose tickled, probably from that pollen she was allergic to. She rubbed her nose and sneezed once, twice, three times.

Katy hurried along the steep path that dove through the trees. She held her Cuddle Bunny stuffed rabbit close. The plastic soles of her house shoes slipped on wet leaves, but she caught herself and plunged on.

Another few steps. This time, when she slipped, she fell forward, off balance.

Katy tumbled. She screamed as spiny brambles caught and sliced at the skin of her bare arms and face. She gasped when thick bushes slowed her fall, and then screamed again when they released her. She plunged deeper, down toward the rushing stream at the bottom of the rock-strewn ravine.

\*\*\*\*

Twenty minutes before, Katy had been alone in the bathroom at Emily's house, sitting on the toilet with the seat lid down. She didn't need to go to the bathroom, but it was the only place she knew of to get away from Em. She couldn't think clearly when her friend was talking all the time. And Em had been talking non-stop ever since they had left Pizza Hut with her family.

It was after nine o'clock, and there was no sign Em would ever let her say a word. She hadn't even been able to tell her about the black dog who had joined her family today, the one she had named Monique. Her heart ached. She missed the dog. She needed to be with the dog—all the time. Otherwise, something bad was going to happen.

Katy left the bathroom, tiptoed down the stairs, and out Emily's back door.

A chorus of croaking frog voices filled the night. The partial moon had risen above the trees. This past year at school, she had learned that when part of the moon seemed to be gone, it was really covered with the earth's shadow.

An owl whoo-whooed from the wooded lot beside their house. A breeze tickled her cheek, and the smell of wood smoke floated past. Somewhere, someone had a bonfire. Crickets chirped from the flowerbed, and off in the distance—was that a coyote?

Surely the black dog wouldn't go where the coyotes were.

A dog barked.

"Monique? Where are you?" she called into the night. She didn't think Mom and Dad would have let the dog sleep inside the house tonight. They didn't know her yet. She was probably outside, sleeping under a bush. "Here, girl."

Sounds of night—birds, frogs, crickets—filled the air, but no dog responded to her call. Maybe her parents *had* let the dog sleep in the house, maybe even in the boys' room.

Now that the dog had come, Katy hoped she might finally be able to relax and not have to listen quite so hard at night when she was alone in her bedroom. Nothing could slip into her room if the dog was guarding her as she slept. She would be safe.

But having Monique in their house wouldn't help with the other thing bothering her. She didn't like what she'd been hearing whenever her parents were together in the same room. Mom's voice was too quiet; most of the time she looked and sounded like she was going to cry. Dad seemed to be talking from far away, if he said anything at all. It was like part of him was somewhere else, like part of the moon seemed to be gone from the sky although it really wasn't.

Maybe adopting Monique would make Mom herself again and bring Dad back into the room from wherever it was that part of him went.

Emily's voice floated through the open back door. "Katy, where are you?"

Katy rushed up the back steps and darted into the kitchen where the aroma of fresh-baked cookies still clung to the cabinets and countertop. Em's mother had let them make the cookies after they got back from dinner at Pizza Hut.

"Were you outside?" Emily asked from the bottom of the back stairs. "Why'd you go out there?"

"To look at the moon and to call my dog."

"But Cleo and Caesar stay in the house."

"A new dog. She came today. Can I get a glass of milk?"

"You didn't say anything about a dog before." Emily poured two small juice glasses full of milk and took three of the chocolate chip cookies. Katy drank her milk in a couple of swallows and snatched two cookies of her own. They climbed the stairs to the second story, and Em's bedroom.

"We just decided to keep her tonight, right before you picked me up."

Emily squinted at her. "Truth?"

"Truth. Her name is Monique. Moe for short. She's a stray."

Emily's eyes widened. "I can't even get my mom to let me keep *one* dog—and you've got *three*." Emily threw herself down on her bed, hugging a round pink-and-blue-striped pillow.

Katy swallowed the last of the second cookie and then pulled in a deep breath. "Em, I've got to go home," Katy blurted. "I can't be gone all weekend, not when Monique just came to live with us. I'm sorry."

Emily threw the pillow against the wall and jumped off the bed. She stalked around the room, arms tight against her sides. She glared at Katy and stomped.

"I'll make it up to you," Katy pledged. "I'll go with you to the lake as many times as you want over the summer. And you can borrow any of my outfits. Even my new swimsuit. I can't go this weekend. Okay?" She waited for Emily's response. Nothing. "I'll let you play with my plastic horses. Even the black stallion. And the spotted appaloosa. You know I never let anyone else touch either of them. But you can. You're my best friend."

Emily folded her arms and stomped her foot again.

After what seemed like forever, Emily looked up with narrowed eyes. "If you promise."

"I do." Katy tucked Cuddle Bunny under her arm. "It's only 9:45. Mom and Dad are up. I'll ring the

5

doorbell, and Dad'll let me right in. I'm going to sneak Monique up to my room. The next time you come over, she can sleep with us." Katy giggled. "It's going to be so cool."

"You better tell my mother good-bye."

Emily's mother had already gone to her bedroom, the faint sound of the Jacuzzi rumbled through the walls of the master bath. Katy said good-bye to Emily's father, who was downstairs in the den watching boxing on HD-TV with the surround sound on.

He muted the volume. "Want me to take you home? Wait a minute until this round is over." He sat forward in his chair, watching the boxers circle the ring.

"That's okay. It's bright enough to see outside, and as soon as I start home, I'll call my dog, and Monique will run down the road to meet me."

"You sure?" Emily's dad asked. The boxers locked together and started punching. His look was glued to the flat screen.

"Yeah. Don't worry."

The sounds of the fight blared from the speakers again.

Katy hurried out of the house, and Emily followed. "Call me Sunday, Emily, okay?"

Katy made Cuddle Bunny throw Em a kiss as she started down the driveway to the street. Little cloud boats sailed across the starry sky, and a breeze ruffled the dark leaves of the black trees.

****

Now, only a few minutes later, the same breeze ruffled the leaves of the trees towering over the spot where Katy lay alone, far down in the bottom of the ravine. She groaned, but no one heard.

## Chapter 2

Thirty-five-year-old Lynn Werling leaned forward in the blue vinyl-covered waiting room chair, her hands clasped over her knees. The brightly lit room was full of people—some reading, some with eyes closed, some stretched out—waiting to be seen by whichever doctor had drawn the Friday night shift at the hospital's ER. A baby wailed, and the mother leaned toward it and cooed.

"He'll be all right, honey. It's the first of many breaks," Randy said, leaning back in the chair next to Lynn. "The kid wants to play sports. This is part of it."

She raised her eyebrows. "Oh? I didn't think you knew much about sports."

"So I wasn't an athlete. You fell in love with my brains, right?"

Lynn looked at her husband and saw large brown eyes behind thick lenses, too long brown hair, some gray strands curling over his ears and down onto his neck. His beard and mustache were neatly trimmed. The spicy scent of his cologne tingled her nose. Their youngest son, four-year-old Will, sat in Randy's lap, leaning back against him.

Where had the years gone? For an instant, Lynn saw Randy as he had been in college. Too skinny, too shy, too absorbed in his studies. But she had managed to distract him. He had the most beautiful eyes. They sparkled when he talked about the subject he loved most, anything historical.

Except lately. Last night, as they sat together in the family room watching television, she'd glanced at him during a program on the History International Channel and his look was somewhere else, his eyes glazed over. He had something on his mind. And he didn't share it with her.

"What happened at practice anyway?" Randy asked.

Lynn blinked, pulled herself out of her head. He was talking about Ty, wasn't he? She considered how to say it. Truth was, their son Ty had not been paying attention, which wasn't unusual. He was out there in the backfield waiting for the soccer ball to come to him. Then, when the ball finally rolled his way, he got run down by the rest of the team. But if she told Randy, he'd end up making some comment later and hurt Ty's feelings. Their seven-year-old son didn't need a guilt trip on top of a broken arm. "It just happened—you know how things move pretty fast out there on the field with those kids."

"Hmmm." Randy looked down the hallway.

A voice spoke over the intercom, paging a doctor. A cart full of equipment clattered past, pushed by an orderly in a white uniform.

"Mr. and Mrs. Werling?" A nurse in blue scrubs stepped up to them, her thick-soled shoes squeaking on the waxed floor.

"How's Ty?" Randy asked.

"The arm's been cast, and we're cleaning up. Not much longer and he'll be ready to go home. He's doing fine."

"Thank you." Lynn rubbed one hand across her forehead. "What a relief." She smiled at Randy; he was checking his watch. The nurse hurried away.

"Yeah. The sooner the better," Randy said.

"I can't wait to get out of here. I hate the smell of hospital disinfectant," she mumbled, touching her stomach. "And it's not just the disinfectant. I hate hospitals." She hadn't been in a hospital since Will was born. In fact, she could count the times she'd had to come to a hospital for any reason on one hand. Lynn didn't count the times she'd had to go to the hospital with her mother.

"You can wait in the car if you'd like," Randy said. "Take Will with you."

"No," she said quickly. "Ty will want to see us all when he comes out. We need to stay here. I'm okay." She hadn't felt the stomach pain in, what, two hours? Maybe it was going away. Maybe it was nothing after all. She could cancel the doctor's appointment she'd made for Monday.

Randy let out a long sigh and Lynn glanced at him. He peered down the hallway, looking for...? Their son, of course. Who else?

"Honey, take Will for a minute, would you? I have to find the men's room."

He handed Will over. She sat back against the uncomfortable plastic cushion and her youngest child snuggled against her.

Randy hurried away.

Lynn had noticed a men's room as they came in, right by the triage desk—the opposite way from where he was headed. "Randy?"

He didn't turn around. She supposed there might

also be a bathroom farther down the hall, maybe around the corner by the bank of phones.

In her mind, Lynn retraced the events of the day. Who would have guessed she would end up here, in the emergency room with Ty? Earlier, she'd been fairly certain she would be the one being brought to emergency for treatment. The stomach pain she'd been having the last week or so was sharper, more intense, and more frequent.

Earlier today, it had stabbed her gut after she almost hit a stray black dog with the car. And Katy had seen the pain in her face when she had dropped her and the boys off for the last day of school.

Lynn ran her fingers through Will's hair. He pulled away and looked up at her, then lifted one pudgy hand and touched her cheek. "Think Moe's still at home? Dad let her out."

*What was it with the kids and that stray dog?* She didn't want another animal—but the dog did have a certain appeal, even to her, partly because of its resemblance to the dog she'd had when growing up, her German shepherd, Lucy. Physically, this new dog was much smaller, but she had that same look in her eyes, as if she had known you forever and knew everything that ate at your heart both now and ten years from now.

Will's elbow jabbed into her stomach and she flinched, expecting pain to stab her. She relaxed when the pain didn't come. "We'll have to see when we get home, honey."

This morning, the last time pain had pierced her, she had fallen to the carpet, pulled her knees up to her chest, gasped for air. The pain drilled into her, and when she thought she would faint if it got any worse, it finally eased.

She'd stumbled into the bedroom, then collapsed on the side of the bed next to the phone. It had unquestionably been the worst pain yet.

She'd immediately called and made an appointment with her internist for Monday.

So, here she sat with Will in the emergency room, waiting for Ty. It would be a perfect place for the pain to return, a perfect time. Someone would take her to an exam room. They'd figure out what was wrong. She'd get the diagnosis.

*Cancer?*

## Chapter 3

Katy groaned. Her leg hurt sooo bad. Her head pounded, and her back itched.

The pain got big, then small, then big again. Something crawled across her cheek. She swiped it away. Her mind wandered. Fog drifted in and out of her thoughts.

*She was having trouble walking through the school hallway. Voices vibrated. Summer vacation plans. Beaches. Lakes. Disneyworld. Way in front of her someone shouted; behind her someone laughed.*

*Her heart beat like the wings of a little bird against her ribs. Had been ever since Mom dropped her off in front of the school.*

*The Dog. They had almost run it over. Mom would have, if Katy hadn't screamed. Then, those big, wide-set yellow-brown eyes had watched them drive away. She should have told her mother to stop right then, to go back. She should have.*

Blackness swirled.

*Someone—something—jabbed her arm.*

*"Katy, where're you going? You didn't wait for me by the library." Emily fell into step beside her. "Hey!" Em called out to someone else, then giggled. "Last day of school. I can't wait to get out of here." The lights above the hallway dimmed, shimmered, brightened.*

*Katy didn't look at Emily.* You think you can't

wait.

*Someone jostled against her on the other side and she stumbled into the boy in front.*

Pain reached in and pulled at the memory, but the starry blackness swirled and sucked her back in.

*The boy glared. The stink of his sweat wafted around her, mixing with the floor wax smell and disinfectant odor of the nearby bathroom. The beige tile walls of the school hallway wavered. A musky, damp smell tickled her nose.*

*She'd seen that same black dog in her very worst dreams. She always woke up with a pounding heart ready to burst.*

*In those dreams she was lost and hurt, trapped in some damp, dark place. No one could help her, not Mom or Dad, or Mrs. Jordan's husband old Mick. Not even Mr. Tilton—and he was an honest-to-goodness war veteran. As much as he knew about guns and saving people and handling scary situations, she didn't think even the kind of smarts Mr. Tilton had would do any good.*

*In her dream it had been the dog who came. The dog had saved her.*

*She stepped into her home room classroom and—*

A thousand pins jammed into her back. Her eyes flashed open to black pain. Stars whirled.

*"Katy? What's the matter with you?" Emily bumped against her on purpose.*

More needles, stars, blackness.

*Ashley Spencer joined them on the other side of Emily, and Emily's voice rose in a giggle as she told Ashley the plans she had with Katy for the weekend.*

*Katy could care less about her plans with Emily.*

*Maybe, if she took an extra-long time at her piano lesson, Emily's family would go on to dinner without her, maybe even decide not to take her with them for the first weekend of the summer at Grand Lake. Sometimes the lessons did run long. Sometimes, Mrs. Jordan told stories about when she was young, or when her kids were young, and half of Katy's thirty-minute lesson was spent listening instead of playing. And sometimes, when that happened, Mrs. Jordan didn't stop the lesson at four-thirty, but went right on to five o'clock.*

Something tickled her nose. Her head swam. It hurt soooo bad.

Fog closed in around her, but her mind churned.

*Usually, Katy minded staying late at her lessons, but tonight she wouldn't mind if it meant she didn't have to go with Emily for the weekend. Maybe she wouldn't budge from that old piano bench until the antique mantel clock bonged five-thirty. That is, if the dog was around, waiting for her. She would be. She had to be.*

*No one else could possibly understand how important the dog was to her. She was the one having the dreams. And if her dreams were more than dreams, if they were telling the future, then the dog would save her family. If anything happened to it—like if Mom had killed it with the car—*

*She couldn't bear to think about it.*

*She wasn't ready to die.*

The thought beamed through her mind-fog. She opened her eyes.

The unbearable pain in her leg overwhelmed her brain.

*Make it stop!*

She tried to scream, tried to move. Darkness. Dirt.

The nightmare she'd been dreaming for months was real.

Chapter 4

Eighty-year-old Mick Jordan sat in his overstuffed reading chair in the evening light. He could hear the television in the living room playing an old sitcom. It sounded like *Happy Days* on some cable channel. He didn't find any joy in remembering those days, while his wife of sixty years, Jo, seemed to want to relive the past over and over again.

Canned audience laughter from the other room broke into his thoughts. "Oh, Archie," Edith Bunker whined from the TV. Jo cackled. He looked out the window and blocked out the noise.

Maybe he should get up and go outside where it was quiet. No TV noise, no car horns honking, no traffic sounds. The trees ate the sounds, unless the wind was right and the air was crystal clear, like in the deadest week of winter.

Peace and quiet was good, and when he was outside the house, he had it all the time. His neighbors were easy to get along with. Of course, there was this latest deal with Al. He said someone had stolen something of his, but he wasn't even able to say for sure what it was. And he'd been pointing his finger at Mick as he said it. Ridiculous. This was the closest thing to real animosity the hilltop had ever experienced, at least as long as he'd lived here—thirty years.

Al hadn't always been like this. A little weird,

maybe, but then he was a war veteran. And Al's wife Betsy had given his problem a name—even though he wouldn't see a doctor about it. She'd called it "post-traumatic stress syndrome." The old-timey name, shell shock, fit just as good.

Jo's high-pitched cackle jerked him back to the present. Had she turned the television up even louder? For years, the sound of her cackling laugh had made him smile. Now it split his eardrums. He got up from the chair and eased across the room and over to the patio door, slid it open, and stepped through.

A squirrel dashed across the yard. He clicked his tongue. The varmints stole all the birdseed, but they were entertaining, running the wires like circus performers and swinging from the bird feeders. Quite the acrobats.

Would the black dog go after the squirrels? Lots of dogs chased squirrels, and he didn't reckon this one would be any different. Katy would probably try to convince the animal not to chase them, but it was unlikely to work.

He pictured Katy as she'd been this afternoon, sitting at their piano, her eyes on the sheet music, the muscles of her face tight with concentration. A quick check of her fingers to see if she was going to hit the right keys, and then a glance at the notes on the page. Then, when the tune was finished, her straight back relaxed and she turned to Jo seeking approval. He'd been watching her from the other room for years, thinking what a beautiful little girl she was. Still so innocent. Still willing to spend time with her family, even her brothers. Not yet interested in boys.

He remembered those days in his family. They

were gone before he had time to appreciate them. And soon after, both of his kids had started their own lives someplace else. These days, Annie and Matthew rarely came home—and he didn't think they stayed in touch with each other outside of their visits on an occasional holiday. Children grow up, he reminded himself. The distance between them all was normal. At least, he wanted to believe it was. Someday, they would get close again. His children would get old enough they would begin to see the old folks were still important and that blood was thick. In the end, you didn't have much else.

At least he hoped it would turn out that way.

His mind drifted back to the dog. He'd seen it early this morning, when he'd been out clipping the hedges around the back patio. It reminded him of something in the distant past. Another dog…He shook his head. The dog had dashed across the yard like something was chasing it. But nothing came. Later, he'd seen the animal lying out by the driveway.

That morning, Jo had checked on him a few seconds before he saw the dog. "Mick! Where are you?"

"Here, Josey. Be there in a minute."

"Mickey? What're you doing?" Jo had sounded alarmed.

Mick had started over to the cement pad that extended his driveway past the garage and into the yard. A tattered net hung from the metal hoop on the basketball goal at the edge of the pad. Something huddled near the bushes beside the cement. A black trash bag?

Mick stopped short of the bushes.

"What is it, Mickey?" Jo's voice had carried across the yard.

"A dog."

"What's wrong with it?" Hands on her hips, she yelled across the few feet of grass and sidewalk separating her from her husband.

The black dog stretched in the leisurely way dogs do to give every muscle in their legs, shoulders, and torso an adequate pull. The animal was about the size of a lab but thin and wiry, more like some kind of hound, or maybe a terrier. The dog's tail wagged in a circle as it followed Mick across the pavement to the garage.

"Come on, girl."

The dog had followed him into the garage.

Now, sitting on the patio in the evening light, he wondered where the animal was at this minute. Probably at the Werlings. Katy meant to adopt her. He remembered what Katy had said after she'd finished her piano lesson. She'd rushed past him and out the patio door, throwing words over her shoulder.

"My dad's home, and he's going to meet our new dog. I've got to get over there."

"Is she a black one?" Mick had asked.

"Yes! Have you seen her?"

He didn't remember ever seeing Katy so excited. "She's beautiful. She'll be a good friend, Katy. You take care of her."

"Oh, I will, Mr. Jordan. I'll bring her over so you can meet her. Mrs. Jordan would like her, too. You used to have a dog, didn't you? I think I remember, but I was so little."

From the corner of his eye, Mick had seen Josephine lingering in the kitchen doorway. "Yes, we did. Mrs. Jordan called her Baby—but she's been gone awhile. Maybe five years. You get on home to your new dog. And you be sure and bring her over soon so we can get to be friends."

Katy shut the door. Through the sheer curtain, he'd watched her run across the yard.

The door opened, and Mick looked at Jo from his yard chair as she peered out into the darkness of the yard. "That dog back?"

He shook his head. "The dog's got a home. No need to wonder about her, Jo. Katy will take care of her."

Jo sniffed. "No doubt she will." She crossed the patio and put her hand on his shoulder. "Katy takes her music seriously and not many of them do anymore. She was 'off' this afternoon. Lots of mistakes. Thinking about the dog, I imagine." Josephine touched the top of his head with her other hand. "I hope she doesn't drop the lessons. I'll teach her as long as she's interested, I promise you that."

He reached up and patted her hand. "She won't quit, Josey, and neither will you." Stiffly, his wife walked back into the house.

A few minutes later, Mick shuffled in, moved across the carpet to his easy chair and lowered himself into it. His back was damned sore. He'd been trimming bushes all day, stooping and straightening. Then he had piled up the small branches blown off the trees by this morning's gusty wind.

He closed his eyes. Today had been a good day. Outside in the warming, late spring sun, there'd been a rare cool breeze, frisking around out of the southeast. Ruffled his hair whenever he took off his cap.

He needed a haircut. You'd think when hair turned white it would stop growing. Instead, it started growing out of your nose and your ears. Odd things happened when you got old, whether you liked it or not.

He was glad the dog was staying on the hilltop.

In the living room, the announcer previewed the late news. Dinner had been nothing special, but he'd eaten every bite of stew from his brimming bowl. Jo had made him a cherry cobbler for dessert. He wanted another serving.

He pushed himself up from his chair, crossed toward the kitchen, but then stopped in front of the sliding door. Even through the glass, he could hear raised voices. He shoved the door open and stared out into the dusk.

Al's voice blared loud enough to wake the dead.

Chapter 5

"You're trying to poison me, aren't you?" Al Tilton barked at his wife, Betsy. "Raw fish! Don't pull that again. Don't you ever tell me something's one thing when it's somethin' else. Sushi whooshi. Ain't havin' none o' that in this house, ever again. You hear me, woman?" Al barreled through the back door. He stomped around the side of the house, cursing under his breath, then started out onto the lawn.

*What a day. What a day. And now this crap for dinner.*

He rubbed one hand over his scalp, feeling the stubble of his so-short gray hair.

He couldn't get them out of his head—those crazies at the parking garage. Why couldn't it have been another old boring day, with the regular parking permit owners rolling steadily in like usual?

Instead, he'd had a whole bevy of the oddballs, starting with that gone-to-seed ex-high school football player with a beer paunch. Could be he'd come to pay a fine at City Hall, but most likely he had come downtown for jury duty. The "fined" used the parking meter lot if they had any sense. But then most of them didn't.

"Three dollars," Al had stated.

The man handed over three worn dollar bills and sped on.

Another car rolled up to the window. Middle-aged broad smiled at him, brown hair striped with blonde. Her thick makeup glistened, and blue eye shadow shimmered. Her makeup pooled in the deep wrinkles at the outside corners of her eyes.

"Three dollars, all day." He'd twitched his lips in a quick smile.

She turned her back to him as she dug in her purse for the money.

What was this thing the women were all doing with their hair? Why, she was tri-colored: brown, red-brown, and nearly white. Weird, that's for sure.

Another car drove past in the middle lane, another monthly permit parker. He lifted his hand in a wave. As if he could stop them from driving on in if they didn't have a parking tag. As if he had any kind of side arm, was any kind of security. Not like when he was a soldier. He shook his head.

"Hey, here's the money," the woman said.

Al took the money and then handed her the receipt. She snatched it and crammed it into her open purse without making eye contact.

*Yep, that's me, the parking attendant. Not human.*

He watched her drive on, then glanced toward the clock and sighed. Four hours to go.

He'd wondered then what Betsy would make for supper. He'd hoped for sweet and sour pork. Betsy did a good job with that. But no, he'd been poisoned with some new crap that tasted like shit.

Another car rolled up to his window. Exhaust belched from the tailpipe. Royal blue hair, spiked all over his—her?—head, plus black eyeliner. Five—he counted them again—five earrings on each ear and one looped through the left eyebrow.

"Hey, dude. I got like this fine," the person said, as he/she tapped on the steering wheel of the faded-blue Mercury. "Where do I go, man? Do I have to pay to park here? No way! I'm payin' a fine already, man."

Al decided "it" was male. He narrowed his eyes at the creature. "Three dollars or turn it around."

"You gotta be f-ing crazy!" the thing said.

Al smiled.

The alien in the car floored the accelerator and peeled away into the parking garage. Exhaust billowed from under the car and filled Al's booth with gray fumes. A coughing fit doubled him over.

The brake lights came on fifty yards in and the Mercury made the turn, squealing. He frowned. The squealing stopped. He peered at the window facing the exit ramp. He waited. Nothing.

From his patio, Al raged. *Damn ignoramuses!* He'd complained for years that people should pay when they left, shouldn't get out of the place unless they paid. *But do they listen to me?*

Al shook his fist at the starry sky. "Damn it all to hell. Damn Betsy! Damn those idiots at City Hall! Damn, damn, damn."

His eyes narrowed as he remembered what came next.

"Hello? You want my money or do I just drive in?"

Al turned to the old man in the big, gray Lincoln. The old woman in the front seat beside him leaned forward and looked at Al.

"Three dollars," he'd growled at them.

Al again glanced at the window to the exit lane behind him. The "thing" and its car had not left the lot like he'd told "it" to. What was he going to do?

He knew exactly what he would have done if he would have had his Army revolver with him. His mouth dried out and his heart thudded. His revolver? *Where is my revolver?* He couldn't remember the last time he had seen it. Sweat popped out on his forehead.

"Is that for all day?" the white-haired woman asked.

"Yup, all day," he said in a shaky voice.

The old man looked at him, then reached inside his suitcoat and pulled out a wallet. He opened the bill section, fingered a lone bill, and handed it to Al.

*A freakin' hundred!* No way did he have change for that. "Got anything smaller?"

The woman retrieved her purse from the floorboard, opened it and dug around.

Cars were stacking up behind them, and others were whizzing by in the permit lane before he could even have a look to see if they were displaying their parking permit. Somebody down the line honked. A sweat droplet traveled down Al's nose and hung on the tip.

The old man thumped the steering wheel. "Come on, Inez. Do you have it?"

Slowly, the woman withdrew three ones from her purse and handed them over. "Have a nice day," the old lady called as the Lincoln crept forward.

*Sheesh.* Things weren't getting any better. From the minute the day began, things had been wrong. That Betsy!

"Damn it! Where's breakfast?" Al had been standing on the patio, smacking the folded newspaper into the palm of his hand. Waiting.

In a flash of color—magenta, black, and royal blue—Betsy had stepped out onto their patio. Her black hair swung nearly to the belted waist of her kimono.

"You grouchy. What wrong?" she had said in her clear musical voice.

"I'm hungry. Breakfast's late," he boomed.

"No cook. Clients this morning. You make own eggs." She rose onto her toes and kissed the back of his neck, then whirled and disappeared into the house.

"Damn."

The drop of sweat on the end of Al's nose dripped off as the next car pulled forward. His heart pounded and his hand shook. *Three and a half more hours.*

At least the afternoon had passed without another "it" or patron with blue-streaked hair.

Six hours later, from his spot in the back yard, Al rued what his life had become. He spent his days at the parking garage, sweating, dealing with all slices and flavors of people. His life had no purpose.

The most he could look forward to when he was at work was that maybe, when he got home, the Werling girl would stop by with fresh cookies. Maybe even oatmeal raisin.

Behind him, the back door slammed.

"You no talk to me like that, Albert. You hear?" Betsy shrieked. "This last time. I had it with you. I pack bags tonight. Leave you. This marriage no work for me." She rushed across the yard toward him.

"Yeah, yeah, yeah. You ain't goin' nowhere, woman. You got nowhere to go, no one to take you in. Thinking about going back to Thailand? Your family's dead, remember?"

Betsy stopped in the middle of the yard and stood,

her arms lifting and dropping as if she was contemplating flying away. She looked ridiculous. Those wide sleeves, that blouse with every possible color in it, and gold threads and fringes. He still didn't like to take her out where people could see her, not even after all these years. He would be better off if she would pack up and go.

"I leave you, Albert," she repeated.

But still she stood there, flapping those arms at him.

"Then go, crazy woman! No skin off my back. Get out, and take that wok and all that crap you put in it with you. I ain't gonna be needin' it!"

Her arms stopped flapping. She folded down onto the ground, sobbing. Her body rocked back and forth. Her hair so dark, spread across her back and covered her head. She looked like some big black beetle squatting in the middle of the yard.

"I'm gonna go out and get somethin' decent to eat," Al muttered as he stalked past her and around to the front of the house. Let her be gone when he got back. He didn't care. Things had been fine with the two of them for a while, far as he remembered. But then...? He didn't know when it had changed. She looked different, she acted different, her clothes fit different. He couldn't stand it anymore. She had to go. And if she didn't pack all her crap, it was going to the dump come Sunday.

Be nice to have the house to himself. Just him. Do what he wanted when he wanted. No clutter. He'd be able to keep track of stuff. Wouldn't be any of this losing things. If something was missing, he'd know who to blame. There wouldn't be any wondering if she'd put it away, or thrown it away when it wasn't even hers. *Good riddance.*

He thrust his hand into his pocket and dug for his car keys. After he slid into the front seat of the car, he jabbed the keys at the ignition, and then jabbed again. *Jeez. What was the problem?* He peered down at his hand, saw his fingers shaking. Set his hand in his lap for a moment and took a deep breath.

The next time he slid the key into the ignition, the engine turned over.

As Al backed down the driveway, the headlights caught the black dog standing by Mick Jordan's mailbox.

*Too bad it wasn't standing in the street.*

He'd take it out.

## Chapter 6

Katy opened her eyes again to the blackness. Pain shot from her leg. She tried to scream. The croak coming from her throat was not a scream. She needed a drink. She needed her mother. She needed the dog.

*I need Monique. Where is she? She's supposed to save me. Where is she?*

"Monique?" she moaned. What if the dog didn't know her name? But the dog had been there when Katy and her brothers had agreed. She had surely heard them talk about what her new name was.

Why didn't she come? *I need you, Monique.*

Earlier today, Dad had opened the car door after pulling into the driveway when he got home from work. Katy had raced up and grabbed his free hand as Will pulled him out of the car. Katy grinned at her dad, echoing Will's urgings to come and see the dog. "See, there she is. Isn't she beautiful?"

The dog sat next to Mom on the cement step by the front door. Her long whip of a tail thudded up and down.

Will pulled away from Daddy and dashed for the pair by the door. "Can we keep her? Huh? Can we?" he screamed over his shoulder. He threw himself down on the step and wrapped his arms around the dog's neck.

The dog looked from Will to her to Daddy with her wide, yellow-brown eyes, and her thumping tail slowed.

It thudded once, and then again a few seconds later. Dad and the dog stared at one another.

"Can we keep her?" Ty asked again.

"She's a nice dog." Will pouted.

"Look how beautiful she is!" Katy added. "She's so well behaved."

"Can we keep her?"

"She'll protect us."

"Hush, all of you. Where did she come from?" Dad had looked at his family. Mom's arms were folded tightly across her chest.

"Her name is, um, is, uh, Blackie," Ty said. "Can we keep her?"

"Blackie? Her name's not Blackie. It's Midnight," Katy corrected.

"No, it's not! Her name is…is…" Will thought for a few seconds. "Moe!"

"Moe?" Ty and Katy had hollered at the same time. "She's a girl dog."

"Her name's Moe," Will had insisted, his lower lip jutting out.

"That's a stupid name. She's a girl." Katy had locked eyes with her little brother and did not back down.

His left foot kicked at the doormat.

"Katy," Mom warned. "Maybe Moe could be short for something."

Katy had thought hard about this and then, she had known. "It's short for Monique. You know, like Monica from that old show you watch sometimes. But our dog doesn't act all bossy and hyper. Monique is better. Will that make you happy, Will? You can still call her Moe for short."

Katy was pretty sure the dog knew her name. She'd called her the name over and over again before she had left to go with Emily's family for pizza.

But then her mind argued with her. The dog didn't need to know her own name. She was a magic dog. She'd come to save her. Every time Katy had dreamed the nightmare, the dog had been in it. She'd been there to rescue her.

Katy groaned again. The pain overwhelmed her, the edges of her vision blurred, and she lost the stars. She wanted to keep her eyes open, but when she pinched them shut, the pain eased a little.

*Where was Monique now that the nightmare was really happening?*

## Chapter 7

Mick Jordan eased down onto the woven fabric covering the metal glider and turned his left side, his best ear, toward the back yard abutting his property line. Betsy screamed at Al, threatened to leave him. Maybe she would this time, but Al had a point, where would she go? No one ever visited. And the two of them never went anywhere.

Jo was as friendly with her as anyone on the hill. He'd seen them out there, Betsy at her water feature or working the raised vegetable beds and Jo in her butterfly garden. Little Katy Werling was often out there helping the women plant, then she picked a few flowers to take home.

Doubtful Betsy would make good on her threat to leave Al. She was still a huddle in their back yard. Al was long gone.

Mick shifted in the glider, tried to find a position to ease his backache. He took another long draw off his pipe.

Tough months of hot summer to get through. Green and lush would give way to yellow and dry. The bushes were thick with leaves, flowers were all blooming, birds were twittering. Another few weeks, a little more hot weather, and the yearly cicadas would tunnel up from underground for a few weeks of life as a flying insect. They'd vibrate their wings from mid-morning to sunset and fill the hilltop with summer sound.

He knew the sound so well, he could close his eyes and imagine it. For six weeks the odd screeching would last, and then, nearly overnight, it would be over. Summer would end. The wind would shift and the sunlight would soften. The leaves would turn yellow, gold, red, and finally brown, and then catch the breezes and shower to the ground.

The aroma of burning leaves would waft through the open windows, and sunlight would sift down through the bare branches. He loved the fall. Before he knew it the year would be gone.

Mick sat on the patio and thought about the black dog. Most nights, packs of coyotes yipped as they raced through the ravine. An occasional cougar might even pass through. That possibility had worried him some when he and Jo had first moved out here, but the kids had graduated high school by then, and grandkids seemed a long way off. Now he had the grandkids, but none of them lived here.

Then there was Katy Werling and her brothers, Will and Ty. Could be the grown up Werlings worried about their young 'uns and what might come up out of the ravine. Hard to say.

Mick pulled himself from the chair and stepped past the hedge toward the shady east flowerbed where his wife Josephine's red begonias and purple impatiens bloomed. He and Jo had planted their usual annuals a couple of weeks ago, but they had already doubled in size and were heavy with buds.

He squinted and then pulled off his golf hat, the frayed rim fuzzy soft under his fingertips. He smoothed his thinning white hair and then jammed the cap back onto his head.

The leaves above him rustled in an odd night breeze. A big bird—some kind of owl?—flapped up from one of his trees and soared low down into the ravine. Goin' after a mouse, no doubt, or maybe a rat.

"Mick, what're you doing?" The breeze carried Jo's voice from the back porch around to the place where he stood.

"I'm here, Josey. Be there in a minute." He took the first few steps across the back yard slowly, then built up speed.

Jo stepped out onto the patio, her hands stuffed deep into the pockets of her green gingham apron, her mouth pinched into a narrow line. "You're looking for that stray." Jo made that same "tsk" sound she had made close to a million times since they'd met all those years ago. Jo's hands were out of her pockets and on her hips now. "You don't listen to me," she said in a quiet voice.

"Yes, I do, Josey. It was just a biscuit."

"First a biscuit, then we're buying bags of dog chow—and I don't want another dog." Jo stomped her foot as she marched back into the house.

A sudden breath of breeze followed him from the back yard into the house. In the den, he fell into his chair and reached immediately for his pipe tool. He scraped the pipe bowl clean, then dipped it into the can of tobacco, stuffing the shredded strands of sweet-smelling leaves hard into the wooden bowl. He struck a match and then lit the pipe, sucking at the stem, pulling air up the throat of the pipe and into his lungs.

Mick puffed on his pipe, squinted, and blinked as the fragrant smoke swirled around his head. He cleared his throat, then went to puffing again.

"Mickey, had you ever seen that dog before?" Jo bustled into the den with a dusting cloth and a spray can of polish.

"Nope." He spoke with certainty, but something tickled at his memory.

"You give it any more than that biscuit?" Her voice had that edge to it; she shook her head at him.

The gray curls didn't even wiggle. She'd been to the beauty shop yesterday, and the operator had sprayed Jo's hair so stiff it sprang right back when you touched it, like the top of a fresh-baked angel food cake.

"Now why'd you go and do that?" Jo continued, although he hadn't answered her. "You *want* it to stay around. Another critter that somebody will have to feed. It's not going to be me." Jo ran the dust rag over the dark walnut shelves and tabletops and around the chrome and wood picture frames. She moved toward the piano.

Mick let his teeth scrape over the end of the pipe stem as he pulled it from his mouth. She didn't want an answer. This was some kind of ritual she went through every so often. If it wasn't a question about their dog, Baby, it was whether he loved her, or loved daughter Annie, or son Matthew. The woman's mind never stopped with the questions. What he wouldn't give for an hour or two of peace and quiet. Between her questions and the piano lessons she couldn't quite quit giving, it was enough to drive a man crazy.

"So where'd the dog come from? Got a collar?" Jo ran the dust cloth across the windowsill. With her left hand, she held the brown and gold drapes to one side as she worked.

"Nope."

Mick crossed his arms and peered out the bank of windows on the back side of the house. The dark wasn't so thick yet; he could still see Tilton's yard. The leaves on the neighbor's banana trees flopped in the wind.

"Girl dog, too, and there's trouble. Probably pregnant, gonna have pups. Somebody'll have to take her in. I can't do it, Mick. It'll break my heart all over again."

Mick watched Jo bustle around the room going over the same shelves she'd just dusted with the already dirty cloth. Had he said anything about adopting the dog?

"Don't you go to worryin', Josephine. The Werlings will take her in. Or maybe Annie—"

"With three kids and no husband, what does our daughter need with a dog? Heaven forbid—and a pregnant one at that. What would she do with all them pups, anyway?" Jo bustled out of the room, and there was immediate silence on the other side of the wall.

He closed his eyes and eased farther down into his worn, gold-upholstered reading chair, holding onto the arms to take some of the weight off his knees. He'd done it now. She'd be in one of her "states" the rest of the night. At least she'd had a few good minutes earlier. Katy Werling always seemed to raise Jo's spirits.

He rubbed his nose. Damn furniture polish. He sneezed, then listened to the silent house for a while before he opened his eyes and peered out the back windows again.

Something thumped somewhere in the house. "Jo?" he called.

No answer.

Mick pulled himself up and shuffled across the room. He was stiff, too many hours of yard work today, followed by too much sitting. He took a couple of steps, tottered. Then he got his sea legs and forged across the looped brown shag carpet to the doorway of the family room, where he grabbed the doorframe and held on.

"Josephine?"

She wasn't in her chair. He moved a couple of steps into the room. Where was she?

Something had fallen to the carpet in front of Jo's blue chair. That crocheted afghan. The one she'd made while her mother was in the nursing home.

He blinked, then rubbed at his eyes behind his glasses and peered again at the lumpy afghan. "Jo?"

He staggered across the room, bent over her, reached quivering fingers to touch her shoulder. His crooked, arthritic fingers prodded. Jo lay still.

A shiver shook him as he turned on the table lamp, and then grabbed the phone beside her chair to punch in 9-1-1. He gave the address.

"Oh, Josephine!" he groaned as he replaced the receiver. He bent over her again, touched a gray curl on her temple. CPR. He should do CPR. He started to drop to his knees, but a pain shot through his lower back. He grabbed at Jo's blue chair, sucked in his breath. The room swam, and the pain blinded him. He couldn't do it. He couldn't kneel down on the floor and bend over to breathe in and out for Jo. His back was ruined. Blast it all. What could he do? Sixty years of caring for each other—it couldn't be over. Not like this. Not with him standing here, a useless fool.

Someone else would have to save her.

Betsy, out on the lawn. Maybe Betsy could do CPR

until the ambulance got here.

He grimaced with the pain as he straightened himself, and then charged across the room, gritting his teeth. He crashed against the patio doorframe, still reeling from the pain in his back. Outside, twilight threw shadows and the gray sky darkened. Mick flicked the yard light switch and pulled the door wide.

"Help! We need help!"

Out in the yard in the thickening darkness, a shape rose up. It ran toward him.

"Help! It's Jo. Hurry!"

The shape grew into Betsy as it ran into the circle of light. She dashed up to the porch, then pushed past him.

"In the living room. Can you do CPR?" His voice caught and cracked. His legs trembled. "I called 9-1-1."

"Yes. I do CPR." Betsy darted into the living room, then threw herself onto the floor beside Jo and checked her pulse. Betsy leaned close to see if Jo was breathing. Using the heels of her hands, one on top of the other, she pumped on Jo's chest.

Mick leaned against Jo's chair. His own heart hammered. What could he do? What should he do?

"Oh, Jo," he moaned. "Stay with me, Josey. Don't go."

As he said the words, he was back there, more than sixty years ago, meeting Josephine on V-J Day. It was a celebration, the end of the war. He had been too embarrassed to go to the celebration, bitter he had not been old enough to enlist and fight. If the war had lasted another year, he could have gone. But it was over, and everyone was cheering and dancing.

He'd first seen Josephine at the dance, the prettiest

girl in the room. Maybe a little on the thin side, and so petite. She caught his eye instantly. Her fragility drew him. Uncertainty beamed from her.

"One-two-three," Betsy counted as her hands pushed on Jo's chest.

Mick blinked. "Josey, Josey-Jo. Don't go," he pleaded.

He'd said those same words that first night. They'd met and had one dance when she turned to go. For him, both the night and his life were just beginning. He pulled her out onto the dance floor again, told her that she couldn't leave, should forget her curfew. She'd jerked away, blushing. But when she looked back at him, when he refused to let go of her hand, the light in her eyes made his heart pound.

Betsy huffed quick breaths into Jo's mouth. Mick rocked on his feet, clutched the chair back. Damn. There must be something he could do to help. He shuffled around the house, turning on the lights as he went. He opened the front door and the garage door, turned on all the yard lights. The ambulance must not miss the house.

There was an emergency strobe light in the trunk of the car, one of those things you were supposed to use so cars didn't run into you when you had pulled over onto the road shoulder with a flat tire or a dead engine. He could set that on the driveway.

He hurried to the car and dug through the trunk until he found the flashing light get-up. Then he rushed back out to the end of the driveway and turned it on.

They would not miss the house. He'd stand out here and wave.

A siren wailed in the distance.

"Hang on, Jo! They're on the way. Hang on, girl!" he hollered back at the house.

Chapter 8

"You'll be a celebrity tomorrow at school, Ty. Bet no one else has an arm in a cast," Lynn said, accelerating the car up their driveway. As she pulled into the garage, she glanced next door at the Lopez's house. Drapes closed, the house appeared abandoned. The lamp they had left on must have burned out. She made a mental note to replace the light bulb tomorrow if she went over to water the plants.

Lynn hoped Gwen and Jim were having fun on their cruise to Alaska. She made another mental note to put an Alaskan cruise on her personal bucket list. She turned off the motor, then slid her arm around Ty's shoulders. His lower lip quivered. She hugged him gently to her. "What do you say we go inside and get you ready for bed?"

Randy's headlights lit up the garage as they beamed on the driveway behind them.

"Here we go, Ty." They got out of the CR-V as Randy turned his Civic into the parking space next to the garage.

"Moe?" Will called as he leapt from Randy's car. "Moe!"

Lynn stepped out on the driveway and scanned the shadows around the house. She followed Will to the side yard, where he called the dog again.

Behind their house, the Jordan's house and yard

lights blazed. Ty took her hand and pulled her back to the driveway.

"Where's Moe, Dad?" Ty whined as Randy got out of his car. "You should have left her in the house. She's gone."

"I couldn't leave her inside," Randy said. "We don't know that she's house broken. If she's still around, she'll come back. If not tonight, maybe tomorrow."

"What if she went down there?" Will asked, pointing one finger at the forested ravine across the street. "What if something gets her?"

"That's silly," Lynn huffed. "Ty, quit scaring your brother. First of all, there's nothing scary living in that ravine, and second, nothing has happened to the dog. She'll be back tomorrow." She hustled the boys through the garage, unlocked the back door, and led her family inside. She flicked on the lights and pulled the blinds closed as she walked from room to room. At the breakfast room window, she stopped. It was nearly ten-thirty. Mick and Jo never left their lights on this late. And their drapes were still open.

"Randy? The lights are all on at the Jordan's house." Lynn peered through the open wood blinds and then pulled the cord to close them. "Seems strange. Randy?" When she turned around, he wasn't there.

He hadn't been with her mentally all evening. Worried about Ty? Maybe he was more upset than she knew about the broken arm.

"Mommy? Where's Moe? What if she's gone? How will we ever find her again?" Will tugged at the hem of her capris, then clutched her left knee.

Lynn bent down to look him in the eyes. She

gasped at the sudden pain from her abdomen. "Ooh," she breathed out. Then, in a few seconds, when she could speak in a normal tone, she said, "I don't know, honey. It'll have to wait until morning. Her fur is black. How could we see her in the dark?"

Will pondered the question.

She ruffled his hair. "Let's all get ready for bed. We can still go to Ty's tournament tomorrow, to cheer on the team. And it's past your bedtime. Come on."

\*\*\*\*

Randy sat on the side of the bed and stared at the bedroom extension phone. Jennifer had not answered when he'd called from the hospital. He'd stood her up. Or whatever the kids called it these days. He had no clue. He was nearly twenty years older than most of his students, on the wrong side of the "generation gap." A few weeks ago it hadn't mattered. Now it did. He slipped off his loafers and put them in the closet, then unbuttoned his shirt and slipped it off.

Randy plodded across the room to the master bath and leaned over his sink. He took off his glasses, splashed cold water on his eyes and rubbed some over his neck. Then he toweled off his face and put his glasses back on. He looked in the mirror.

*What would Lynn do if she knew?*

He couldn't believe this was happening to him. He, Professor Randy Werling. How many times had Jennifer been in his office before? And then today, when she had walked past him and he had closed the door, her scent, exotic and intoxicating, had filled his small office and soaked into the pages of his books.

Remembering, his heart pounded and so did the blood in his lower core. He sucked in his stomach. Not much there in the way of muscles but at least he watched what he ate. He still looked pretty good, didn't he?

She had stood only inches away. He could have taken off his glasses and still seen her clearly. He could have placed his hands on the sides of her arms and caressed her. Instead, he had stepped around her to the desk.

"Jennifer," he'd said.

She tilted her head back and smiled up at him.

What would it be like to kiss her? Fifteen years in the classroom and never before had this happened. Why was it happening now? Oh, it wasn't that he hadn't wondered what sex would be like with some of them, especially the ones who openly flirted, probably thinking they could get a better grade if they showed cleavage, or wore tiny shorts or skirts. He'd never even considered taking it beyond the student-professor relationship. But that was before Jennifer had walked into his class.

He imagined their lips touching. He would open his mouth. Their tongues would roll over each other around and around, over the smooth, slick surfaces of their teeth, melding the warm wetness of their mouths. Her arms would circle his neck and his hands drop to her buttocks, then move up her back and over her ribs to—

"Randy? I'm going to need some help in here," Lynn called.

He opened his eyes and peered into the mirror, where he saw Jennifer's eyes, like an ocean with white-capping waves, focused on him. The apples of her cheeks turned pink as she smiled.

His insides melted. He ran his hands through the

too-long graying hair over his temples. This afternoon he had wanted, more than anything, to reach across the desk and pull Jennifer into his arms.

He had watched her look shift, and followed it to a photograph propped up on the cluttered bookshelf to his left. Lynn, Katy, Ty, Will, and himself, gathered in front of the fireplace with Katy holding Caesar and Ty holding Cleo, while Will petted Angel, the rabbit, in Lynn's lap. The only family member missing was the goat.

Jennifer had looked down at her books. "This intercession fast track on the Civil War is hard for me, Professor. Do you have anyone—like a graduate assistant—who might tutor me?" She looked at him through long silky lashes; a shy smile turned up the corners of her perfectly formed mouth.

She didn't think he would just hand her over to a graduate student, did she?

He closed his eyes, remembering what he'd said. "Did you have a time in mind? My evening is free. Could we say…seven-thirty outside the campus library?"

"Tonight would be great. I'll be bored and lonely. My housemate is driving home to New Mexico for some long weekend family celebration. I have no plans."

Here, in his bathroom, his brain exploded. An empty house, and three entire days and nights. His face blazed with heat. Perspiration popped out on his lip. He shoved back from the vanity sink and clenched his fists.

Randy walked out of the bathroom and across their bedroom. Through the door, he could see Lynn pull the sand-colored bath towels from the linen closet in the hallway. He pulled on a T-shirt.

"Randy?" She looked over her shoulder at him. "The lights are all on over at the Jordans'. It worries me. Would you go over there and check on them? I'll get the boys ready for bed."

Randy stared at her. She wanted him to go over and check on the neighbors because their lights were on? When had Lynn become the neighborhood busybody?

"Okay," he mumbled. He slipped on his flip-flops and shuffled downstairs.

Outside, the just-past-full moon was rising, bathing the neighborhood in soft light. He stopped and looked up at the stars. Tonight hadn't turned out like he'd expected it to.

He didn't really believe in fate. He didn't think much about why things happened. Jennifer had happened in his life. He hadn't asked for it. In fact, he had tried to keep from reacting despite his attraction to her.

He turned his attention to the Jordan house and crossed the grassy back lawn to the Jordan's well-lit acre. Barney, the goat, bleated at him from his pen as he walked past. Landscape lighting led the way up a brick walk and through a series of raised flowerbeds, then around to the front porch. Light poured from the front windows.

He rang the bell and waited. He rang it again and looked through the front window. They'd probably gone to bed and left the lights on. Why was Lynn so worried? Randy walked around the house, peering into windows as he went. The television was on, and so was every lamp he could see. But no Mick or Jo. He continued around the house.

As he stepped onto the driveway, his foot brushed against something; it crashed over. He picked up the emergency flasher light. Randy flicked the ON switch and stared at the throbbing red strobe. Wasn't like Mick Jordan to leave something out to get kicked or broken. He glanced at the house again.

He'd seen the news clips about the home invasions. They were creeping nearer to his neighborhood. He took another peek through an open window. Seemed like leaving the drapes open and the lights on was an open invitation. But on the other hand, maybe an invasion had already happened, and something was really wrong.

He went around the house again, trying every window and door, ringing the bell, calling out. Nothing. They weren't home. There was probably a simple explanation—they'd gone somewhere, not thinking it would be after dark when they got back. That was all it was. No need to make it into any big deal.

He headed for home. The trees frogs' chorus shrilled from the woods. Something touched his cheek, and he swatted around his head with his hand. Mosquitoes. Why did they always want to suck his blood?

Had Jennifer found someone else to study with when he didn't show up? Someone else to take her home to her empty house? Beads of sweat formed on his forehead. Another something brushed against his cheek, and a sudden itch started on the back of his neck.

Something bigger than a mosquito shoved against his leg. Startled, he dropped the emergency lamp he'd carried with him since finding it on Mick's driveway.

The black dog looked up at him and whined.

"Geez, you scared me," he scolded. "Where'd you come from?"

Her tongue hung out of her mouth as she panted.

"Go home, get something to eat," he said. "Shoo." He had no intention of letting the kids keep this animal. They already had Cleo and Caesar. He didn't want another dog. He didn't care how much the kids wanted this one, he didn't. "Go on, dog."

The dog trotted toward the blackness of the wooded lot on the other side of the house, where another shrill chorus of tree frogs competed in a different key from the others. Randy continued toward his house. In a day or two, his kids would have forgotten all about the black dog.

Jennifer would no doubt forget all about him once she'd finished his class.

\*\*\*\*

Heavy footsteps pounded up the stairs.

"What's going on at the Jordans'?" Lynn called.

"Looks like they went out and left all the lights on." Randy entered the bathroom.

Lynn squeezed extra water out of the bath sponge and then swiped it across Ty's back, careful not to let the water dribble down onto his pajama bottoms. She set the sponge on the edge of the sink. "There. That's as clean as we can get you tonight."

"Doors and windows are locked. Doesn't look like anything inside has been disturbed. I think they went out, forgot to pull the drapes. They'll probably be home before long."

Lynn wrapped the big fluffy towel around Ty's shoulders and rubbed his back. "Okay, here's one ready to be tucked in. I'll plop Will in the tub."

48

"Did you find Moe, Dad?" Ty asked.

Randy shook his head.

Lynn watched her husband steer Ty out of the room and thought about her neighbors. Mick and Jo never left their lights on, never left their curtains open after dark. She thought of the rash of home invasions in the area featured in the news. If someone had broken in, wouldn't a door or window be open? Wouldn't there be some sign that something had happened? Apparently, Randy hadn't seen anything to be alarmed about.

She shoved the stopper into the tub drain and turned on the spigot, watched the water pour out and begin to fill the tub. A sharp pain jabbed her abdomen. She grabbed the edge of the bathtub to steady herself.

The pain was getting worse.

She eased down to the floor and rested her head against the side of the tub.

In her mind, she saw the black dog, looking through the window. Like this morning. She remembered it clearly: she had just finished her Pilates exercise tape and sweat had beaded on her upper lip. Outside, in the yard, the dog was looking into the house. The animal's tail wagged in a circle.

"Hi, dog," she had said as she opened the atrium door. The animal raced to her, tongue lolling out of the side of her mouth. Lynn's heart lurched.

The dog rose up on its hind legs and put its front paws on Lynn's chest, then licked her face. Lynn pushed it away, but the dog came at her again, leaping and yipping. She shoved the dog away; it yipped some more. Laughter rolled out of Lynn's mouth, coming all the way up from her stomach. Still the dog came at her, leaping and woofing, running circles around her. Lynn dodged to one side, let the animal chase her. Then, she chased the dog. She laughed until she had to bend over and catch her breath.

The black dog collapsed on the grass and rolled over on her back, legs high in the air. Light-headed, Lynn let her knees fold and dropped down to the ground. Her face ached. She couldn't remember the last time she had laughed like this.

The dog rolled over, stuck her hind end up in the air, and wagged her tail. "Arf!"

Crazy dog! She pranced over to Lynn and threw herself down on the grass next to her, once again rolled onto her back and thrashed the air with her legs. Lynn rubbed the dog's tummy.

But then, her smile had drained away. *Lucy. This dog acts like Lucy.* Lynn had scrambled to her feet and hurried into the house.

Now, waiting for the tub to fill, her mind raced through the Lucy years. She'd taken the German shepherd to obedience school. Spent every spare moment of her fifth grade year with that dog.

Lynn had pitched the neon pink Frisbee into the air, and then, when it got close to where the dog waited, Lucy leaped. Her strong shoulders lifted and her jaws opened, then clamped down on the disk. She caught it! She always caught it.

Fast-forward three years. Eighth grade. She and Lucy and her older brother Mark were walking in the park across from their house. Lucy trotted beside them, without a leash.

"Heel," Lynn commanded. The dog dropped back. "Stay," she said, and the dog stopped, sat down and waited as Lynn walked away. "Come!" she called. The dog ran eagerly to her.

"Give me the Frisbee! I'll throw one she can't catch," Mark had insisted. Lynn had pulled the Frisbee out of her backpack and handed it to him.

Mark had tossed it hard. The disc flew low and long, flying over the grassy lawn and into the street beyond. Lucy raced after it.

The driver of the moving van didn't even have time to hit his brakes.

Chapter 9

Katy startled awake. Her brain screamed—her leg! *Ooooh.* Blackness pressed in around her. Where was she? What had happened? Stars spun in lazy circles.

She remembered.

"Dog," Katy had screamed that morning. The picture of the animal on the road played in her memory like something on YouTube. "Don't hit it."

Her mother had slammed her foot on the SUV's brake. The car had squealed and skidded sideways toward the ravine that snaked through their forested neighborhood.

Time slowed.

Katy's heart pattered in her chest, and so did her breathing. *Please, please, please let the dog be okay.*

The car shuddered to a stop. The car engine hummed.

Katy had swiveled in her seat. A black dog stood off to the side of the road by the mailbox, looking after the car. "There it is, it's okay. You didn't hit it, Mom." Kay's heart gradually slowed, but her brain sped up. She knew that dog. She'd been dreaming about it for weeks.

"If it's a stray, can we keep it?" Ty asked, before Katy could ask the same question.

The car coasted down the hill. "Cleo and Caesar might not like to share the house with another dog,"

Mom had said. "Besides, that black dog must belong to someone."

Katy stared out the window toward the thick green line of trees edging the ravine. The dog didn't belong to anyone. The animal had come because of *her.*

Katy peered into the side mirror before the car turned the corner. A half block away, the black dog, still watching the car, had moved to the side of the road and lain down.

In the ravine, Katy tried to shift her body. Pain shot up her leg all the way to her head. A shiver slid down her arms and the sky shimmered, mixing darkness and moon and stars and more darkness. The memory pulled at her.

The dog. They'd wanted Mom to tell them they could keep the dog.

They'd been trying to talk her into it most of the way to school after she'd almost hit it.

Katy couldn't see the dog in the side view mirror anymore. Ty giggled in the back seat. Katy glanced over her left shoulder. Gross. Each boy had a wiggling finger stuck deep up one nostril. Another "Biggest Booger" contest.

Sweat popped out on her forehead. She wanted to get out of the car; there wasn't enough air for the four of them to breathe.

"Can we keep it, Mom?" Ty had asked.

Mom hit the brakes as they coasted down the hill to the flatter land and the road to school. "What are you talking about?"

"That black dog you almost hit. If it's still here after school, can we keep it?"

"Yeah, Mom. Can we keep it?" Will chimed in.

"That dog might not even be around tonight." Mom's voice sounded stern.

"I know it's a stray," Katy said in a quiet, firm voice. "It's another dumped dog, like Caesar and Cleo were before they adopted us. It will starve if we don't feed it. Besides, we've never had a black dog before." Her mind raced. They *had* to keep the dog.

"I want a fierce dog, not another wimpy dog," Ty insisted. "I bet that dog would go after the garbage man."

"Yeah, and the UPS man, too." Will's head wobbled up and down.

"Boys, we don't want a dog to go after the garbage man or the mail man. We want nice dogs." Mom stopped the car at a corner and waited on traffic.

"We need a protector, a scary dog that bites." Ty slammed his right fist into the palm of his left hand.

"We *don't* need protection or a dog that bites."

A motorcycle zoomed across the intersection, out of turn.

"Then why did you have an alarm system installed last week?" Katy asked, using a quiet voice that sounded more like her mother than herself.

Her mother turned the corner and accelerated. "I've told you. Your dad will start teaching classes this summer at other campuses, and he'll be getting home late. It's a precaution, kids."

"A dog doesn't cost as much as an alarm system." Katy had seen the bill lying on the kitchen counter.

"Animals aren't cheap. We'd have to feed the dog, take it to the vet for check-ups, buy it bowls, a bed, a collar, and take care of it for as long as it lives. Fifteen years, maybe."

"Still," Will pouted, "wouldn't be that 'spensive."

'Spensive. 'Spensive. 'Spensive. The word swam around her, along with the darkness, and the weird, wet smell of the hard ground beneath her.

Her leg hurt soooo bad.

*Owwwwwwww.*

Chapter 10

Close to midnight, Al unlocked the door and stepped into the dark house. Betsy's Akia was in the driveway. She was probably curled up asleep in their bed. So much for her threat.

He stopped in the kitchen doorway, then eased down the hall. He walked silently on the balls of his feet, quiet as a panther in the forest. The blackness closed in around him and the hair prickled on the back of his neck. His heart ka-thumped against his ribcage. The house was so silent. A roar started in his ears and shook his brain. His lungs stopped working. His fingers and hands tingled. The tingling crept up to his wrists, then to his elbows.

*Breathe, man, breathe.* He closed his eyes, denying the blackness was real, and that there was someone— *who?*—just beyond, waiting with a knife, or bayonet, or ax, or a sharpened bamboo spear clutched in grimy, blackened fingers. He gulped, then swallowed to wash the lump down his throat. He was at home. He wasn't *there*. This wasn't *then*.

Count: One...two...three...four.

He ran his hand down the wall and then forced himself to take a step.

His footfall sounded on the wooden floor.

A siren went off in his head.

He intentionally bumped the wall as he moved

forward.

Goosebumps raced across his back.

His hand shook as he reached first to flick on the lights in the hall, and then inside a doorway to turn on the lamps in the guest bedroom. He moved on down the hall, repeating the process in Betsy's sewing room, and finally, their bedroom. Soft light filled in the shadows.

"Betsy? Betsy-girl?" he called.

He turned in a slow circle, then stepped to the closet. As his hand rested on the knob, he remembered. At dinner, he'd had too much to drink. He'd said something wrong. But he couldn't remember what it was. *Oh, Jesus.* "Betsy?"

He opened the closet door. Her clothes hung in rows, haphazard, shirts next to dresses, slacks next to jeans. He glanced up at the shelves. Her small overnight bag was gone, but everything else was there, sets of green, blue, and colorful patterned scrubs. His breath whooshed out.

She'd be back. He knew she didn't mean to leave him. She wouldn't. Where would she go? She loved him, didn't she? He rubbed at his forehead.

The woman was crazy about him, had been for thirty years—ever since—? His mind failed him, a hole had been burned in the gray matter.

She wouldn't just up and leave him, would she?

The hospital. They'd met in the hospital. He could almost remember. Yes, a hospital. She was a nurse, wasn't she? He reached in and touched the sleeve of a shirt with cartoon animals leaping across it.

He hurried down the hall to the kitchen. The back door stood open. Had he left it open? He shook his head. Was he losing his mind? When had he last taken one of those pills?

Al peered outside as he stepped to the open door. He jerked to a stop. The light poured out into the yard. Yellow animal eyes stared at him from a few feet away. He flipped on the porch light and the yard lights with one hand as he grabbed the doorknob with the other. A black dog sat at the edge of the sidewalk a few feet away. The animal wagged its tail.

He recognized the dog he'd seen earlier, hanging around his neighborhood.

"Hey, get on home, you. Go on!" he yelled. The dog's tail stopped wagging.

An uneasiness crept back into his mind. His heart stuttered, and the lump grew in his throat. He looked away from the animal and behind him into the house. The lights were on, and yet it still seemed...

He turned back to the dog. The hound panted in the way dogs do that made it seem like it was smiling. He didn't believe dogs knew how to smile. How can an animal with no sense of humor smile?

"Git!" He tried to shout, but the sound died in his throat and came out as a squeak. The dog stood up and trotted toward the house. He ought to shut the door. The dang animal was headed straight for him, as if he was holding the door open so it could come in. But his hand didn't push the door closed. He held the door open and let it trot by. The animal stepped around his legs and into the hall, then headed straight for the kitchen.

"Whoa, there! Where you goin'? Don't be making yourself at home in my house and peein' on everything!" He followed the dog into the kitchen.

The animal stepped around the corner and into the half-bath/laundry room. "Hey!" When he stuck his head into the room, the dog was lapping out of the toilet as if it was a water bowl.

"Hey!" he yelled again. The dog lifted its head out of the toilet and trotted right over to the jeans and work shirts that Betsy had sorted into a pile onto the floor. Then it circled around and around and around and plopped down, giving out a big sigh as it closed its eyes.

"I don't think so—!" Al said. He ought to cross the room and give the dog a kick, kick its ass all the way out the back door and into the yard. But his skin prickled again. He turned and looked past the kitchen to the dark living room.

"Betsy?" he called but his voice cracked. She wasn't here. She wasn't going to be here tonight. He had said something, done something. He was alone.

He spun around to the dog.

The black dog had settled in. Its tongue flicked out, up over one side of its muzzle, then it grunted and tucked its head into the curve of its body and sighed again.

"Hmmph," Al muttered. He flicked off the laundry room light and stepped back into the kitchen. "Guess it has water, but what'll it eat? No dog food. A bowl of cereal? Maybe some eggs?" He looked around the empty kitchen.

"Betsy'll be back tomorrow," he said to the dark living room. "She will." His voice sounded strange to his ears.

Al put his hand on the light switch and slowly pulled it down, turning the lights off. The lights he'd left on in the bedrooms softened the dark of the kitchen. In the laundry room, the rhythmic sound of the dog's breathing vibrated the silence. He walked into the laundry room, eased himself down to the floor and braced his back against the dryer. He put a hand out and laid it on the dog's chest, watching his hand move up and down with the gentle motion of the animal's breathing. He left his hand there, feeling the movement, listening to the snoring. For the first time in a long time—how long?—he felt...safe. He closed his eyes.

Chapter 11

*Saturday*

The bedroom door snapped shut, and Lynn's eyes opened.

Randy was up. Could it be that he was really going to go in and check on Ty, or Will, without being asked? She lay there, warming to the idea, but expecting any moment to hear Will or Ty call for her.

The cream swirls in the green and blue curtains glowed with the sunlight behind them. She glanced at the radio alarm clock. Six-thirty. Randy was up early for a Saturday. Lynn rolled to one side, threw her legs over the edge of the bed, and sat up. No pain. A good sign.

She stood and stepped quickly to the dresser, then pulled on a T-shirt branded with the elementary school PTA logo and a pair of black shorts.

After a fast stop in the master bath to wash her face and brush her teeth, Lynn stepped out into the hall and walked the few steps to Ty's room. Randy was helping him pull on a short-sleeved T-shirt, stretching the material up and over the cast. "How we doing, hon? Need any help?"

"Got it covered." Randy straightened Ty's shirt and then reached down for Ty's shoes. "I've got some things to take care of on campus today. Shouldn't take more than a couple of hours. You still thinking of going to the tournament with the boys?"

The muscles in Lynn's face tightened. She should have known he was up this early for a reason, and there it was. Work. On campus. Even though it was Saturday, early summer. This intersession seemed to require a lot of him—certainly more time than she remembered from previous years.

Lynn watched Randy comb Ty's hair with his fingers. "Okay," she said slowly. She wanted to remind him that when they had talked about taking Ty to see at least one of the tournament soccer matches she had meant they would go as a family. Had Randy forgotten or did he even care?

"But Daddy, the soccer tournament."

Randy's brow creased and then quickly smoothed out. "I know, son. But you need to rest. You shouldn't be out there all day long. How about making one of the semi-final matches later this afternoon? Or even the finals tomorrow?"

Ty's lip jutted out. He wasn't happy, but Lynn could tell he wasn't going to argue, or even push about this one. No doubt his arm was hurting.

"Whatever," she said. "Let's go downstairs, honey. Soon as you've eaten something, Ty, I'll get you some aspirin."

"Don't overdo it, Lynn. He can handle a little pain."

Lynn cocked her head at her husband. Words hung on the tip of her tongue, but as usual, she bit them off. She didn't want to argue, or say anything negative in front of Ty. Usually Randy was all about her taking care of the kids, down to the smallest detail. Now, suddenly he was concerned about making Ty tough?

Randy fussed over Ty's hair, touched his shoulders, then his cheek, as he peered down at him. She shrugged. "Okay. Breakfast in fifteen minutes."

Lynn left the bathroom and moved to the boys' room. Will was still in his bed, covers pulled high up around his neck. She paused a moment to look at him. Cherubic. "Will? Time for breakfast. First day of summer, you don't want to miss out, do you?" she called softly as she crossed the room. His big brown eyes flashed open.

He let out a big sigh, then closed them again.

This wasn't like her ball-of-energy boy. She leaned over him and touched his forehead. No fever. "Are you hungry?"

"Is Ty up?" Will murmured.

"Yup. He's getting dressed in the bathroom with your dad."

Will sighed again, threw off the covers, and sat up. She watched as he scooted to the side of the bed, then plopped to the floor. She pulled some clothes out of the bureau and started to help him dress. "I can do it, Mommy!" he protested.

"Okay, then." Lynn handed him the shirt and turned away. She pulled the bedclothes up and smoothed the quilt over them, then tucked it in under the pillow.

Randy lingered in the kitchen doorway, watching the kids spoon in their cereal and cram cinnamon toast into their mouths. Will, rosy cheeks, still with a baby look; Ty, pale face, sandy hair wet around his face from washing. He picked up his briefcase.

Lynn looked at him, and her eyes formed a

question.

"Lots of students are enrolled in this intersession class, and I need to get a jump start on grading the first assignment. I should be back by lunch." Randy kissed Lynn on the cheek and left the house.

\*\*\*\*

He backed the car down the driveway. She couldn't suspect anything. She was wrapped up in the boys, wrapped up in Mommy World.

Would Jennifer show up at his office this morning? Would she be angry? It could be all over. Maybe he had only imagined her attraction to him as well as her intentions with the study meeting he had missed last night.

A small ache began behind his forehead. He didn't always get the right message from women. Lynn told everyone it had taken three "accidental" meetings to get him to notice her, and another three before he asked her out. Even then he had been petrified she would say no, never realizing she'd set everything up from the beginning. In the end, he had been certain as all get out he wanted to marry her. He had wanted that above all else at the time. Eleven years ago.

He turned onto the asphalt street, glancing only briefly at the green forest of the ravine. *Looks cool down there. Gonna be a scorcher up here.*

Thirty minutes later, his breath came in short gasps as he trudged up the stairs into the faculty building. His heart had an odd rhythm to it. Jennifer. In the back of his mind hovered Ty and Will and Katy and Lynn, but up there in front Jennifer's image glowed. She made him feel so alive. So it had been with Lynn once, and he wanted it again. He sensed he was the most important thing in Jennifer's life right now. He'd seen in her eyes the unbelievable look Lynn had once given him that meant, "I WANT YOU!"

Randy unlocked his office and then pulled the door shut. He pushed his back against the closed door and breathed deeply. Yesterday's scent of Jennifer still hung in the air. How was it the clean, sweet smell lingered so long after she'd been here? The first time she had walked past him after class, the first time she had glanced up at him and smiled, the aroma had awakened him.

He crossed the room and picked up the picture of his family. They smiled out at him. His little family. He put them in the top drawer and closed it. Here, without guilt, he could think about Jennifer. He sat down in the chair and let his mind go wild.

****

Maybe Will was right. Maybe, if she had some kind of guard dog, it wouldn't be so hard to let Randy take on these extra night classes at the other campus, even with the worry of the increasing home invasions. But then, they were talking about that black dog. Black, like her dog Lucy had been, and probably smart, like Lucy had been.

She swallowed the lump in her throat. She didn't want to think about what had happened to her dog all those years ago. Just like she didn't want to think about Randy and his new workload. He seemed excited to have the chance to spend more time away from home. Away from her and the kids.

Last week, for three nights in a row, she'd gone to bed before Randy. She's been asleep when he finally slid into bed. The other four nights he'd gone to bed while she was giving the kids their baths, and was snoring softly by the time she crawled in.

He'd been too tired to have dinner with their friends Beth and Mark two weekends ago. And when their former neighbors, the Bauers, had invited them and the kids over to dinner last weekend, Randy declined; he had to grade papers.

*Randy and I are both thirty-five years old.* She felt ancient; life was moving on without her. Things were happening in the world, but all she saw was this neighborhood, this house, this family. Perhaps those things were all there was to life. She was no longer sure they were enough.

Lynn rubbed her stomach, pushing her fingers deep into the flesh. It didn't hurt when she pushed, didn't even feel sore to the touch. Instead, she was faced with fierce, unpredictable stabs of pain at the oddest times.

Lynn hurried into the living room and kicked off her shoes. She shoved the loveseat to one side and slid the DVD into the player. The electronic sounds of the game the boys were playing in the family room echoed, even in here.

She reached her arms high to stretch and then yawned. Maybe a nap would be better than exercise. It was tempting to fall into the loveseat and curl up to sleep, but it wasn't even nine o'clock in the morning. She straightened her shoulders.

And closed her eyes. Outside the school yesterday, she had wanted to turn the car the other direction, away from home. She'd wanted to run away, like she had her senior year in high school. If it wasn't for the kids… She shook her head back and forth as if she could shake the idea of running away out of her head. It wouldn't make anything better to abandon her life.

Caesar padded over to her, and she reached down to push the wiry white hair away from the terrier's brown eyes. His tongue darted out to lick her fingers, and then he sat at her feet, his long fringed tail sweeping the floor behind him.

"Okay, then. Exercise it is."

Lynn rushed over to the thermostat and flicked it down a few degrees. She intended to sweat, and maybe she could kick her mind into gear at the same time.

Exercise was a stress release, wasn't it? She touched *play* and stepped back a few feet.

On the DVD, a slim, red-haired woman, who looked like exercise was the last thing she needed, greeted her imaginary audience. "Thank you for joining me. Before we get started, I want to introduce you to someone who is working very hard to accomplish their goals. Someone who knows what it feels like to want something and to have to make sacrifices for it. I want to introduce you to—the new you."

The perky woman grinned at the camera and clapped. Lynn grimaced. Right. The new me. What is *wrong* with the old me?

From the corner of her eye, she saw something move beyond the window, out in the yard. Was it Monique? Had she come back?

She hurried over to the patio door and slid it open. "Here, dog. Nice dog. Here, dog—" Behind her, Caesar barked. She stood for a minute, watching, and then slid the door closed when the black dog didn't appear in the yard.

"Now, breathe with me and let's stretch!" the instructor said behind her, on the DVD.

Lynn gasped and doubled over as the stabbing pain sliced through her stomach.

Thirty minutes later, Lynn turned off the DVD player. She wiped the sweat off her face with the small towel, and then dabbed the back of her neck. She'd made it through the entire DVD once the pain stopped. And sweat was still pouring from her.

Cool air from the a/c vents whispered over her face and arms, but the green world outside the window, where leaves played in the wind, drew her attention. She breathed deeply, then let the air out, breathed in again and then let it out. Muscles warm from exercise, she relaxed.

Lynn stuffed the last load of laundry into the dryer, filled her glass up with ice and poured herself more raspberry tea. The phone rang. Sharon Bauer, the caller ID read. She settled in at the kitchen table.

"So, you got that alarm system in, didn't you?" Sharon asked. "There was another robbery last night, west of you about five blocks."

"The alarm system is in, and I'm still getting used to turning it on and off. I'm forever forgetting to set it when I come into the house. Five blocks, huh? That's scary."

"Yeah. And this time they pistol-whipped the husband and came close to raping the woman. Gets worse every time. I can tell you, I'm not having any trouble remembering to set my system," Sharon exclaimed. "When Ted's not here, I'm locked in like a felon in maximum security."

Lynn frowned. She wasn't even sure their alarm system was on.

"So, is Randy still going ahead with teaching at the

other campus? You tell him how you feel?"

"I've told him how I feel. He wants tenure. Thinks this is what he has to do to get it."

"You don't believe that?"

Lynn chewed her lip. *No. I don't think the extra teaching hours have anything to do with tenure.*

"Why else would he want to spend all that extra time on the road and in class?" Sharon asked.

Lynn didn't want to talk to Sharon—or to anyone—about this. If she didn't talk about it, it didn't exist, did it? "I don't know. I'll miss him, that's all."

"So find something else to do. A hobby. And don't say you don't have time. You have to make time to do the things you love. How about gardening, or tennis, or volunteering? Or a job?"

Lynn bit through the edge of one fingernail. *Who'd want me? I haven't worked since Katy came along. How could I compete? These kids today are so far ahead of me with their computer know-how, it's scary.*

"I'm saying you should think about it. Maybe Junior League would be a good thing. I know some people. I could find you a sponsor if you're interested."

Cleo padded into the kitchen and sniffed at the empty dog bowl. Then the little brown dachshund marched over to her, toenails clicking on the floor, and nosed her leg. Lynn bent down to scratch Cleo behind her ears. Across the room, Caesar leaped from his sleeping pad under the kitchen window and reached her in three bounds. The black and white terrier pushed his head under her hand. She stroked his wiry fur. The two dogs plopped down at her feet.

"No, Sharon, thanks. Hey, got to go. The pest control guy just showed up to check the termite stations. Talk to you later." The phone landed too hard in the cradle. She squeezed her eyelids closed. Hobby? No mother she knew with kids at home ever had time for a hobby. *Will's in school, I have time.*

She loved to read, especially mysteries. How long had it been since she read the current best sellers? These days, she read to the children before bed and fell asleep as soon as her head hit her own pillow. For years before the kids came along, she played the piano nearly every day. Now Katy played and she listened. Could she still read music or play the right key with the right finger?

Her brain was too full of things like robberies, stabbing pains, stray dogs and absent husbands to have anything resembling a *hobby.*

Lynn opened her eyes, and her look flew to the window. Once, another hobby had been her dog. She loved dogs, Caesar and Cleo included. Painful as the Lucy-memory was, she let it play.

Mark had thrown the Frisbee, a long, low one, and Lucy had dashed after it. The wind carried it over the grass, over the street, and into the path of a moving van. Lucy leaped and the grill of the truck caught her. It had happened right in front of their house.

Lynn let out a sob. She'd never adopted another dog. Cleo and Caesar—strays—had adopted *them.* And it looked like Monique had them pegged as her future family, too.

She moved closer to the window and scanned the yard. Where was Monique? Maybe the dog knew Katy wasn't home. Was that why she hadn't come back to the house, yet?

And Katy hadn't called from the lake. That

surprised her, too. It wasn't like Katy not to call, and especially since she would want to check on her new best friend.

A tiny seed of worry planted itself in Lynn's head.

## Chapter 12

Al could sense the room was lighter than it should have been. For a moment, he listened to the silence. The bed was hard, his pillow flat as a deflated balloon. He opened his eyes. But it wasn't his bed. He was lying on the laundry room floor. He got to his feet and stumbled into the kitchen. Where was…Betsy?

He looked around the kitchen, his mind fuzzy. He touched his face. It was there. He placed his hand on his chest. There were ribs that rose and fell as he breathed. But inside, he was a void, as if nothing existed there.

The woman had been here. He scanned the room—there was evidence of her everywhere. A single pink zinnia in a glass vase on the granite counter. A black onyx penholder, with the pen inserted, placed on the small chrome desk by the kitchen phone. Simple white towels with black edging hung from the door of the black oven.

Where had she gone? His brain throbbed as he tried to remember.

Where was the damn coffee? He jerked open the cabinet by the sink. He tried the next cabinet and the next, slamming each door when the coffee wasn't there. Where's the frigging coffee?

A cannon boomed in his head.

Al stumbled down the hallway to the bathroom. The house was too quiet. He could hear his footsteps on the carpet, his fingernails dragging along the painted walls.

He washed his face, dried it, and then leaned in toward the mirror to study the mug that stared back at him.

*Ke-rist!* He jumped when a cold something touched the back of his left knee. He shifted his weight to the ball of his foot, and jerked quickly around. The dog.

He'd forgotten about the dog.

She'd settled down to sleep on his dirty clothes pile last night. And she was still here. Damn. What kind of mess had she made? He sniffed the air, moved cautiously on his bare feet into the kitchen, and then through the den and the living room. He pulled air through his nostrils, seeking the acrid scent of dog urine or feces. Nothing. The dog padded along behind him, toenails clicking on the shiny wood floor.

He unlocked the patio door and slid it open. The dog dashed past him and out the door. He closed and locked it.

There, the dog was gone. He wouldn't let it in again. Didn't need a dog hanging around, wanting to be fed and petted and spoiled. Good riddance.

Back in the kitchen, he opened the refrigerator and took out the milk carton. He removed the lid and sniffed, paused and sniffed again. Smelled okay, but heck if he could read the expiration date. Betsy took care of that.

Where were his glasses? Betsy always brought them to him. He'd taken them off last night. Where had he been since?

He spied the red can of coffee behind where the milk had been.

Where were his damned glasses?

He barreled into the living room, pulled cushions from the black leather sofa and the recliner, ran his fingers over the black lacquer tables and the arms of the chairs. The wire rims of his glasses had a way of blending in, losing themselves against the slick, shiny black of the table or the granite counter surfaces.

*Where were they?*

He stalked from the living room to the bedroom, and then into the bathroom. No glasses. His blood surged through his veins and pounded into his temples.

"Betsy!" he bellowed. If she was here, she'd find his glasses in two shakes, hand them to him, and smile. But she wasn't here. She'd probably hidden them before she left.

The phone rang.

He stomped back to the kitchen. "Hello!"

"Albert? Richard. You working the booth today for the convention? You're late."

The cannon in his head boomed again.

"Albert?"

"Yeah, yeah. I'm here."

"You're there? You're supposed to be here, buddy. You coming in?"

"Um. Geez, my head."

"You sick? Okay, then. I'll cover it for you. You put your twenty in this week, right? See you Monday."

The dial tone buzzed in his ear.

"Fine," Al said to the quiet.

The cannon in his head blasted again.

Chapter 13

Katy's whole body shivered. Her mouth was dry and gritty, like she'd been eating mud pies with Will. Something poked at her back, and her leg hurt really bad. Her head ached so much she didn't want to open her eyes. She tried to shift her position.

"Oh!" That hurt worse than anything, ever. Worse than going to the dentist. Worse than a shot or falling off her bicycle. "Mom?" Her voice came out in a squeak.

She held still, afraid to try to move again. "Mommy?"

Katy opened her eyes. Above her and all around, bathed in the odd gray light of early morning, the world was green. Her mind was empty of the memory of how she had come to be here. It was too hard to think with the pain. The green all around, above, beside, could only be the forest. She pushed back into her mind. She'd been walking home from Emily's in the dark. She'd heard Monique barking. She'd turned down the path into the ravine and called the dog's name.

She tried to move again. The pain—it was her leg—hurt so bad!

"Caw, caw, caw."

A crow peered down with black eyes, cocked his head, and hopped a few inches farther down the low branch, only a few feet above her. Crickets and grasshoppers chirped in the bushes.

Katy forced her eyes open. Tall skinny trees with dark bark and green-white patches of moss grew everywhere. Somewhere, water gurgled. Off in the distance, a dog barked. The crow flapped its way to another tree and cawed again. The damp coolness beneath her crept through the thin fabric of her pajamas. The back of her neck itched.

"Help!" She tried out her voice, but it sounded more like a croak than a word. Dryness had shriveled her throat, and her tongue had ballooned to fill it like a wadded up dry rag.

How far away was that water? Katy moved her head. Leaves rustled beneath her. She reached her left arm over the ground and touched an edge. She stretched her fingers a few centimeters farther. Empty air. The stream bank? If she rolled over, could she reach the water? She used both arms to lift herself up so she could see over the edge.

The ground dropped away. No telling how far. How could she ever get down there? The pain in her leg hurt so bad. And her head felt like a giant sewing needle had been jammed into it. She closed her eyes and dropped herself back down onto the wet earth.

She screamed with the awful pain and tears squirted from her eyes as she gasped for breath. What was wrong with her leg?

Katy had to look at her leg, had to see why it hurt so badly. She used her forearms to lift herself up again and looked toward her feet. The legs of her pajama bottom were splotched with dirt and ripped. Oh, Mom would be so mad that she'd ruined these pants. They were brand new, first time she'd ever worn them.

Her right leg—the one that hurt so bad—was folded under her. It looked funny, and there was something—a branch?—sticking out of it. If she could unfold it, maybe the pain would go away. Once again, she tried to shift.

She screamed with the incredible, terrible pain and began to cry.

"Help me! Help, help, help, somebody!" she moaned.

She tried again, louder. "Help! Please! Somebody? Mommy? Daddy!"

The woods all around her were silent. The birds and squirrels were listening to her, but was anybody else?

She called out again, but her cry faded into a sob.

Then, something crashed through the underbrush at the top of the ravine, far above her.

"Help! I'm here. I can't move. Please help me!" She twisted her upper body, trying to see above her, to the top of the ravine.

The bushes jerked. Something was coming down. She couldn't see it. The shadows were so dark, and it was moving through the black patches toward her.

Her heart pattered. What if it was a big mean dog? Or a coyote? Katy tensed and shut her eyes. She lay still.

"Help me, dear Jesus. Please send an angel to help me. Please, Jesus!" Oh, she needed help. She reached out, feeling around her for Cuddle Bunny. Where was it? She'd had it last night, at Em's. She remembered she'd made Cuddle Bunny wave good-bye to Em before she headed up the street, at the start of her two hundred and fifty steps. "Cuddle Bunny? Where are you?"

The bushes above her crackled as something pushed its way down the slope. Katy shivered. She closed her eyes. If she was going to be eaten, let her die with the first bite.

The woods were silent.

Something cold touched her face.

Chapter 14

Mick Jordan's eyelids popped open. His heart fluttered, but he wasn't short of breath like he would have been if he'd really been running with the dog, laughing in the sunshine like he'd been dreaming. He wasn't sure how many years it was since he'd been able to run. Still, it had been a good dream. A good dream of a good day outside with the dog, running home to Josey-Jo.

The beeping noise nipped at his mind, urged him to open his eyes. When he did, he saw he was stretched out on some hard recliner with plastic upholstery, still wearing his clothes, a white thermal blanket draped across him. He looked around. The long, blue fluorescent bulb on the wall illuminated Jo in the bed. One tube snaked into her arm from a plastic bag suspended on a metal stand. He supposed the nearby monitor machine—the beeping he'd heard—was measuring blood pressure, maybe heart rate. The faint scent of disinfectant tickled at his nose.

Jo lay bluish-white there on the bed, nearly the same color as the pillowcase on the flat hospital pillow. He averted his eyes, not wanting to see the oxygen tube running up her nose or the hospital paraphernalia arranged meticulously on the tray table near the bed, on the side closest to the window.

Someone was stretched out in another reclining

chair, covered with a blanket twin to his own. Not Annie. Who? Long dark hair. He remembered. Thank God for Betsy, who had come a-running when he had hollered, and had known how to do CPR. She'd kept Josephine alive until the ambulance got to their house.

"Betsy?" he asked softly.

Instantly, she sat up. "Mr. Mick? You okay? How's Miss Jo?" Betsy threw off the blanket and vaulted out of the chair, leaving it stretched out in the reclining position. Mick sat up and slowly brought his recliner into chair position, then stood. He stepped toward the bed, reached out, and smoothed the blanket over Josephine's feet.

"She's asleep. The monitor's beeping, so she's alive. Thank God—and you—for that."

"She very lucky. She have heart attack, and you right there to help. I'm glad you call for me. Anything you and Miss Jo need, I help."

Mick scratched his head and tried to remember last night. It was a blur, from the time he heard the thump until the minute he woke up. Vaguely, he remembered the emergency flasher, and an image of Betsy, bent over Josephine, giving mouth-to-mouth resuscitation.

"Did you call Al last night? He'll be worried," Mick said.

Betsy lifted her chin and reached out to touch Jo's right hand where it lay on top of the thin blanket. "He no worry. I tell him I leave him."

He remembered something had been going on out in the yard last night. Not all the words had carried across to him on the wind. But he knew, from the way the Asian woman had waved her arms and then dropped to the ground, she and Al had had an argument.

"Oh, Al, he's got a short fuse. This morning he's probably regretting his words," Mick said soothingly.

Betsy shook her head back and forth. "I no stay there, with him, any more. Maybe someone else be better. Al not take medicine. Not right…I help you and Jo. Stay until she better." She paused and looked at him. "If you want."

Mick stared. "You'll stay here? At the hospital, with Jo? Don't you have to go to work somewhere?"

"Somebody need to stay here. You too tired. I stay, watch over her. I have days off. When she come home, I come with her. If you want me, Mr. Mick. I will care for her until she up and around. I care for my grandmother in Thailand. I care for…many people. This easy job for me." Betsy smiled, and her eyes nearly disappeared under the folds of her eyelids.

Mick frowned. He wasn't sure about relying on this woman whom he barely knew. But Josephine had always liked her. "You work as a nurse, Betsy? Is that what you do?"

She nodded, then picked up a white washcloth from near the room's small sink, wet it, wrung it out, and wiped it across Jo's brow. She wet it again and swabbed at Jo's lips. "I know what to do." Then she turned to Jo and leaned close to her right ear. "Miss Jo. Betsy here. I take care of you. Mr. Mick, he right here, too. You rest, now, Missy Jo." Betsy slowly swabbed Jo's face and then laid the cloth on the bed tray. "I nurse for long time. Before Al. In Thailand."

Mick peered at the woman, trying to read the expression on her face, but the shadows were too deep. A nurse in Thailand? She didn't look old enough to have been a nurse when Al was in the service. Al had never talked to him about her. If she was a nurse, what else mattered? Jo needed her help. And he did, too. "Betsy, I would expect to pay you."

Betsy shook her head again, her eyes closed. "I happy to help, Mr. Mick. For little while, it okay. No pay."

Mick patted Jo's feet again, then turned and sat in the recliner. He'd gotten little sleep last night, and his back and legs were aching and stiff. He rubbed at his neck, a crick had set in. His eyelids were heavy.

A middle-aged nurse, black hair cut close to her head, bustled into the room. Her thick thighs, covered in checkered scrubs, rubbed against each other and made a swishing sound as she walked. "Good morning. How are we today?"

Mick grunted. How did she think they were, anyway? His wife of nearly sixty years was unconscious after suffering a heart attack.

The nurse picked up Jo's hand, curled her fingers around Jo's thin wrist, and kept an eye on her watch as she timed Jo's pulse, then checked the monitor. She pulled out a gadget, inserted one end into Jo's ear canal and waited a few seconds until the instrument beeped. She wrote something down on Jo's medical chart. "Anyone need breakfast in here? We serve to family members of patients. You family?" The nurse raised her eyebrows at Betsy, and then looked over at Mick.

He nodded. "Yes, close at it gets. Like a daughter."

Family. He'd forgotten to call the kids last night. Been in a fog. Jo would recover, wouldn't she? With Betsy living with them, taking care of Jo, everything would be fine in no time, wouldn't it? Still, he had to call Annie and Matthew, even Marilyn and the kids.

They needed to know what had happened to Jo.

The nurse's head jerked in a nod. "Good enough. Eggs, toast, jelly, bacon. Work for you?"

He hadn't thought he was hungry, but when she said the words, his stomach rumbled. He glanced over at Jo in the bed.

It was the first time in so many years he wasn't having breakfast with Jo. Even when he'd been in the hospital for back and knee surgeries, Jo had always come to eat with him, or to keep him company. He wished she would open her eyes. He needed to know she was still inside her body, still Josephine.

"I'll let the floor nurse know. They'll bring breakfast in within the half hour. Coffee, tea, me?" The nurse laughed.

Mick didn't feel like laughing, but Betsy smiled. Did she understand the nurse had made a joke? Asians seemed to smile and nod at everything, funny or not.

"We eat, see the doctor. Then you go home to rest," Betsy said.

It sounded like a good plan. He had no strength for arguing. In fact, he might just lean back in the chair again until breakfast arrived. The room swam around him, and his arm throbbed. He supposed he had slept on it wrong last night.

After he got home, he'd call the kids and let them know what had happened.

Breakfast came thirty minutes later. He and Betsy ate in silence, and then he balled his napkin up and pushed the rolling tray table away. Mick stepped over to the bed. "Josephine? Jo, I need you to wake up. We gotta talk about some things. Come on." Mick stood by the edge of the bed and stared down at his wife.

He reached out one hand to touch the filmy-thin skin on her forehead. He could see the blue blood vessels there, under the surface. She looked like a doll made of rice paper that would crumple with a single hug. "Jo? Are you going to wake up?"

He had always believed he would be the one to falter first. He was the one with the bad back, the bad knees, the high blood pressure. Jo was the one who golfed every day, weeded the flowerbeds, cooked the meals, and still managed to clean house. This couldn't be real. It couldn't be Jo lying there.

He reached out again, but this time he let his finger trail down over her face, down her neck to her shoulder, and then down to where the IV invaded her vein. "Oh, Jo, Josey-Jo."

He had not planned for this. He thought he'd planned out what to do in every scenario. He had their money budgeted and invested, planned for retirement and planned trips they had yet to take. But he hadn't planned for his wife to be lying unconscious in a hospital bed.

"Mr. Mick? We should go home, you need rest." Betsy's voice came at him from the doorway. "We come back late afternoon. They call if something change. Miss Jo, she sleep now. She know you need rest. Come with me, Mr. Mick."

Mick looked at Betsy, hooded eyelids, smooth complexion, long black hair. She must be about the same age as their Annie. She was kind, and Annie was often too preoccupied with herself to be kind to others. If she were here, would she be as kind as Betsy?

Startled, he remembered again that neither Annie nor Matthew knew their mother was lying here in the hospital, hooked up to tubes and wires. He needed to get home to call them. Would they come to be with him, come to hold their mother's hand even though she was unconscious? If they did, there would be no need for Betsy to stay with him, although she had very kindly offered. His mind started to work through it, to determine if the kind of love his children held for their mother was great enough to bring them here from a distance, if they would see this crisis in Jo's life as surpassing the perceived difficulties in their lives which kept them anchored to cities far away. He wasn't sure of the answer. What did that mean, not to be sure of his own children?

"Mr. Mick?"

He pulled easily away from those thoughts. "Yes. You're right, Betsy. We should go home." He glanced over at his wife. "I want her to wake up. I don't understand why she's not waking up. Will she...ever...wake up?"

"They run MRI and other tests today. Miss Jo will go to labs soon. We should get out of way. Ready?"

He nodded, raked his hand across the circle on the top of his head where his scalp was balding, and murmured a low "Be back later, Josey" before he followed Betsy out of the room and down the corridor. Then he stopped. "Betsy, will we call a taxi?"

The woman reached out and took his hand. "I drive your car last night, Mr. Mick. 'Member? You ride in ambulance with Miss Jo. I drive your car behind. We drive home now, in your car."

Of course, that's what had happened. The night was a blur. His mind chewed on the lost hours. He'd been at the windows, searching the deepening shadows, thinking of the black dog. Jo had been alone in the den, having her attack for heaven-knows-how-long. Hurting. Unimaginable pain, probably. Would she die because he was piddling at the window, thinking of the dog?

Chapter 15

Katy's eyes jerked open. Large yellow-brown eyes stared into her face.

"Monique," she whispered. She slid her arms around the dog's sleek neck.

The dog licked her cheek, and then sniffed her. Slowly, she backed out of Katy's grasp and sniffed all the way down to her toes. She sniffed an extra-long time at her leg, where the constant pain roared.

"Oh, Monique, it hurts so bad, all the time." She worked her fingers through the dog's coat, feeling her warmth. "Will it go away if I imagine something else, like I do when I'm at the dentist's?" She squeezed her eyes shut. "I'm thinking about the lake, and swimming with Em." She chewed at her lip. "It's helping a little."

The dog scooted closer.

"Thank you. Oh, thank you." She hugged Monique around the neck again. The animal sat close to her, so warm. Katy let her body relax into the dog, and Monique braced her legs and took her weight, eventually lowering her body so that Katy used her like a pillow.

"I don't know what happened," she told the dog. "I remember yesterday, when you first came and I saw you. I remember piano lessons and coming home so Dad could meet you."

She pinched her eyes shut. Last night. At Em's.

Then, starting up the hill—and the barking dog.

"Was that you, Monique? Were you out in the forest last night? Did you hear the coyotes?"

The dog whined, lifted her head. As Katy's body shifted, pain zapped her. Katy groaned. Monique lay back down.

"I knew you'd come." She shifted, resting her head against the dog's belly. The animal breathed beneath her, lifting her up and down. Her body was…floating. On a cloud. Up in the blue sky. Safe.

Her mind floated, too, and she imagined Mom, calling from where she stood by the kitchen sink.

"Katy—did you find your bag? It's by the front door, all ready to go. Emily's mom will be here soon to take you out for pizza."

Katy remembered stepping up next to her mother and patting her hand. She had told her what she had decided. "I'm not going to go to the lake with Emily. Monique has just come to live with us, and I think it would be better if I stayed home."

"Oh, I don't want you to do that, Katy," Mom said. "I know how much you love going to the lake with Emily. I've already packed overnight things in your backpack and put Cuddle Bunny beside it."

"But Mom, this is Monique's first night. What if she gets lonely?"

"You think there's any chance of that with Ty and Will? She'll be fine. And she'll be here when you get back on Sunday. Get your bag. They'll be here any second."

Mom had that tone in her voice. No matter what Katy said, her mother would not change her mind.

She had trudged down the hall toward the front

door. Behind her, in the den, she could hear the boys laughing. Will and Ty were playing with Moe.

Katy had chewed at her lip. Outside, a car horn honked. She picked up her backpack and tucked Cuddle Bunny under her arm. "Bye Mom, bye Dad, bye Monique."

She had pulled the door closed behind her and walked out to Emily's mother's red Toyota 4-Runner.

****

Deep in the ravine, Katy groaned as the dog shifted. Katy adjusted her body, pushing herself up close against the warm, black fur. She fell into an uneasy sleep but didn't notice when, an hour later, the warmth beside her disappeared.

Chapter 16

Randy Werling locked his office, then ambled down the hall. He tried to look normal, although he felt anything but. All morning he'd waited for the knock on the door or for the phone to ring.

No word yet today from Jennifer. In his office, he worked half-heartedly on a paper for publication. He probably wouldn't see Jennifer again until Tuesday's scheduled test.

As he walked down the hall to the building's vending machine for more coffee, he caught a whiff of Jennifer's perfume. He whirled. Two co-eds giggled as they stood whispering with heads close together. Neither looked at him.

Two hours later, on the sidewalk in front of his classroom building, he stopped. He'd told Lynn he would be home by lunch, but he didn't want to go home. If he stayed here, there was a chance—albeit a slim one—Jennifer might show up. At home, the least he could hope for was a phone call on his cell.

After a group of students rushed past, he followed them toward the Student Union. His stomach growled, and he pictured the Taco Hut concession in the main eating area. It wouldn't help to eat; this gnawing in his stomach was not food hunger.

He forced himself to eat half of a fajita chicken salad and to drink a glass of ice tea, but the food didn't erase the hollow feeling. Randy closed his eyes and rubbed his fingers over his eyelids, pushing slightly. He remembered the family picture. He'd pulled it out from the upper drawer of his desk twice that morning, then returned it. The boys looked mischievous, Katy wiser than her years. Lynn smiled in her secretive, Mona Lisa way.

Randy opened his eyes and scanned the tables. Jennifer wasn't seated at any of them. Wasn't in one of the lines, wasn't standing in a group with friends. What would he have done if she was?

She made him feel alive in a lustful way, in an "absence of responsibility" way. Somebody loved him, wanted him, but didn't need him to take care of children, or make money, or fulfill any need.

What if he had imagined that look in Jennifer's eyes?

Randy carried his tray to the return area, threw away the trash, and stacked the tray.

The cell phone in his jacket pocket buzzed against his upper thigh. He jerked the phone out of his pocket and checked the caller ID. Home. Lynn?

"Hello." His voice came out soft.

"Randy? I thought you'd be home by lunchtime?" Lynn's voice sounded strained, breathless.

"Um, well, I got tied up here. Had something to eat at the Union. Is something wrong?"

"I don't think I'll be able to take Ty and Will to watch the tournament. I'm having this stomach pain, and—" She gasped.

"Lynn?" He waited for her to continue. "Lynn, are you okay?"

"I—d-don't—know."

The words came out in between gasps.

He started down the hall at a fast jog, exited the building, and then raced along the sidewalk to the parking lot. "Did you call the doctor? Do you need to go to the E.R.?" His brain shifted to memories of last night, the hours spent at the hospital with Ty. And now Lynn? She had never gone to the E.R. for anything, and only to the hospital for giving birth to their children. Both Ty and Lynn within two days?

"I've got a call into the doctor. I'm sure she'll call back. Soon."

Randy glanced at his watch. "I'm on my way home. Call me on my cell after you've talked to the doctor."

He was moving so fast that he barely registered the young blonde woman who stood in the shade of a tree not far from his car.

\*\*\*\*

"No, stay in bed," Randy said to Lynn. She looked so white; pain pinched the skin around her mouth. "I can take care of Will. He's complaining a little, and I think it's because he played too hard with the black dog and ate too many cookies when you weren't looking."

Lynn grabbed at her stomach, pulled her knees up to her chest, and groaned.

"Has to be gallbladder. Didn't the doctor think so?" Randy asked.

"Yeah. But that pill's not working."

"It will. Give it a little time. Rest."

Randy closed the bedroom door and stood outside in the hallway. Gallbladder. That wasn't such a big deal, was it?

He walked slowly down the hall to the stairs.

"Dad, where's Moe? Did you see her when you came home?" Ty asked from the sofa in the family room.

Randy reached the bottom of the steps. "No, Ty. I didn't see her around the house after I drove to the drugstore for your mom, either. Don't know where she is."

He wasn't sure if it was good or bad the dog had not yet appeared.

How should he handle this thing about the dog? Katy and the boys were determined to keep the animal. They insisted he and Lynn had already given their approval. He didn't want to argue. It was a battle he wanted to win, but at what price?

The best thing would be if the dog didn't come back. Then, no decision would have to be made, the animal would make it for them. Maybe it had understood him when he told it to go home last night. He scooped some ice out of the icemaker tray and into a glass, filled it with tap water.

After he'd come to bed last night, Lynn had told him Katy had wanted to back out of going to Emily's and then on to the lake because of the dog. She'd be upset when the dog wasn't here on Sunday afternoon. She'd probably think it was her fault and feel guilty she'd gone away with Emily.

Behind him, Will groaned. "Daddy?"

Will was holding his stomach. His eyes were huge and his face greenish-white.

He's going to hurl, Randy thought. He started to grab for the trashcan under the kitchen sink, but vomit shot out of Will's mouth and all over the tile floor. Then the leftovers dribbled down Will's chin and onto his shirt.

"Oh, crap, Will!"

Tears streamed down Will's face; he gasped for air between retches. Randy grabbed him up and dashed for the bathroom.

Will crouched in front of the commode while Randy wet a washcloth. He wiped his son's face and mouth. The retching subsided. Will groaned.

"Okay, upstairs with you." He picked Will up and climbed the stairs. Will clutched his neck and pressed his head against his collarbone. Randy carried him to the bedroom Will shared with Ty, then over to his twin bed. He pulled back the quilt and the sheets and tucked Will in.

There, that wasn't so bad. But what next? Should he ask Lynn what he should do? There was something good about a cool damp washcloth, wasn't there? He'd seen Lynn do it a dozen times.

As Randy stepped out of the room, he turned to look at his son. That very second, Will threw up all over the bed.

"Randy? Is Will sick?" Lynn called from their bedroom doorway down the hall.

"Yep. I'll take care of it." Inside the boys' bedroom, he gagged from the smell of vomit. Will looked up, his eyes dark holes in a green face. Randy braced himself, tried to breathe through his mouth and not his nose, and then crossed the room. "Do you think you're done?"

Will moaned and doubled over, holding his stomach with both hands. Randy picked him up and carried him across the hall to the bathroom. "Okay. Lie down right here on the bathroom rug. I'll pull the yucky sheets off your bed and get your pajamas. Be right back, kiddo."

When he turned to leave the bathroom, Ty stood in the doorway, feet wide apart, hands on his hips. "Is he puking? I'm not sleeping in there with him. No way."

Randy couldn't argue—he wasn't sure he would want to sleep in there, either.

He braced himself for the odor when he re-entered his sons' room. Randy stripped the vomit-spattered sheets and blanket off the bed, wadded them up and carried them to the top of the stairs. He took Will a fresh pair of pajamas, grabbed a can of disinfectant spray from the closet, and then went back to the bedroom. The mess had been contained on the bed. Lucky. He felt a little queasy himself.

In the bathroom, Will vomited again. Randy covered his mouth and nose with one hand, then squatted behind his son and stroked his forehead. He swabbed Will's face with the damp washcloth.

"It'll be over soon, champ. Get it all out. Sorry you feel so bad."

Tears streamed down Will's face.

Finally, the boy pushed away from the commode and turned in his arms.

Randy flushed the toilet for the fifth time and then picked up the boy and set him on the tile counter next to the sink. He pulled a paper cup from the dispenser, filled it with water and handed it to Will. "Rinse."

Randy swabbed his son's face with the cloth again. The green tint had left Will's skin; he looked exhausted and feverish.

Randy carried him down the hall to the master bedroom. Lynn sat up.

"I think it's over," Randy said.

"Bring him here. He can snuggle with me while you remake his bed." Lynn smiled sweetly and opened her arms for Will. Randy handed his son over, then headed for the linen closet.

Downstairs, his cell phone rang. He stopped in the doorway to the boys' room to toss the clean, checkered blue and white sheets across the room at the bare twin bed. Then he dashed down the hallway and took the stairs two at a time. The ringing stopped.

He grabbed up the phone. The caller ID listed Jennifer's number. He punched a button to call her back and got her voice mail.

Damn. He closed his eyes. Jennifer. *Where are you? What are you doing?* Only hours ago, he'd smelled her scent. Remembering, he inhaled deeply. Now, all he could smell was the faint stench of Will's vomit. His shirt was spotted with it.

"Can I go outside and look for Moe?" Ty had his hand on the back door knob. "She hasn't been around all day. And I'm going to sleep down here tonight, on the sofa. I'm not sleeping with Pukey in the same room. No way."

Randy carried his cell phone as he walked outside with Ty. He'd call Jennifer back as soon as Ty and the dog were racing around the yard.

"Moe! Here, girl," Ty called. "Moe!"

Several seconds later, a streak of black dashed toward the house from the forest, barking, yapping, running in crazy circles. Randy grabbed his son's arm.

"Whoa. Wait a minute. Something's wrong with her."

The black dog ran right up to them, stood only a

few yards away, and barked furiously.

"Nothing's wrong. She wants to play." Ty struggled to break Randy's hold. The dog barked, then darted across the yard. She stopped and loped back, still barking. She raced in circles.

"She wants me to chase her!" Ty insisted.

Randy wasn't sure. The dog seemed different. Intense. Not like she wanted to play, but something else. He'd never seen a dog act quite like this.

"I'm not sure about that, Ty. She's not right. Why don't we go inside?"

He guided Ty into the house, watching over his shoulder to make sure the dog didn't race in when they opened the door. She stood feet from the back deck, whining, watching them, looking over her shoulder and then at them. The dog yipped.

In the house, Randy watched from the window as the dog barked, sat down, yipped and whined, stood up, circled, and barked some more. Something was wrong with her. There was no spit drooling from her mouth, but she was acting crazy enough to be rabid. No need to take chances.

He pulled the drapes and covered the window. The television came on in the family room as Ty settled in on the floor with his enormous bear TV pillow. Randy laid the cell phone down on the island in the kitchen and climbed the stairs. Will's bed had to be made.

His callback to Jennifer would have to wait.

His crotch tightened as blood pumped through his nether regions. She had called. Jennifer wasn't angry at him. She would still visit his office and come to his class next week, even after he had stood her up with no explanation.

Randy shook his head as he climbed the stairs. A new feeling fluttered in his stomach. He didn't want it to go away.

Thing was, right this minute he had to deal with Will's vomiting and Lynn's stomach pain. He hoped the worst of it was over; he wasn't sure he could handle the horrible smell if the boy kept throwing up.

And Lynn's stomach. He'd never seen her in such pain—not even when she had gone into labor with any of their three children. This pain today had gotten so bad, so fast, it was hard to imagine. Wouldn't she have told him if the pain had bothered her before?

Chapter 17

At home in his living room, Mick closed his eyes and tried to focus on the frantic voice of his daughter, Annie, his eldest child. "I don't know. The doctors haven't said. Yes, I'm home for a little rest. I'll go back with Betsy, my neighbor. Remember? She's going to help your mother and me get through this."

The pitch of Annie's voice had gone up. Of course he realized he was expecting a lot from her on the spur of the moment. Yes, he knew she had a family and other obligations and couldn't drop everything.

"No. The doctors don't know when she'll wake up." He said the words and one part of his brain was screaming, *she may never wake up.* He swallowed and tried to concentrate. His shaking hand rubbed his right eyebrow.

"No. I don't know if she will know you are there." His voice cracked. He cleared his throat, then took a deep breath.

As if through a tunnel, he heard Annie ask, "She's not going to die, is she, Dad?"

One possible answer screamed through his brain.

He coaxed out the words. "It will depend if she has another heart attack, but so far, so good." A huge lump blocked his throat. Blood rushed to his face, burned. Damn it. Why had this happened? How could Jo have let this happen?

"Dad, I can make some calls, arrange for John to keep the kids so I can fly home. It's expensive, though, with no advance purchase. I want to come, it's just that if she's going to wake up and be fine tomorrow…"

"If it's the money, Annie, I'll pay for your ticket," he said. She knew he wanted her to come, her mother would want her to come. Lord, it had been six months since her last visit, and the pair of them were getting more and more decrepit every day. Who knew when it would be the last sunrise for either of them? *What if Jo had already seen her last sunrise?*

"I'll get back to you. Wish you had a cell phone. How can I reach you at the hospital?" Annie sounded irritated.

"Call the main St. John's number, and they'll transfer you. If I'm not in her room, I'm here or somewhere in between."

Gently, he replaced the receiver. Next, a call to Matthew. No time to think about it. He planted his feet, as if a punch would come through the phone line and knock him for a loop.

The phone rang and rang at his son's home, and then the answering machine picked up. Mick didn't leave a message.

Best Mick knew, his son still saw his kids regularly, and someone—Marilyn?—made sure that they called their grandparents each month and sent emails with pictures. Marilyn would know how to reach Matthew. They were only divorced, not completely out of touch. He dialed the phone number that had been his son's for ten years, until the separation a year ago.

His granddaughter, Lacie, answered the phone. "Hi, Grandpa. What's up?"

"Hi, sweetie. Is your mom home, or would your dad happen to be there?"

"Mom's here."

The phone clattered as Lacie dropped it onto the table. "Mom!" she yelled. "It's Grandpa Mick."

Seconds later, his former daughter-in-law picked up the phone. "Mickey? You all right?"

"It's Josephine, Marilyn. She's had a heart attack." He heard the gasp on the other end of the phone. "She's in the hospital. There's no answer at Matthew's house. You know how I can reach him?"

"He doesn't have a cell phone anymore. Short of asking the highway patrol to watch for his car in the tri-state area, we'll have to wait until tomorrow. He calls the kids on Sunday evenings."

Maybe Josephine would be awake by then. She'd be awake, and maybe in the rehab unit, like Betsy had said. "We have to wait for him to call?"

"I'll leave a message on his home phone. Ask him to call you. Tell him it's urgent. Maybe he'll check messages before Sunday night."

"Thanks for your help."

"Mickey, should I bring the kids?"

Marilyn didn't ask the question Annie had dared to ask. Instead, it hung in the air above the phone like an invisible dirigible. "Let's wait till she wakes up. I'll tell her that you want to bring them. If she hears that, even unconscious, it will warm her heart."

"We'll pray for her, Mickey. And for you, too. Let me know how she's doing."

Mick hung up the phone. Betsy's father had been in a rehab unit once. When Betsy had told Mick about it this morning, it had calmed his worries, given him some idea what to expect when Josephine woke up. Now she had to wake up.

In the living room, Betsy watched the bald psychologist with the TV talk show. Darn if he could ever remember his name.

Betsy smiled and patted a spot on the sofa beside her. "You sit down, Mr. Mick. Rest eyes. We go back to hospital soon. Catch doctor when he go round. Get report. Rest, okay?"

He nodded, but instead of sitting down beside her, he crossed the room to his humidor and scooped tobacco into his pipe. Somehow, even with shaking hands, he managed to tamp the tobacco into the bowl without spilling too much onto the carpet beneath the end table. He looked out the window, eyes blurred with moisture. What was that out there? The dog?

Mick shuffled to the patio door, slid it open, and stepped outside. He scanned the yard, but nothing moved except for a bird flitting from tree to tree, squirrels high in the branches, and something—a rabbit?—under the bushes back by his property line. He hoped Angel, the rabbit, hadn't escaped its cage at the Werlings again. If so, it was a goner. That red-tailed hawk had been soaring around the last few days, and Angel was probably still small enough the big bird could carry her off.

Mick sank down into a chair, pulled his lighter from his pocket, and huffed at the pipe until the fire caught and a whiff of fragrant smoke curled up around his head. He pulled the pipe from his mouth and cleared his throat.

"Here, girl, come here," he called. What was it Katy had said she'd named the animal? The name had left his mind. Rustling leaves drew his attention to the forested lot on the side of the house and as he looked, the black dog burst through the undergrowth.

The dog raced over, panting. She ran right up to him and pushed her muzzle against his leg. He stroked her skull and scratched at her ears as she whined. The animal was quivering.

"You miss Katy already? She's at the lake, but she'll be back tomorrow to play with you." Mick rubbed the dog's head, and the dog looked up at him, still and silent. Their eyes met and locked. She whined low, like an idling engine. "I wonder when Jo will be back. If she'll be back." The dog pushed closer and laid her muzzle on his leg. Mick's heartbeat slowed, the muscles in his neck relaxed. He let out a long breath. "I hope everything's going to be all right. I don't know anymore." A sob caught in his throat.

The dog pressed even closer and halfway closed her eyes as he rubbed at her ears. "You know Jo had a heart attack? Last night—and I was thinking about you. Wondering what you were doing, where you came from. I should have been in there with Jo."

The dog let her breath out in a huff, as if she'd been holding it in. Mick wasn't sure dogs ever did that. At least no dog he'd ever known.

"Oh, I know, there isn't any way I could have known what was happening. But I haven't had the kindest thoughts lately, and I'm not proud of it."

The dog tilted her head, leaned into his fingers as they probed at her ears.

Then, she jerked her head up and glanced over her shoulder, toward the forest and the ravine beyond.

"I know it's all got to change, girl. I'm old, Jo's

old. But hell, this is hard to accept. I was young just yesterday, you know?"

The dog whined and peered at him.

"I'd swear you understand what I'm saying."

The patio door rolled open on its track.

"Mr. Mick? Telephone." Betsy stepped quickly to his chair and handed him the wireless receiver.

He stiffened and his mind raced. Was it the hospital? Another attack? He scooted to the edge of the chair; his heart beat faster. "Hello?"

"Pop? Is Mom okay? I'm coming home."

Tears sprang to Mick's eyes, and a lump manifested in his throat. "That'd be good, Matthew. Real good." His eyelids pinched closed. Overwhelmed and relieved, he bowed his head.

Mick reached his hand out to scratch behind the dog's ears, but he groped empty space. She was gone.

When he and Matthew finished talking, Mick punched off the phone and sat back in the padded patio chair. His mind replayed the last time he'd seen his son. August, was it? After Jo's home-cooked dinner. Matthew announced that he and Marilyn had separated. Mick had said things he regretted—accusing things.

He remembered the look on Jo's white face as she stood in the doorway to the kitchen, her hands reaching first toward him and then toward Matthew as she implored the two of them to stop yelling, to calm down and talk like grown-ups. He knew he'd been too harsh, and he knew Matthew would remember those words. One didn't forget that sort of thing. Word for word he could recall things his own father had shouted at him as a young man—and more than fifty years had passed since those days.

"Matthew's coming home, Josey," Mick said, looking up at the sky, transmitting the words through space to where his wife lay in the hospital bed. "You'll see him soon. Everything's going to be all right. It is."

Chapter 18

Light reflected off a car windshield as a pickup truck turned the corner. It flashed into Al's eyes as he sat at the table on the side patio. His hand moved to the top of his head where coarse hairs spiked.

Not needed at work today. He ought to be doing *something*. Uneasiness started deep in his groin and inched its way up to his throat. What was it he had done before the parking lot days? He blinked, searched his memory. Damn strange. Some days he was a man without a past. Then, next day or next hour, it all came rushing back. He shook his head. Sixty years old, and losing it. Getting old was hell. Especially for a soldier. He studied the fruit bowl he had brought outside and selected an orange. Not much in the house that didn't need cooking, but the fruit was good. He thrust his thumbnail into the spongy peel and began to strip the orange.

The black dog seemed to appear from thin air beside the chair.

"Where you been all morning?"

The dog lifted a paw and put it on his knee.

"Shake hands?" He reached for her paw. She pulled it away, then placed it on his knee again. She whined, then yipped. "I don't speak dog. Don't know what you want."

Some sound—unidentifiable—scratched behind

him. Inside the house. "Betsy? Did you sneak in here, woman?"

Silence. Al rose from the chair and slithered through the house. He stopped at each doorway to survey each room. He pulled together his observation skills, looked for some change that would tell him something was different, someone else had been here. Because someone else HAD been here—the placement of the air was different, like something was missing or rearranged.

"Betsy?" he called again, softer.

He checked all the rooms, then traipsed back to the rear patio door.

His eyes came into focus. The dog was gone. He scanned the back yard for her, but instead of the dog, he saw that some of the fescue had grown to five inches tall, especially around the flowerbeds where it got lots of water from both the spring rains and Betsy's nightly watering. His lawn looked like crap next to the flowers Jo and Betsy had planted. Blooms stood tall red, purple, and yellow in a central flowerbed.

In the yard behind his, where Jim and Gwen Lopez lived, he caught a glimpse of movement. Was that where the dog had gone? He remembered the couple had left last week, gone on vacation, but hell if he could remember where they'd gone or when they'd be back. He'd learned that bit of news from Betsy; she'd talked to Gwen in the back yard before they'd left town. She should have kept her mouth shut. Her reward had been to be asked to keep an eye out for things at their place. But she wasn't here to do it. Damn if he'd step in to help with that chore.

Had that movement been the dog? One minute she

was whining—next she was gone. She'd eaten well enough last night, but was no doubt hungry again. He stuck two fingers into his mouth and whistled. He didn't really like the dog, but...He'd had his first good night's sleep in months. Years. And no nightmares.

"Here, dog!"

She didn't come. Something caught in his throat. He jabbed at his eyes. Pussy. He didn't need a damned dog. What was he crying about?

A flash of color beyond the arborvitae hedge drew his gaze. There was Mick on his own patio staring up into the sky with his mouth open as if a UFO was hovering over the back yard. Mick leaned on his cane, and his mouth moved as if he was talking to someone.

Betsy stepped out onto Mick's patio.

Al's breath swooshed out. He hopped back to the shadowy doorway.

His wife patted Mick's shoulder, then hooked her arm through Mick's and helped him maneuver across the patio toward the driveway.

Al returned to the edge of the patio, watching as Betsy helped Mick get into the passenger side of his car, then Betsy got behind the wheel and backed the car down the driveway.

Al peered after the vehicle. Where were they going?

Betsy would have a fit if she knew he'd let a dog spend the night in their house. He didn't care. She'd walked out on him, hadn't she?

Since when did she and Mick get so buddy-buddy?

When the two of them got back from wherever they'd gone, he'd go knock on the door. He'd go over there to talk to Mick. They used to talk a lot, the two of them both active service Marines, different wars. His brain reminded him they'd had that argument. He couldn't remember what they'd argued about.

Whatever it was, it had been serious. Damned if he was going to go over and apologize for something that was most likely Old Mick's fault in the first place.

He'd sit by the front window and watch for their return.

Betsy had gone no further last night than next door to Mick and Jo's house.

He smirked. Some runaway she was. She'd run less than a hundred yards.

Chapter 19

Lynn pulled her knees up closer to her chest and let out a long breath. Outside the bedroom, in the hall bath, Will retched again and Randy repeated, "It's okay. Just get it all out."

There shouldn't be any more in his stomach for the poor kid to get out. One half of her brain told her she must get up to help care for her son, but the other side spoke more insistently. *There's nothing more you can do. Let Randy take care of it.*

She concentrated on breathing deeply and encouraging her body to relax. The pain eased. And it was such a relief to have Randy here at home where he belonged, taking care of the boys. Too bad they couldn't be doing it together, but at least it wasn't her doing it alone like usual. Not that she could do it today, anyway.

Her thoughts looped around. One second it was the boys, seeing them like they had been yesterday, fighting in the car as she drove them to the last day of school. Then her thoughts turned to Sharon, their brief phone call, and the last time they'd been able to get to lunch alone. Such a good talk, they'd had. All about mothers, and daughters, and working, and staying at home, and careers and fulfillment.

She pulled in a breath and let it out slowly, trying to ride the pain. Her mind jumped to the recent robberies. She couldn't defend her family in her weakened state, if somebody barged in. She'd done what she could, bought new dead bolts, hired someone to install them on all the doors, and made sure that the battery in her garage door opener worked. She'd even had that alarm system installed last week.

Lynn hadn't been completely truthful when Katy brought it up yesterday. She hadn't had the alarm system installed because Randy was trying to expand his teaching at the other campus. But she had not wanted the kids to know anything about the home invasions. Hearing it on the ten o'clock news, learning that it was happening somewhere else in town was one thing; fearing that the invasions were creeping closer, maybe into their own neighborhood, was something different. People were being hurt, pistol-whipped, raped.

Lynn had been thinking a lot about those self-defense classes she'd taken back in college. Could she remember any of that stuff when she needed it? Remembering the moves was easy, actually being able to do them was the big question. She'd had three babies and gained twenty pounds.

She pushed out her breath and closed her eyes, wishing she could will the pain in her abdomen to go away. But it wasn't that simple. Tears filled her eyes, and her throat swelled. She didn't ever remember feeling this kind of pain, not even when she was in labor with the kids.

She recalled a comparable pain only one other time. The accident with Tony. Before she met Randy. For a second, she let her mind recall that pain, and then the medication she'd gotten so dependent on.

Dependent? Addicted. What she would give to have just one of those pills to take the edge off this...Tony had loved her so much that he had wanted to spare her the pain. He'd gotten her what she needed then. Where was Tony now?

She hugged her knees to her chest even harder and turned her face into the pillow. These thoughts could take her nowhere good. She was a different person, living a better life. Tony would have dragged her into a dark world.

Sharon was the one person in her life who knew about Tony—and she never brought him up, didn't talk about the "good old days." In reality, those days had been anything but good. They had been dangerous, and the two of them had been lucky to escape whole, both mentally and physically.

Her mind moved on to Katy, at the lake with her best friend, zipping along behind the boat on the old inner tube. Having the best time of her life, Lynn hoped. But then she remembered how much Katy had wanted to stay home with Monique. Could be she wasn't having such a good time after all.

Where was the black dog today? She hadn't heard her bark, didn't think she was in the house. If Randy had let her outside and she had somehow gone back to where she had come from, Katy would be heartbroken. She would blame herself.

Cracks of sunlight beamed around the edges of the drapes. Sunny. A good lake day. Lynn wished she had the energy to go outside, feel the sun on her face, play with the dog—Katy's Monique.

For no apparent reason, her throat closed and her windpipe constricted. The air smelled of vomit and urine and some unknown earthy scent. The urge to vault from the bed and run outdoors overwhelmed her. She threw off the covers and jerked open the bedroom door.

"Randy? Randy, where's Monique?" She swayed, unbalanced, and grabbed at the doorjamb to steady herself.

"What?" Randy's voice floated up the stairs. "Are you up, Lynn?"

Lynn closed her eyes and held on tight as the hallway and the bedroom tilted. "Monique?" she called, but she wasn't really sure that her mouth moved. She eyed the undulating bed, then launched herself back toward it, letting her body fall onto the hump of sheets and quilt. She turned onto her back feeling as if she was floating in liquid.

"Lynn, honey, what are you doing?" Randy's face, wavy, appeared above her. She blinked, opened her eyes wide so that he would solidify, so that she could see him clearly.

"Monique? Katy will be so upset." The words spilled out of her mouth. To her own ears, she sounded like a drunk.

"Something's wrong with that dog. Got bit by a skunk or something. She's outside, and I'm keeping Ty in. We're downstairs, playing a game on the X-Box. You need anything?" He pulled the covers up and tucked them around her.

"A skunk? Rabid? Oh, no."

"She's acting crazy. If we don't feed her, she'll move on."

Lynn turned her face into the pillow, her eyes full of tears. Bitten by a rabid skunk? No, that can't be. Monique didn't come all the way here to find them only to be bitten by a skunk. They needed her protection. How could she protect them if she was rabid?

Chapter 20

Katy wanted to throw up again. And she was going to have to pee soon, or she might explode. Her teeth had been clenched for so long her jaw ached. And her leg. This morning, she couldn't have imagined it could hurt any worse, but as the shadows of the leaves had moved across her with the shifting sunlight, the pain had grown and grown until her brain roared with it.

"Monique?" Her shaking voice sounded so small. Who would ever hear her?

She scanned the hillside for the dog, searched along the shadowy forest floor, and along the black silhouettes of the tall trees. Nothing moved among the gray rocks, green moss, fallen branches, and lumps of brown mushrooms. Monique had found her once. She would come back. She had to.

"Help!" she called.

"Caw!" a crow answered.

She looked up through the tangle of limbs and into the leafy canopy. Splotches of blue sky danced among the dark leafy shapes. Shimmering dust showered down like glitter in the scattered light beams. Maybe it was fairy dust, maybe her fairy was coming down to save her. Her entire body throbbed with the pain in her leg.

She wanted to believe in fairies, but she knew she was too old. Just a year or two ago, she had believed. But now she knew fairies were fake. And a lot of what grownups told her was fake, too. They wanted her to believe everything was all right, people were happy and safe. But at school, the teachers had been whispering about something called a "home invasion"—and it was happening a lot everywhere. And then, at home when Mom and Dad's door was shut and they thought she was asleep, their voices did not sound like everything was all right.

She had a bad feeling that sometimes nightmares did come true.

Monique was sort of like a fairy. She had come to save her, hadn't she, like in the dream? But she wasn't here this second, and Katy was hungry and thirsty and hot and cold all at the same time.

"Help! Monique? Help!"

A fly buzzed across her forehead and then landed on her leg. She swatted it away. An itch began on the back of her bent leg. As she scratched the spot, the itch began to crawl all the way up her legs, then her bottom, and then up her spine. It finally stopped on the back of her neck. She couldn't reach every place at once.

Her whole body itched like one giant mosquito bite. She shivered. If she didn't scratch it, maybe the itching would go away. She held her breath and counted. One...two...three...

When she reached forty, the itch had subsided, but the fly was still buzzing her. Another fly joined it and the two of them buzzed around over her like the planes she'd seen last year at the Bartlesville air show.

She imagined the flies were the planes. Ty and Will had leaned way back to look up at the planes as the pilots waved their wings at the crowd and turned loop-de-loops. The flies weren't turning loop-de-loops, but they weren't flying in straight lines either. One fly zipped down to land on her, and when she waved her hand it chugged up like a really old plane at the air show, the one with two sets of wings. It had sputtered across the sky above the cheering crowd, then dipped down over the runway before looping up, engine roaring.

At the show, she'd held her breath as the plane climbed higher and higher, and then the engine had cut off. The crowd had gasped as the plane fell back toward the earth. Katy had covered her eyes, not wanting to see the pilot slam with the plane into the ground. When the crowd cheered again, her eyes had flashed open to see the plane nose point up and the chugging engine push the plane higher into the sky.

Her heart hammered against her ribs as she watched the flies, just as it had hammered as she watched that plane. She had dived to earth like the plane. She'd slipped off the path and tumbled down to this rock ledge above the stream. The water gurgled below her. She was so thirsty, and it was so close. When she swallowed, her throat was all sandpapery, like the rough stuff Dad used to smooth the front doors before he had repainted them last year.

She didn't want to die down here. Katy remembered the man who'd been in the news—and even had a movie made about him. The man had cut off his own arm to save himself when he got trapped while climbing rocks somewhere. He had been all alone. He had thought he was going to die, but he didn't want to. He had sawed his arm off, all the way through the bone. She'd wondered at the time, what would I do if I got trapped like that? Could I saw through my arm or my leg?

Thing was, she wasn't trapped. She thought maybe she had a broken leg, and it really hurt. Surely, she could crawl out of here. She didn't have to cut anything off. She still had two arms and one good leg, right? She could crawl.

Katy took several deep breaths then reached up to grab some tree roots jutting out from the eroded soil bank. If she could pull herself to the rock above her, maybe she could crawl back up the bank.

When she tried to lift her body, the pain in her leg exploded. She let go of the root and dropped. The world blackened.

Chapter 21

The hospital door swung shut as the nurse left the room, and Mick Jordan turned back to where his wife lay in the hospital bed.

"Jo? Josey-Jo, it's me, I'm here." His heart pounded. He couldn't believe what the nurse had told him.

Jo's blue eyes opened and she smiled. "Mickey. I'm glad to see you."

"Oh, not near as glad as I am to see you."

"Where are the kids?"

Mick blinked. Matthew was coming, but not Annie. If someone had asked him to make a bet about which of their kids would rush home, he'd have put money on Annie. He still couldn't quite believe it. Wasn't this serious enough for Annie to drop whatever it was she was doing and rush home?

"Mickey? I asked you, where are the kids?"

"They're both fine, honey. They send their best. Annie's tied up, but Matthew—well, I think he'll be here later today. They both know you'll be up in no time and back at home. Annie and the kids will come visit then. The grandkids wouldn't be allowed to come in here to see you. What use in making the trip?" That was right, he told himself. If it truly had been serious, the grandkids would all come, wouldn't they? Their parents would make sure they came. Jo was going to get well, going to be at home, back in the kitchen and the garden in no time.

"Okay." Jo closed her eyes and sank back into the pillow. "I'll rest…so tired."

"I'll be right here. And Betsy's down the hallway getting a coffee."

Jo's eyes half opened. "Sweet of her to help. She's good company for you. Quiet. You like that." Her eyes closed again.

Yes, Betsy was quiet company, a comfortable person who exuded peace and safety. It was good to have someone else in the house and not be alone, good not to be pressured to start or continue a conversation. She was an easy person, and he was so grateful for her. Kind of like that black dog. They'd both showed up in the nick of time. Just when he needed them.

He remembered the feel of the dog's head under his fingertips as the EMTs worked on Jo. The animal had leaned against his leg as if she knew he needed comfort.

The dog would stay in the neighborhood. She'd make her home with the Werling family, like Katy wanted. The dog surely had more sense than to pick him to live with. His days living on the Hill were numbered.

"Mickey, promise me you'll find us someplace else to live. The house—the yard…I can't do the work anymore. So tired."

Mick blinked. His fingers rubbed across her hand again. "What do you mean, Josey? You and I aren't done yet. We'll talk about a move later, maybe spring."

"Let's do that, Mickey."

He leaned over her. "I will, Josey. I will. You sleep

now. Rest."

"He'll come back around," Jo mumbled with her eyes closed.

"Who?"

"Al. He'll come back around. Always does. He has a good heart. Betsy knows it."

What was she talking about Al for? Here she'd almost died, and she was talking about weirdo Al. Didn't have anything to do with anything. Jo was talking nonsense, but at least she was talking. He picked up her limp hand and stroked, feeling the fine bones beneath the film of her age-spotted skin. "What do you mean?"

"She'll know what I mean. Tell her." She molded her fingers around his thumb and squeezed.

The beep from the machine startled him as the heart monitor alarm sounded.

\*\*\*\*

"She be okay, Mister Mick. You see. Now you need rest. Come home with me. I fix you soup. Good dinner. Then nap. Matthew be here in no time."

Mick leaned forward in the waiting room chair, his hands clasped on his knees. "I don't know, Betsy. Don't know. I feel like I shouldn't leave. I feel like something—oh, Lord."

Another alarm sounded down the hallway and two hospital staffers dashed on their thick-soled shoes from the nursing station toward Josephine's room. Mick pulled himself to his feet and stepped to the doorway where he could see down the suddenly empty hall. He couldn't be sure if the alarm had come from her room. He grabbed the wide railing nailed onto the wall and took a step in that direction.

"Mister Mick? You wait, please."

He waved one hand back at Betsy and shook his head. He kept moving. He had to see, had to know what was happening. Was he losing her? Was she going? His heart raced.

As he neared the doorway, two nurses walked out, followed closely by a doctor. Inside Jo's room, another nurse adjusted the blanket over Josephine's still body.

Mick's heart raced even faster as he shuffled toward the bed. "Is she…? Is she…?" He couldn't bear to say the words. He stared at her white face. "Oh, Josey." He closed his eyes and saw, played across his inner eyelids, the story of their life. Their meeting at the dance, their first kiss, the night of their engagement. She'd looked so innocent in that pink dress, with those thin, fluttery sleeves. Like a princess. He could hardly believe that out of all the men in the world, she loved him.

He'd had to beg her father for her hand in marriage. The old man had frowned, then grumpily muttered something. Finally, after Mick had asked again, the old man had agreed to the marriage, but there was a threat implied behind his grumbled words, "If you ever…"

And he had never. He loved every fluffy hair on her head, despite the way his thoughts had been lately, his wanting peace and quiet, his occasional seeking of solitude in the yard or with his pipe out on the patio.

"Oh, Josey." Tears leaked, wetting his cheek. He lifted one hand to wipe them away and placed the other on the hard hospital bed, next to her shoulder. His body swayed.

"Mickey? What's wrong?" Her voice was low, but

it was her voice.

His eyes flashed open. "Josey?"

Her eyes were open too, and intent on his face. "She's alone. Someone needs to look for her."

His brow furrowed. "No. You're not alone, I'm right here with you."

"Let her mother know, Mickey. Send someone. The dog can't do it alone. She's hurt."

Mick stared at Josey, at her wide open eyes. He'd thought she was looking at him, but when he straightened and put his weight squarely on both feet, her look didn't shift to stay on his face. She was looking where he had been. But she wasn't looking at him.

"Josey, who are you talking about? Josey-Jo?"

Her eyes closed. He stepped back from the bed and lowered himself into the blue plastic easy chair where Betsy had spent last night. Jo was dreaming, or reliving some moment from the past.

Who was she talking about?

Chapter 22

About three p.m., Al groaned as he got up from the wooden armchair in the dining room where he'd been sitting off and on all day. His butt was numb; he rubbed at his lower back. He'd seen Betsy and Mick get in the car and leave, watched them come back a few hours later. Betsy had carried sacks of groceries into the house, and Mick had leaned hard on his cane, head down, legs as bowed as ever. Mick moved slower than slow.

What was going on over there? And where was Jo? He couldn't imagine why Betsy would hang out with Mick if Jo wasn't there. The two women were friends. Maybe they were best friends, the way Betsy talked about her. Talked about her like Jo was her mother. Not a day went by that the two of them didn't spend at least an hour gabbing out in the yard.

Al trudged over to the desk and pulled out Betsy's bird binoculars. He lugged them back to his chair at the dining room table. When he finally got them focused on his neighbor's kitchen window, he could see someone inside. He wasn't certain, but it might be Betsy in the kitchen, moving to and fro. But why would Betsy be cooking dinner? Was Jo sick? If Betsy was cooking, it was probably something stir-fried, with chopped vegetables.

Betsy stopped moving in front of the window. Still

no sign of Jo.

His stomach rumbled. Had he eaten today?

Any minute, Betsy would come out of the house, cross the back yard, and come home. She'd want to talk to him, or else get more clothes or something. At the least, she'd probably call and tell him where she was.

He would NOT call the Jordan house.

Something moved in the backyard. The black dog again. That dog had been racing around their little area—The Hill they liked to call it—all day, barking at the Werlings, whining over at Mick's. She'd not been back here though. And hadn't he told her not to come back when he kicked her out this morning?

He meandered to the back door and turned the knob, then pulled it open. The dog stood in his backyard, her tail low, nearly tucked between her back legs. She whirled and raced his way, barking as if she was on the attack.

"Shush, you. Stop that barking."

The dog kept it up. Crazy barking. She looked straight at him and yapped her head off.

"Shut up!" He slammed the door. He'd be damned if he'd stand there and let that animal bark at him. He should throw something at her to get her to shut up.

If she would have padded over to him quiet-like he would have rubbed her side with the edge of his shoe until she grunted and let herself fall over, then stretched out, and invited him to rub the whole length of her back. He'd have let her in, fed her, even fluffed up the pile of dirty clothes and towels so she could make a bed on the laundry room floor again.

He glanced over his shoulder at the interior of his house, it was filled with late afternoon shadows. Silent.

His neck prickled. Long ago, before Betsy, television noise filled any house he lived in whether he was watching the tube or not. He always kept the TV on for the noise, like he often left the water running in the kitchen sink, or the clothes drier going even when there was nothing in it to dry. He couldn't stand the silence. He heard "things" in the silence.

The barking stopped. Al rubbed at his neck; his stomach muscles tightened. He looked out the window. The dog peered up at him. As soon as she saw his face, she tilted her head and whined. She turned and looked behind her at the ravine, then turned back to him. What was she hearing? Danged if he knew. Whatever it was, it seemed to worry her. She yipped up at him.

Betsy came out onto the Jordans' patio. She sat down, facing their house. Maybe she missed him. *Good.*

The black dog raced across the lawn to the Jordan's. Betsy stood up and bent over, patting her thighs as she encouraged the animal to come closer. But the dog barked, ran back and forth across Al's yard and the Jordan's yard and then back to Betsy, barking all the while.

Betsy threw her hands up in the air and retreated to the sliding patio door. Al could make out Mick standing in the doorway. Betsy went inside; the drapes closed. For a minute, the dog stood at the edge of their patio, her tail drooping. Then, she trotted off.

Al slipped through the shadowy house into the living room, moving past dark shapes that morphed into furniture when he turned on the lamp. He settled into his black leather recliner and turned on the television. Still couldn't find his glasses. Couldn't see the TV

Guide to tell what was on.

Well, he'd find something to watch. He wouldn't be lonely. She'd chosen to leave him, hadn't she? Let Betsy pay the price.

Chapter 23

Randy brought Lynn another glass of lemon-lime soda.

"Still hurting, honey?" he asked.

"Not quite so bad. Did you fix something for the boys for supper?" She sipped the soda. Pain had etched lines across her forehead.

"Not yet. Maybe I'll order pizza delivery."

Lynn's face paled. "Just the idea of pizza makes my stomach hurt. And I can't imagine Will would want pizza either. Maybe some chicken noodle soup."

Randy shrugged. Even lying in bed sick, Lynn corrected him. She knew everything, after all. "You sure you don't want to go to the hospital?"

She shook her head. "Only if it doesn't get better soon. You might give the Bauers a call, let them know we may need to drop the boys off. I'll rest easier knowing we've got someone to watch them for us if it gets any worse." Lynn drained the rest of the soda from the glass and lay back on the pillows. She moved slowly, her features pinched as if she were expecting pain.

"Need some more to drink?"

"Mmmm." She nodded, her eyes closed.

He touched her forehead and ran one finger along her jawbone. "I'm sorry, baby," he said.

She murmured and kept her eyes closed. In a few

moments, her breathing deepened and slowed. He slipped out of the room but left the door cracked. He carried her glass downstairs for a refill.

Too bad she was sick, but at the same time it was damned inconvenient.

He glanced over at his cell phone on the table in the family room where Ty was watching television. He could call Jennifer. His heart pounded. The world around him tilted and dipped like a roller coaster ride whenever he thought about her.

*It doesn't mean that I don't love my family.*

The risk of discovery increased the excitement but also made him feel a little nauseous. Just not nauseous enough to stop thinking about it.

What would it be like to be with another woman after all these years?

The image of his daughter's face hovered like a morning mist in his mind, and he couldn't explain it. Why did he have a guilty conscience for something that hadn't even happened?

Katy was ten, still engulfed in her own innocent world. She didn't think about Mommy and Daddy in any way except as the people she loved who protected and cared for her and her brothers. Life was so simple when you were a kid.

Katy was swimming and skiing at the lake. Hopefully she'd escaped catching Will's stomach bug. The other three of them might not be so lucky. Better that Katy wouldn't be exposed until late Sunday.

He walked by the kitchen extension phone, paused, then picked it up and punched in Jennifer's number. It was early evening; she was probably out with friends. He'd leave a brief message, to let her know he was thinking of her and sorry he'd missed their study date.

She answered the phone, breathless.

Quickly he turned his back to Ty and the family room, and brought the phone even closer to his mouth. "Hi. Um, it's Randy. I'm calling to let you know I could probably meet you tomorrow, if you still need help."

"Oh," she breathed. The sleepy sound of her voice made his heart race. "Thank you. I was so disappointed last night. I thought maybe you..." She paused, and swallowed. "I'm glad you can make it tomorrow."

"Me, too." Saliva balled up in his throat, and he choked on it with his next breath. He coughed, cleared his throat, and then coughed again.

"Are you okay?" she asked. "Randy?"

"Fine. Just got something stuck in my throat." He swallowed again, and got it right this time. "Tomorrow then, Jennifer. Bye."

"Good-bye. Tomorrow."

His heart swelled at her sweet voice. The phone clicked, but he didn't put down the receiver. Instead, he breathed into the phone, as if she was still there, on the other end. "'Til tomorrow," he repeated.

"Randy?" Lynn's shaky voice came through the phone loud and clear.

Chapter 24

Rustling leaves. Cawing crows. A fly, on her nose.

She had to pee so bad she ached with the need.

Katy's thoughts floated amid throbs of pain. So thirsty. She should be looking for something. No, not something—the dog! Her personal YouTube went into action again.

They were in the car. Mom was driving. It was Friday, after the last day of school. Katy scanned the street, the yards, and even the bushes for some sign of the black dog as her mother pulled the car into the driveway.

Then, she spied the dog standing in the deep shadows under the tree in their side yard.

Katy shrieked and vaulted out of the SUV. The black dog raced toward her. "Hi, girl. Hi, hi, hi! Where have you been?"

The black dog licked her hands and danced around her, hopping on her hind legs. Will and Ty both jumped from the car and ran to the dog. Her tail went around and around in a circle.

Mom walked toward the house. "Katy, get your music and head to Mrs. Jordan's," she called over her shoulder. "Boys, in the house! Ty's got his practice tonight for the tournament games tomorrow. I'll get dinner started. We'll barely have time to eat before we have to go. Ty, move it!"

She was using her stern voice, but it was not yet stern enough to pull Katy away from the dog. "I love you. Yes, I do. Stay here. I'll be back. You wait for me. We'll go for a walk, and I'll fix you a treat. I love you."

"Katy Marie! In the house! Will, Ty, come on."

"Oh, Mom," Katy muttered. The dog trotted beside her as she dragged herself toward the house, where her mother waited beside the front door. She patted the dog's head as they moved. "She wants to come inside. Can she? Mom, please?"

Her mother frowned; she was holding her stomach. "No. Get inside. The dog probably isn't house trained. And I don't know how Caesar and Cleo will react."

"She wants to go in, Mommy. Please?" Will begged.

"Please? Can she, huh?" Ty pleaded.

Katy knew Mom would give in. "Please. Let her in the house. She'll like Caesar and Cleo."

Her mother unlocked the door and pulled it open. She was giving in. Her mother's frown was still there, and her face was pale. She still had one hand on her stomach.

"Your stomach hurts again, doesn't it?" Katy asked.

Her mother looked over at her; her eyes seemed huge. "No."

Katy recognized the lie. Her heart hammered. Had it started? The nightmare? Had her mother had a stomachache in the dream? She couldn't remember. Katy sighed. She didn't feel scared, more relieved the dog would be a part of her family. If the dog was part of their family, maybe those horrible dreams she'd been having would stop.

In the ravine, Katy opened her eyes and groaned. She looked into the leafy green tops of the trees, and saw bits of blue sky beyond. Beneath her, the ground was hard and rocky. She wanted to shift positions. But she remembered. If she moved, the horrible pain came.

The vomit-smell was all around her. She retched. Nothing came up. Her stomach was empty. Her throat was on fire. And she *had* to pee.

Where was Monique? She had been here earlier. She had been right here, beside her, the dog's warm body pressed up against her.

"Monique? Here, girl." Her hoarse voice didn't sound right, not even to her own ears.

*Why didn't Monique come back?*

Chapter 25

One hand clutched her stomach, the other clutched the phone. Lynn gasped, the sudden jabbing pains came in a steady rhythm.

As soon as Randy had left the room, the pain had sliced so deeply through her midsection she could hardly gasp for a breath. She'd hollered for him, but he had not responded. He was probably with the boys, where the noise from the television drowned out her cry. She had picked up the phone to call an ambulance. Randy was on an extension. Talking to a woman. Making plans to meet tomorrow.

He was having an affair.

"Hang up the damned phone," she growled through the pain. The receiver clicked, the dial tone popped on, she punched 9-1-1. Footsteps thundered up the stairs, and Randy burst into the room.

"Let me explain." Randy hovered over her, one hand repeatedly wiped at the hair on the back of his head, the other reached toward her.

"I need an ambulance." Lynn said to the 9-1-1 operator. "I'm having severe stomach pains. The address is—" She sucked in a jagged breath at the next sudden stab.

"Lynn, please. I'll take you."

"No." Tears spilled out of her eyes, and she doubled over as the spike of pain peaked then receded.

"Something's wrong." She gave the operator the address. "I'll try to stay on the phone, but..." Nausea climbed up her throat. She threw her legs over the side of the bed and lurched, gagging, across the room, dropping the receiver. "Oh, God," she moaned as her stomach roiled.

"Lynn. Honey..." Randy started after her, but she slammed the bathroom door in his face and threw herself to the floor in front of the toilet.

A minute later, exhausted, she lay on the cool tile and held her stomach. She drew her knees up to her chest. The fetal position lessened the pain, at least the pain in her stomach. The tile was icy under her wet cheek.

"Damn him, damn him. Damn, damn, damn!" Her voice got louder and louder.

Randy knocked on the door. "Lynn, honey, please open the door."

"Go to hell!" The power in her voice surprised her. "Go to hell, and take your girlfriend with you!" Tears popped out of her eyes, but her voice was strong.

"Lynn! Come on, open the door."

"Let me know when the ambulance is here," she growled.

"Oh, shit." Randy's voice rumbled on the other side of the door. He gave the address again. Then he tapped on the door. "Lynn. They're on the way. Five minutes?" He tapped three, then four times. "Lynn, please. Open."

The pain crested again; she clamped her jaws together. "Go to hell!" she moaned.

Lynn pulled herself tighter in a fetal position. How long had this affair been going on? How could she not have known? She'd seen the faraway look in his eyes, known his mind was somewhere else. She'd thought he was thinking about his classes or getting tenure, maybe dreaming up a vacation or—anything. But an affair!

Her breath came fast and quick. The room closed in around her. She forced herself to open her eyes as wide as she could and look at the ceiling, at the walls, at the floor, the shower stall, the sink. Oh God! A drum roll played within her chest.

Her body tried to expel something, with no result. She grabbed her knees and held on when the cramps came again. She blew out her breath and tried to simply breathe. No air to pull into her lungs.

Maybe she would die.

For an instant, the worst instant, she thought maybe she WOULD die. Then, like a distant echo that wouldn't completely fade, someone called her name.

"Mommy?"

The voice sounded like Katy's, but couldn't be Katy because Katy was at the lake with Emily and wouldn't be home until late tomorrow. All the same, the voice made her think life could not be over yet. She had to help Katy and Ty and Will grow up. She couldn't die. Her job was not done.

What she needed to do now had nothing to do with Randy. Air poured into her lungs. She sucked in more, breathing deeply, then exhaling. The pain stopped.

Other than the initial deposit of seed that had made her babies, it was clear that Randy had little, if anything, to do with her life. Quite easily, as if their bond had been severed with a knife, she disconnected from him.

She straightened out her body, sat up, and then

stood. She flushed the commode.

Lynn stared into the swirling water, watching it circle the toilet bowl and eventually exit. More than water was exiting through the hole and emptying down into the sewer. She pushed the flush handle again and watched the water circle, then empty.

She'd had this all wrong. How many years had she listened to her mother and father screaming at one another? The result was she never allowed an argument—or even a disagreement—to be verbalized with Randy. The end result? No spark, no chemistry, and no marriage. Both of them had grown sterile, complacent. And she had let her own personality, her desires and ambitions, become absorbed into what she had believed was the more important role of wife and mother.

Bullshit.

Since Katy had been born, she had been asleep. Comatose. Where had those years gone?

Lynn perched on the edge of the bathtub. She shivered. She tried to go over the revelation she had just experienced, but exhaustion fogged her mind. She had come to an important conclusion about Randy, her marriage, and her own purpose. She had to hang on to it. But her body shivered and quivered, and she wanted only to lie down and sleep.

## Chapter 26

"You sure one of us shouldn't go back to the hospital, Betsy? Don't we need to be there?" Mick stood in the doorway of the kitchen and watched as Betsy put away the supper dishes.

"No, Mr. Mick. You need rest. Doctor say so. Miss Josephine is quiet. Her body need sleep. Tomorrow, we know what happen next. Rehab, maybe?"

Rehab. Jo might not be home for weeks, and when she did come home, she might not be able to do anything. No cooking, cleaning, gardening. Mick turned away from Betsy, feeling deflated, exhausted, beat up. How in the world were they going to manage living here in this house on this acre if she couldn't do those things?

"Mr. Mick? You okay?"

He waved his hand at Betsy and trudged into the den, dropped down into his reading chair, and slumped over, his head in his hands. What was he supposed to do? Think about a nursing home for Jo? Think about a retirement village for him? He looked around the room. What in the world was he going to do with their things? All the things they had bought on their travels, all the books he had read over his lifetime, all the photographs and pictures and mementoes. Who would want them? Annie was so busy with her own kids, and Matthew... Neither one of them would care if the house and everything in it went up in smoke.

Outside, the black dog yipped again, then was silent. She'd been barking all day, wanting to play, he supposed. Why weren't the Werling boys out there with her? Of course, Katy was gone to the lake with her friend. Maybe the dog missed Katy. Either way, it was none of his concern. He hoped the Werlings were still committed to keeping the animal. What if they weren't? What if they hadn't given her food or water today?

He pulled himself out of the chair and trudged through the kitchen, past Betsy washing dishes, and into the garage. He dug around in the box of doggy biscuits and picked out two. Then he stepped out into the back yard.

"Here, girl," he called. Then he whistled. The dog didn't come. He laid the biscuits on the edge of the concrete right next to the yard, then shuffled through the garage and back to the reading chair in the den.

Mick wanted nothing more than to sit right here, deep in the cushion of his favorite chair, and sleep. Maybe when he woke up the past two days would have been a bad dream. Maybe Jo would be hustling around the room with her dust cloth, and there'd be a cobbler on the countertop cooling for dessert.

The dog barked again, closer. He could get up to look outside, but his body didn't want to move. Why bother? The animal wouldn't come to him, wouldn't come to Betsy. He was too tired to try again tonight. He needed to sleep but knew as soon as he lay down, his whirling thoughts would prevent it. How could he sleep when Josey-Jo was lying there in that hospital bed alone?

And how could he sleep wondering whether or not

she would ever be back in bed beside him? Who knew if tonight would be her last night on this earth?

Chapter 27

Katy pinched her nose to shut out the smell of the pee that soaked her pajama bottoms and underwear.

She hadn't wet herself since she was a little bitty kid. Would Mom be mad? Her head hurt, and her leg hurt, but at least *that* part of her didn't ache anymore.

Katy tried to clear her scratchy throat. So thirsty. So hungry. Hours since Monique had been here.

Her back itched. She wiggled, trying to scratch the itch in the dirt beneath her. OWWW. Pain shot from her leg.

Night would come soon. Monique would bring help. But what if she couldn't get anyone to come? Katy shivered. Her whole body shook. Alone again, another whole night?

Ty had soccer matches all day. Mom and Dad and Will would have gone to those. Might go to dinner with the team after, if his team won. They might not be home until after dark.

Her eyes filled with tears, and her whole body ached.

Maybe Monique could get Mr. Jordan to come with her, if Mom and Dad were busy. Could Mr. Jordan follow her this far down into the ravine?

She didn't think so. Sometimes he had a hard time moving. She'd seen him walking with a cane. Could someone with a cane make it down here without falling? She had fallen; anybody could.

Monique was smart. She would know better than to bring Mr. Jordan down into the ravine.

Maybe Mr. Tilton or Miss Betsy, then. Monique would figure out how to get one of them to come with her.

Monique had brought her fruit twice today. First the orange, then an apple. Katy was sure the dog had taken them from a fruit basket Betsy sometimes set out on the patio if the weather was right. She'd sat out there with Miss Betsy lots of times, even earlier this week, right after school on Monday. Katy frowned at the darkening sky and scratched her face, remembering their conversation.

"You have big summer plans, Missy?" Betsy had asked as she handed her the fruit bowl and encouraged her to take an orange.

"No. I'm going to sign up for summer reading at the library—and I've still got piano lessons since the Jordans aren't going anywhere."

"Oh, but reading and music—very special. In your mind, they take you anywhere you want to go. Anywhere in world. England, Hawaii. Good places to visit—even if pretend. Right?"

Katy remembered nodding; Betsy was right. She'd been right there in Hogwarts a lot lately, with Harry Potter and Hermione. She loved those books, even though the other kids were reading "Goosebumps" books now.

The ache in her leg sharpened, a sudden spark of pain as if a wizard like Dumbledore had focused his wand on her and said an incantation.

Oh, where was Monique?

Monique barreled through the undergrowth each time she returned. The dog had to be acting weird when she was back in the neighborhood. Betsy would know something was wrong with Monique if she kept barking. She'd know Monique wanted something—and she'd follow her.

But what if she didn't?

An owl hooted in the distance, and closer, a dog barked. Not Monique. She knew her bark. She'd recognize it anywhere.

Sweet Monique.

The tension in Katy's body eased a little. The dog had lain right next to her, letting Katy use her as a pillow. Monique had turned her head and stared into Katy's eyes, and Katy had stared back until she had fallen asleep.

Where was Monique? Katy tried to shift, and cried out when another jab pierced her leg.

Maybe Emily would call her house to talk to her, to let her know how many times she'd been skiing today and whether she'd been able to slalom.

Maybe Em had seen some cute guy on another boat, and they'd waved at one another all day.

Katy squeezed her eyelids closed, imagining the scene at the lake. If she concentrated on the lake, the pain throbbed a little less.

But what if Emily was still mad at her for not going? She might have made a new best friend at the lake. Maybe Sarah Mahoney was at the lake with her parents, and she and Sarah had become *bff*s.

She wouldn't think about it. Pain speared her body. Her back arched, and tears squeezed out of her eyes.

Emily would call her—surely she would. Katy

gritted her teeth, and the sour, dry lump that was usually her tongue stuck to the top of her mouth.

What would Mom and Dad do when they found out she hadn't gone to the lake with Emily? They'd be mad, but they'd also be worried. Then they might decide Monique knew something they didn't know.

Then they might follow the dog.

They might be on their way to the ravine right now.

She listened real hard, fully expecting to hear something crashing through the forest, calling her name.

And something WAS crashing through the underbrush.

"Mom? Dad? Monique?" she called. Her voice didn't sound very loud, and talking hurt her throat. It made her whole body hurt, even though she hadn't moved.

"Help!"

The crashing came nearer. She closed her eyes. It had to be Monique. It wasn't nighttime yet, nothing would be hunting or coming to eat her. And with Monique coming around so much, other things would leave her alone, right?

The cold nose touched her cheek, and her eyes flew open.

"Monique!" She circled the dog's neck with her arm and tugged Monique close.

The dog dropped two dog biscuits onto Katy's chest.

"Oh, thank you. Caesar and Cleo like these a lot. I've never tried one." Katy held one large bone-shaped, bacon-scented biscuit up to her lips and closed her eyes. The meaty smell of the biscuit made her mouth water.

She gnawed off a tiny edge with her front teeth, and chewed it, imagining it was a gingersnap.

In less than twenty seconds, she'd eaten the whole thing.

"Thank you, Monique. You're the best, and I love you more than anything."

The black dog lay down beside her and closed her eyes. Katy rubbed the dog's head, feeling the warmth radiating through her short black fur, and then she scratched her ears with one hand as she ate the second biscuit.

Monique licked her hand. Katy stared into the dog's eyes. She pulled in the animal's warmth, listened to her steady breathing, and fell asleep.

Sometime later, the dog lifted her head, eased away from Katy, and dashed out of the ravine along the same obstacle-filled path she had picked her way down minutes earlier.

An owl hooted as the light of the day dimmed.

Chapter 28

Randy hurried around the car to open the passenger door and help Lynn out. She swayed as she stood, woozy from the medicine the ER doc had given her.

"Easy, honey. Lean on me," Randy said. He didn't want her to fall as they navigated up the front steps and into the house.

She didn't look at him. She hadn't looked at him for hours. Not while they waited for the ambulance, and not when he assured her he would find someone to watch the boys and come to the hospital right away. Not when he got to the hospital and told her Dave and Ellen Keating, fellow professors at the university who lived nearby, had agreed to keep the kids for a few hours. Not even after she got back from having the imaging done, and the doctor had given his diagnosis.

She'd turned away from him when he tried to reassure her and refused to look at him even after the hospital aide had finished loading her into their car.

He couldn't blame her. Lynn had been suffering for weeks. Why hadn't she said something to him? His conscience reminded him she'd told him with her eyes a hundred times, and he hadn't seen it. He certainly should have noticed the way she huddled on the sofa or sat hunched over at the dining room table, one hand over her stomach. She picked at her food. She'd lost weight, and he never noticed.

"Here we go." He put one arm around her as they went up the front steps, opened the door, and guided her into the house. She looked at the front staircase, then closed her eyes and leaned against the wall.

"I could carry you up?" he offered, his hands outstretched.

She turned away from him and started up the stairs. One step at a time, using the handrail, she pulled herself slowly up to the second floor.

"I'm right behind you." He stayed two steps below her, ready to catch her if she fell.

Lynn didn't fall. She trudged to the top of the stairs and then down the hall and into the bedroom. At last, she eased down onto the rumpled bed.

"I'll be back up in a minute with some ice water. Need anything else?"

She turned away from him onto her right side.

What will it take to make this right? He'd already confessed nothing had happened with Jennifer. He'd admitted to lust, and that was all it was. He hadn't done anything.

"Go get my boys." Her voice sounded unnatural.

"Okay. I'll do it right now. Are you sure you'll be all right by yourself for a few minutes?"

When she didn't move or speak, he edged out of the room, bounded down the stairs, and ran outside to the car.

He sat quietly for a moment before he started the car's engine. His brain whirred, his heart pounded. The world was whirling around him, and he knew it was his fault. No one else to blame. He blinked, disconcerted by the lump growing in his throat.

He remembered a time in high school when he had

deliberately failed a math exam to convince the kids who'd been calling him a nerd that he really wasn't one. He'd been unable to eat that night, aware how flunking that test would affect his GPA and might make a difference in what college he got into. The ramifications were far-reaching, and the decision had been made in only a few seconds. He couldn't take the teasing any more. He had wanted to be part of the *in* group, wanted to be invited to their parties, wanted to have the cool girls look at him instead of snickering at him behind their hands as they walked past.

So what was his excuse this time? Mid-life crisis? Lack of attraction to Lynn? No. The answer was simple and lay entwined in the perfume, the husky voice, and the sultry eyes of a nineteen-year-old freshman.

"It might be her gallbladder. The tests were inconclusive, though," Randy said as he sank down onto the Keatings' sofa. "She's got pain medication to get her through tomorrow, and something to help with the nausea. Doctor's appointment set for Monday. Then, maybe surgery later next week, if they think that's the problem."

"Oh, gallbladder pain is so awful," Ellen said. Her arms crossed over her sagging bosom. "She'll feel much better when they've removed it. My sister went through it last year. Diagnosing it is nine-tenths of the battle." She nodded her head firmly. "I'll go round up the kids."

Dave leaned against the arm of the sofa and smiled down at Randy after Ellen left the room. "Glad that's all it is. Could have been cancer or something, you know?"

Randy nodded. Yes, it could have been cancer.

They could be facing a life or death diagnosis.

"Gives you pause, doesn't it? I think about how I'd feel if I lost Ellen. The kids are getting older—won't be long until it's just the two of us again. Know what I mean?" Dave winked. His hair was much grayer than Randy's. And his paunch pulled the golf shirt tight across the middle; it hung over his leather belt. "And Lynn's so beautiful, so devoted to you and the kids. You're a lucky man."

Randy nodded. *I know I'm a lucky man!* He wanted to yell. *And I don't deserve any of it! I can't even keep my freakin' mind on my own family!* He closed his eyes, squeezing the lids tightly down.

"Some guys throw that kind of thing away. You know? Younger woman, different lifestyle. Can't seem to settle down and be grateful for anything. We're the lucky ones, Randy. I can tell you see that." Dave squeezed Randy's shoulder.

"Daddy!" Will scurried into the room, still wearing the Batman pajamas Randy had dressed him in after this morning's commode-hugging episode.

Randy wrapped his arms around his youngest son in a bear hug and when Ty rushed up beside him Randy opened his arms to include him, too, but softened the hug to a simple pat that fell above the cast on his arm.

"What's wrong with Mom?" Ty asked.

"The doctors gave her some medicine. She's at home waiting for us."

Each of his sons took one of his hands and pulled him toward the front door.

"Come on, hurry," Will said.

"I can't thank you enough," Randy called over his shoulder to the couple.

Dave slid his arm around Ellen's ample waist. "Any time. We're glad to see you and the boys. Next time, though, don't wait until it's an emergency to call. Give our best to Lynn."

Randy drove slowly through the curving streets of their neighborhood. As he turned up their street, he caught a flash of black from the corner of his eye.

"There's Moe! Stop, Daddy!" Will screamed.

The dog raced up to the car, barking, as they turned into their long driveway.

"Hi, girl! Where you been?" Ty yelled as he knocked on the car window at the dog outside.

When the car stopped in front of the garage, the boys flew out of the backseat.

The black dog barked. Her tail wound in a circle. She dashed toward them and then away, then back again, barking all the while.

"Moe!" Will hollered as he tried to throw his arms around the dog when she ran past him.

The animal bolted away, and then scampered back, yipping and crying.

"Let's go in and see your mother." Randy put a hand on each boy's shoulder and steered them toward the door. "It's too dark to play with her."

"Can she come in? It's time to sleep." Ty held open the door. "Come on in, Moe."

The dog barked and backed down the sidewalk.

"She doesn't want to come in," Randy said. "Tell her goodnight."

"Later, Moe! We'll play tomorrow," Ty called. He shoved his good arm against the door until it was wide open and he could slip through. "Mom?"

As the boys dashed up the stairs, Randy shut the

front door. The black dog barked at him from the front walk.

What was wrong with it, anyway? Who knew if the dog had ever had a rabies vaccination?

He watched her for a moment, looking for signs of a foaming mouth, or some other injury that might be provoking her. Her barks became more insistent, like yips, and she kept turning away and then turning back.

The animal had gone crazy. Thank goodness she hadn't followed the boys into the house.

Tomorrow he'd call Animal Control and have her picked up.

Chapter 29

The evening shadows closed around Al as he sank into the deep cushions of his recliner. The closed mini-blinds kept everything out. Including Betsy.

Today was Saturday, wasn't it? She had been gone two nights. Hadn't she? Without Betsy here, he wasn't sure of anything. When had he last eaten? Brushed his teeth? Combed his hair? A troubling thought started like seed blown in on the wind and sprouted immediately.

*She might never come back.*

He ran one hand across the rough beard stubble on his jawbone. Then he ran it back the other way, feeling the spikey little hairs. Betsy hated his stubble. She wouldn't kiss him if he wasn't recently shaved. Said it hurt her skin. Surely he'd shaved. Just a few minutes ago. Hadn't he? His beard grew so fast. If it kept this up, in another hour or so it would be an inch long.

Something scratched at the back door. He sank further down into the cushions. Betsy wouldn't scratch, she would walk in. It might be the dog again, scratching at the door or yipping. It had probably been going on for days.

One time, he remembered getting up from the chair and going to the door. The dog was pacing on the patio, holding something in its mouth. It paced back and forth, then dropped whatever it was and yipped. The dog had looked up as if it could see him there behind the thin black curtain Betsy had hung over the back door window so no one could see into the house.

A lot of good that curtain did. The damn dog could see right through it.

Another time he'd opened the door to let the dog in. He'd wanted her to come in. And not to shut her up. He wanted to feel her warm, smooth fur. He had wanted the animal to lean into him, welcoming his touch. He wanted to believe another living creature wanted his warmth. Betsy didn't want his touch any more. She had chosen Mick and Jo over him. Maybe he should let the dog live with him, let it make a nest in the dirty clothes every night.

But the black dog had darted away as soon as he'd opened the door. It ran in circles, something hanging out of one side of its mouth. Wanting him to play? Insisting he play. But his bones were too heavy. His mouth was lined with cotton, and he could hardly keep himself upright at the door much less carry himself through the doorway and out onto the patio. He weighed a ton. How could that be?

Had he eaten since that last disgusting meal Betsy had fed him?

She'd poisoned him. That was it. Nauseated. Dizzy. Bones that weighed a ton. Couldn't even pull himself up out of the chair.

What kind of fancy Oriental poison had she used? Puffer fish? He knew about that one. But if she used that, he'd be dead, wouldn't he? Maybe he was dead. Walking dead. No, sitting dead. He'd gone to the door hours ago. Since then he'd been sitting here, bones getting heavier by the second. That was it, he was sitting here, dead.

Al wouldn't get up to see the dog again. He'd let it in once. Slept with it, even. And what had happened? It had wanted out like Betsy. Away from him. Like it couldn't stand the sight of him. Betsy hadn't come back. Why should the dog?

It wanted to play. That was all. Well, the dog would have to find someone else. He was going to sit here and be dead. No need to do anything else. His bones couldn't do it.

*Was Betsy coming back?*

Outside, the dog's yip had turned into a howl.

Chapter 30

Lynn pulled her knees up to her chest and hugged them.

Damn him. She gritted her teeth. Randy having an affair? Randy with a girlfriend? She would laugh if she wasn't still in so much pain.

She had devoted her life to raising their children, believed her family was everything, and she had made Randy her world. Now she had a houseful of kids and a philanderer for a husband.

Damn Randy! And damn her!

She squeezed her eyes shut so tight that the tears burned through her eyelids.

They said history repeated itself. She'd never, ever believed it would happen to her. She opened her eyes and focused on the soft fern green color of the bedroom walls.

Her mother and father had been arguing in the kitchen when Lynn returned home from a night studying at the library.

"That woman!" Her mother's screaming voice echoed down the hall to the front door. "How could you? You've humiliated me again in front of this whole town. People snicker when I walk down the street. Why are you doing this, Ed? Again? Why?"

That night, Lynn had stopped dead in her tracks, before she tiptoed back to the front of the house, away from her mother's angry shrieks. She had turned off the porch light and the living room lights and gone up the front stairs to her room. She'd shut and locked her bedroom door, then pulled off her clothes and crawled into bed. She didn't brush her teeth or wash her face. More than anything, she wanted to avoid the sight of either one of her parents.

How many times had she seen her father, sheepish, with a glint in his eye and a smile he couldn't quite keep off his lips, and her mother, wide-eyed and crazed, black hair disheveled from running her fingers through it, lipstick smeared or wiped completely away?

The house fell silent. Maybe they realized she'd come home. Maybe they were tired of fighting. Maybe her mother had lowered her voice. Lynn had stared at the wall and wondered what her mother would do.

Even then, in high school, Lynn knew the answer. Nothing.

How many times had she heard the argument, when they thought no one could hear? Breakfast, lunch, and supper were always ready. The house was always clean, and the laundry always done. Mother had her club meetings, did the shopping, and had her hair done. Dad went to work and had his affairs.

Life went on as usual.

Lynn would not go on as usual. Her stomach ached, but that was not the worst pain. Men betrayed their wives and in response, by doing nothing, women betrayed themselves.

When they got married, Lynn remembered telling herself she would allot these middle years to Randy and to raising their children, but she would still have her life. Then she had fallen into the same trap as her mother, believing these years belonged to him and the children. It was a small sacrifice. But, as of this moment, she realized that "allotment" was not right. She had lost most of *who* she was in her effort to be a perfect wife and mother.

The pain cut into her gut again. She pulled in a breath and let it out slowly, trying to relax and let the medicine work. The stabbing pains did seem to be duller, shorter.

She hoped the tests on Monday would tell for certain it was her gallbladder. Knowing what it was, finally, and what the resolution needed to be would make the pain easier to get through. Hopefully, the gallbladder and the pain in her abdomen would be gone next week.

However, the other necessary changes in her life needed much more thought and planning.

Chapter 31

Once again, Randy heard the black dog out in their yard, howling crazy-like at the rising moon. A shiver ran down his back as he peered through the white shutters of the kitchen window. The dog sat down, got up, circled, sat down, got up, circled, all the time howling or yipping. Something was definitely wrong with the animal.

"Sorry, guys. You can't go out." He locked the patio door and stretched to put the key up on the top of the doorframe. "Will, you need to get your strength back, and Ty, with your arm, I don't think it's a good idea."

"But Moe wants to play with us, Dad," Will whined.

"Can't you hear her? She wants to come in," Ty added.

"Oh, yeah, I hear her. She'll stop in a bit. You can't go outside. It's too dark, and she's too excited. End of discussion."

The boys scowled at him, then turned their backs and stalked into the den. In a few minutes, a *Wii* game blared, but not quite loud enough to block the sound of the dog outside. What could make an animal sound like that? Desperate, almost. He took another look through the shutters. She seemed to see him and ran at the house, barking, then turned and dashed down the driveway. She stopped and listened, then ran back at the house, barking again. Poor animal must be rabid. He could think of no other reason for its behavior. It would break the kids' hearts. But for their safety, it seemed clear he had to be the one to have the animal picked up, and probably put to sleep.

Randy locked the front door, too. Good thing Katy wasn't home. She was the only one of the kids who might think to get a chair and reach up for the key. She'd be outside, running after Monique, no matter what he told her to do.

The television blared louder in the den, and then Ty and Will began to argue over what video game they'd play next, or whether they were going to watch TV. Both of them had short fuses tonight. They were tired and not feeling their best. After last night with Will, he was not on top of things either. And Lynn was still upstairs in their bedroom not speaking to him.

On the way through the kitchen, he grabbed a handful of cookies to pacify his sons. He passed the kitchen phone. Instantly, one voice in his head told him he could make a quick call to Jennifer. Didn't he want to hear her voice?

He was startled to realize he was no longer sure he did. He was embarrassed and full of regret about his infatuation with this student. He had hurt Lynn. He had lost his own self-respect. He wished Lynn hadn't found out about Jennifer before he came to this realization.

He hurried through the room and into the den. "Cool it, guys. Either pick a game or pick a video or I'm going to send you to bed. Which will it be?"

The boys threw themselves down in front of the television and Ty slid a DVD into the player. The intro screen to *Spiderman III* popped on. Caesar raced in from wherever he'd been and squirmed his way in between the two boys.

Randy eased down into his favorite chair and raised his feet to the footstool. He noticed the pile of photo albums on the coffee table between his chair and Lynn's usual place on the sofa a few feet from him. He opened the top album.

The faces of his smiling children stared up, each kid years younger.

When had they taken all these pictures? There were dozens from every season of soccer, every dance recital, every family outing and every holiday. Lynn had carefully labeled each one, and put them in the albums chronologically. At one point, she had begun to add all kinds of doodads to the albums. Decorative frames, quotes, titles, borders, and trinkets.

Was this what they called 'scrapbooking?' He vaguely remembered Lynn talking about it, offering to show him one of the albums, but he hadn't taken the time. Hadn't she told him about some scrapbooking "parties" given by some friends?

Will climbed onto his lap. "Daddy? I'm tired." He rubbed his eyes. "Who's that?" He pointed at a picture of himself as a baby. Six months old and sitting up alone on a blanket in the middle of the living room floor, with Chloe stretched out beside him.

Randy ran his fingers through his son's hair. "You! Think you were ever that little?"

Will shook his head. Randy agreed. When had he been that little? Where had the time gone? "Let's go upstairs and get ready for bed. Ty? You coming up?"

Ty rolled over onto his back and crossed one arm

under his head, and the other arm, with the cast, across his chest. "Nope. Not sleeping in the Vomit Room. I'll stay down here on the sofa."

Randy looked at Will's face, his eyes droopy with sleep. Will wasn't going to argue, so why should he? He understood Ty's point, after all. So, if Ty slept on the sofa, it gave him a reason to ask Lynn to let him back into their room. It was either that or sleep in Katy's bed for the night. He wasn't thrilled about sharing her twin bed—or the room—with a dozen stuffed animals and Caesar and Chloe in their dog beds by the footboard.

"Okay, then. At least come up and brush your teeth. Then we'll make up the sofa."

The three of them climbed the stairs together.

As the boys brushed their teeth, Randy stopped at the closed door to the master bedroom. Lynn's supper tray—a bowl of chicken noodle soup and crackers—had been left on the hall carpet, the food half-eaten. He listened at the door; a mixture of relief and dread dropped over him when all he heard was silence. She wasn't crying or moaning. It could be a good thing, couldn't it? He carried the tray downstairs and then came back up to finish getting Will to bed.

Once the bedtime routine was done and Will was tucked into his bed among fresh-smelling sheets, Randy carried another set of sheets and a blanket down to the living room. He unfolded the sheets then tucked them around the cushions of the sofa for Ty's bed.

Ty slipped in. "Moe must've gone to sleep. You think she's okay?"

Randy listened. Outside the house, all was quiet. Faintly, he heard the tree frog chorus, but the dog had either gone somewhere else or quieted down to sleep. "I think you're right."

"She'll be better tomorrow. She wants to play."

"Hmmm." Randy pulled the blanket up to Ty's chin, then bent to kiss him on the forehead. "Love you. Sleep tight."

"Are you going to bed, Daddy?"

"In a minute. After I finish looking through the photo albums. Your mom's been 'scrapbooking.' "

Back downstairs at the kitchen sink, Randy washed the dishes from Lynn's tray. Then he sat down and picked up the last photograph album.

Lynn hadn't changed much over the years; she was still beautiful—thick, golden brown hair, big eyes, and long lashes. She certainly hadn't gained any weight. Maybe the angles of her face had rounded out a little and her hair was a bit shorter. He peered at the photographs of himself and didn't really like what he saw. He was fatter around the middle, and the hair around his temples had turned gray. His eyes seemed smaller behind glasses that kept getting thicker and thicker as the years passed.

*Well, what do you expect? I read all day long and often in the evenings.* Maybe Lasik was the answer here.

About midnight he closed the last album. He listened for any sound from upstairs. All was quiet. He could hear Ty's even breathing from the sofa.

What was Lynn going to say when she finally spoke to him again? He tried to build up courage to climb the stairs and knock on their bedroom door. This could be rough. He wasn't sure he was ready for what she might say. He had to make her understand nothing had happened. It was an infatuation, nothing more, and it had already passed. Jennifer was nothing to him. Really. She wasn't. He closed his eyes.

There was something so appealing about Jennifer. She reminded him of those early days, when he and Lynn first met. The way Lynn had looked. The way she had stepped up so close to him and smiled into his eyes. Did Lynn still have the photo album from when they were dating?

He dug around in the cabinets below the book shelves, certain there had to be an album of their first years together. Lynn's photo album habit had begun long before him and their family. Finally, he found it.

There he was, at least twenty-five pounds lighter, growing a patchy beard. There were photos of Lynn hugging him, and him looking—surprised. Before Lynn, his life had been focused on studying history, reading about it, looking for endorsements of some sort that the version of the history he was reviewing was truthful and unbiased.

He knew history depended on the eyes of the one doing the telling.

It occurred to him that the albums he'd been looking at all evening were his family's history. According to Lynn. The photos were of what was most important to her: the time their family spent together.

"You're too absorbed!" Lynn had said to him so many times. "Life is what's happening now, in reality, not what happened years ago, or months ago, or minutes ago! Forget your damn history. Our family's history is happening, and you're missing it!"

Maybe she was right. He'd given the boys their baths and put them to bed. History was being created.

And his history, like Lynn's, was this family. It wasn't Jennifer. She was some blip on his radar screen, an anomaly in his history. He was not going to change his family's history for Jennifer.

He closed the oldest album and listened for any sound from upstairs. Quiet.

His heart thudded. He had come so close to losing it all—so close to making a mistake that would not be forgotten, and maybe not forgiven. Maybe family history—Lynn's version—had already changed. Maybe this one mistake was all it would take.

Randy closed the album and laid it carefully on top of the stack on the table. He glanced over at Ty. In his sleep, the slight chubbiness of his cheeks was still visible. It hadn't been that long ago when he and Lynn had brought their first son home from the hospital to this house. Time had passed, and he had walked through it in a haze.

He looked up the stairway again and listened closely before he got up from the sofa.

If Lynn was not awake, he would wake her.

## Chapter 32

Mick Jordan stood on his driveway and stared up at the stars. Out here on the outskirts of town, the stars were still clear as ever, even though the city crept closer. New shopping mall going in a couple of miles away, new housing additions all around it, more cars every day on the asphalt two-lane leading to the expressway. Amazing that the stars stayed the same.

"Mr. Mick? You okay?" Betsy's voice came from the patio door.

"Stars are pretty tonight. Bright."

"Yes. They very bright. You need rest. Come in, please."

Mick turned toward the door. His feet shuffled as he walked. Old feet. Old knees. But he'd sure played the golf all these years, all the golf a man could want.

"You feel okay? Miss Jo, she scare us all, didn't she?"

Mick's throat closed up as he remembered the way the hospital staff had shocked Josey back to life this afternoon. Tears had rolled down his cheeks when the heartbeat monitor had finally shown peaks and valleys again. But in those few instants, when he thought she was really gone from him, his own heart had stopped as well, and then started again, with hers.

"They watch her close. She be okay. We pray she wake up tomorrow and ev'thing be good again." Betsy patted his hand.

"We had lots of good years out here. Raised our kids, sent them into the world. It's been just Jo and me for a long time."

"I know, Mr. Mick. You and Jo, you take good care of this place. Lots of work."

"Yeah, but you know what? My back hurts, and my head hurts, and I'm tired." He eased down into his gold chair. "I don't want to mow the yard anymore, or rake up the leaves and cart them to the incinerator. It's been a real bother lately."

"You right. You not have to. I help you find someone do that for you."

"Don't suppose anyone would be surprised at that, do you?"

"No, Mr. Mick. You stop all that work when you want. Only then. I call hospital now, to check on Miss Jo one more time. She be so glad to see Matthew tomorrow. And Annie coming, too. I pick her up at the airport, 11 o'clock, right?"

"That's right."

Betsy slipped away toward the kitchen. From where he sat he could see her at the back door, staring out the window to the west. Her house was dark. What the heck had Al been doing without Betsy? She was tired and worried about the jerk. He could see it in her face.

The doorbell rang.

"I'll get it, Betsy. Likely a neighbor, or some kid selling something." He shuffled down the hallway to the door, flipped on the front porch light, took a peek out the peephole and stopped. He blinked and looked again.

The chain lock rattled against the doorframe as he hurried to slide it free and pull open the door.

Mick grinned at Matthew. His son stood in the middle of the porch and made no move to hug him.

"Hey, Pop! How are you?" Matthew's eyes looked hollow.

"I'm getting better every minute, son. With you here, and Annie coming tomorrow—well, your mom's bound to feel so much better, and quick."

Mick pushed the door the rest of the way open and grabbed Matthew's arm to pull him in. Behind him, on the front walk, a dog whined.

"New dog in the neighborhood?" Matthew asked as he stepped into the front hall.

"Well, I'll be," Mick said. The black dog stood at the edge of the circle of light and whined. He would have said that the dog seemed worried, if he hadn't known a dog didn't have feelings.

"This is my son, girl. This is Matthew. And Jo's doing better. Sure she is. Nothing to worry about there. Go home, go back to the Werlings."

He closed the door and flicked off the light.

Matthew grinned at him. "You sound like you're talking to a person, not a dog."

"Something about that dog is different. You'll see. You'll be talking to her like she's human, too, in a couple of days."

Mick led the way into the living room where Betsy perched on the edge of the plaid sofa.

Betsy went on to bed after a bit. Mick watched as Betsy told Matthew good night, told him she was glad he had come. Matthew's shirt seemed a size or two too big, and his bony feet were loose in his sandals. His face was thin, gaunt, and his eye sockets protruded around his eyes.

Mick didn't want to see what had happened to Matthew. It had been hard enough to hear it on the phone, during a conversation when they were five hundred miles apart. But to see him like this…It tore at his heart.

*And he'd been afraid to tell you why, old man. Afraid of your judgment. Are you still judging him?*

Mick shook his head to get the voice out of his mind. When he glanced at his son again, Matthew was staring at him.

"You okay, Dad?"

Tears welled in Mick's eyes. He should be asking that question of his son, not the other way around. "I'm fine, Matthew. I'm so glad you've come home."

He wanted to touch his son, to put his arms around him and weep. Why had it taken Jo's near-death experience to bring Matthew home, and for him to see his own stubborn prejudices were just that, and had nothing at all to do with "tough love"?

Instead, he reached for the pipe, cleaned it, stuffed it again with tobacco, and lit it. He didn't trust his voice to speak. These thoughts were new, and he wasn't sure that he could follow through so quickly with the actions they required.

## Chapter 33

Al rolled over in bed and groaned. His sleep had been dreamless—so rare. *Keep those eyes closed. Don't get up. No reason to get up. There's no one else here.*

Scratch, scratch, scratch.

The sound was like an emery board rasping on his fingernail, grinding at his brain. Relentless.

Scratch, scratch, scratch.

Al vaulted out of bed; he planted his bare feet on the wood floor, his body tensed into his "ready" position. Where was the noise coming from?

Scratch, scratch, scratch.

Something was at the window. Betsy! Ridiculous. She wouldn't be scratching at the window, she'd be walking in through the door. Something else, then. A squirrel? They were bold, they peered in at him sometimes, but he'd never known them to scratch at the bottom window frame. A bird? In spring, they'd sometimes peck at a reflection in the window. This was summer, wasn't it?

In two bounds he was at the window. He jerked back the drapes.

The black dog stood there, her tail going round and round like a windup toy, and she still had something in her mouth. What the—?

"Go 'way! Get out a-here! Stupid dog!" He yanked the drapes closed and threw himself back into bed.

Scratch, scratch, scratch.

He pulled Betsy's pillow off her side of the bed and jammed it over his head. There. He couldn't hear.

Scratch, scratch, scratch.

He pulled the pillow down harder and yelled, "Stop it, you damn mutt. Get outta here!"

The thick pillow finally blocked the sound. As far as Al knew, the scratching had stopped.

He dozed.

## Chapter 34

In her dream, Lynn was back at college. It was midterm, and she realized she had a final in a class she hadn't attended in weeks. She had meant to go, it was on her schedule, but somehow everything intruded on that time and she couldn't get there. In fact, she was having a hard time remembering exactly where the class was. She knew the building, but was the class in the corner room of the second floor or the third floor? And why was the stairwell so difficult to navigate? If she could get to class a few minutes early, maybe the professor would let her take the test later in the day, after she'd at least had a chance to read the last few chapters.

She turned the door handle to the class. It was locked. She knocked on the classroom door. No response. She knocked again, and again.

"Lynn? Lynn, are you awake?"

The professor had answered with Randy's voice.

"Lynn, honey, I need to talk to you. Can I come in?"

She opened her eyes. Randy. He was outside the door. She had locked him out. She took a deep breath. She halfway expected the pain to slice into her abdomen when she moved, but it didn't. The heavy-duty pain medicine the doctor had given her was working. She sat up, and the room spun.

Randy kept knocking. "Please open the door. I have to talk to you, honey."

She tried to focus on the door. The spinning room slowed so that she was able to slide to the side of the bed, sit up, then step to the door and pull it open. She immediately turned and dove back into the bed and under the covers again.

"Are you feeling better?" Randy's voice was soft, caring.

Did he think she was a damn idiot?

Lynn rubbed her forehead and ran her fingers through her hair to smooth the humps and tangles. "No pain right this minute." Cotton had filled her mouth.

"If you can talk to me, I want to talk to you."

"Mmmmm." Lynn straightened the covers, expecting Randy to sit, like he sometimes did, on the edge of the bed. Instead, he followed her to the bed, climbed up on it like Ty would have, and lay down next to her. He folded his glasses and set them on the nightstand. He laid his head on his pillow, and then turned to face her, their noses only inches apart.

Randy-before-children had sometimes done this. They'd cuddled close and talked into the night, then fallen asleep. No making love, just talking. It was one of the things that had made him different, made her fall so much in love with him.

"I love you, Lynn."

She heard him say the words. How could they still be true? If he desired another woman, lusted after another woman, how could he still love her? She'd always thought their love was unbreakable. But it felt broken now. A giant void filled her chest.

"You may not believe me, honey, but I do love

you. I told you I don't know what came over me with this girl. Nothing happened. We never even so much as touched. It was all in my mind."

Lynn saw concern and something that might be fear in his face. She closed her eyes.

"Lynn? Did you hear me?"

She snuggled deeper into her pillows and the soft mattress. Randy inched closer until their foreheads touched. She inhaled and then breathed out a deep breath like she did in yoga.

She had given everything she had to Randy and to her family, with no hesitation. But something had changed.

She opened her eyes. He looked different, and she didn't like what looking at him made her feel. She sat up. "I want you out of this house. When I wake up in the morning, I don't want you here."

"Lynn, you can't mean that. You're in no shape to take care of the boys should one of them need anything. You're not thinking straight."

"My thinking is fine. You're the one who's not thinking straight. If you want a different life and a different wife, then get out. I won't live with it like my mother did. I told you about that years ago, Randy. I've always been embarrassed to tell anyone what my mother let us both live with for too many years. She was ashamed, and she took all the blame. I won't take all the blame, and I won't smother my own wants and needs anymore just to keep us together if you want another woman."

It was a long speech, and her breath ran out at the end. She paused, every muscle in her body tense. She waited, not only for Randy to speak, but for her body to respond with another sharp pain.

"Honey, how 'bout if I sleep in Katy's bed? Then we can talk about this over breakfast."

She looked at him, then slowly shook her head. Her jaw clenched.

"I...said...get...out...of...the...house. I mean it."

"But where? You can't mean a hotel."

There was a silly half-smile on his face, as if he could talk his way out of this in only a few words.

She let the words hiss out between her teeth. "Not my problem, is it? Maybe your girlfriend has some extra room."

Something flashed in Randy's eyes. For an instant, she wondered if she was making a mistake, pushing him out like this. Maybe she was pushing him right to the place where he most wanted to be.

But then something ballooned inside her chest, filling up this new empty void that her love for Randy had filled for so many years. If he was so quick to rush to that girl, then let him. She could handle things on her own. Wasn't that practically the way things were most of the time, anyway?

Randy got up from the bed and stepped to the door. "You're sure you want it this way?"

"*You* want it this way. Get out, Randy."

He put his hand on the doorknob. "Okay, then. Goodnight."

The door clicked shut. Lynn stared up at the ceiling fan as it whirled around and around and around. A quietness dropped down over her body like mosquito netting. For an instant, she was aware she was headed down a path toward something different. Then the pain medicine fog thickened again.

In the half sleep, she saw the black dog, lying in a pile of green leaves. But the animal wasn't alone, Katy was with her, and Katy was crying.

Lynn came awake, shivering. She remembered what she had seen and admitted it could have been a dream image of herself lying there with the dog. She and Katy really were so very much alike, both in the way they looked and the way they thought.

*Maybe it was me, curled up with the dog. Maybe the dog came in my life just in time to help me get through this development with Randy.* She wouldn't give the development a name, even though she knew it was called *Jennifer.*

Lynn closed her eyes. It was comforting to imagine snuggling with the black dog. It was a sign there could be comfort in her life, and possibilities for the future.

Her breathing slowed.

Chapter 35

The sun was gone. Shadow fingers had crept toward Katy across the forest floor for hours, until eventually, the skinny sunny spaces in between them became gray and then black.

Sweat trickled down her face, and her skin felt like someone had rubbed a glue stick over it. Her tongue had ballooned to fill up her mouth. And her throat had closed up. Must be the size of a soda straw, just a crack. Her shriveled tummy rumbled and growled; it gnawed at her insides, trying to find something to eat.

Pain pounded in her leg.

Why had Mommy and Daddy not come looking for her? By now they knew she hadn't gone to the lake with Em. Surely someone had missed her.

But what if they didn't know? What if they didn't care? What if Mommy and Daddy were happy to have Ty and Will and no longer wanted her in the family?

Panic rose up in her narrowed throat.

Her breath hitched, loud in her ears. She closed her eyes to block out the darkened forest and tried to breathe slowly. Slowly.

Monique would come back with help.

The dog had given her a bath with its tongue. Mommy would be disgusted if she knew, and Ty would be jealous. Monique had licked her face and her hands until she started to giggle. The dog had nuzzled her with its nose and licked and licked.

She laughed out loud as she remembered. After that, Monique had settled close, practically on top of her, her body warm like a heating pad in the cool night air. Katy had shifted as much as she could with her hurt leg, so that her body curled around the dog.

Monique had licked her cheek in the same rhythm as the pain throbbed in her leg. Lick. Lick. Lick.

When she woke up again, the dog was still there. Monique sniffed her all over, and sniffed a long time at the hurt part of her leg.

"I'm hungry, Monique," she told the dog.

Monique had looked around, almost as if there might be some food for Katy growing right there. But other than lots of old acorns, and some tiny red berries from some of the bushes, Katy didn't think there was a thing she could eat in that forest.

"I bet you're hungry, too. Back home, I bet Mommy remembered to fill your bowl with food. And I bet she left it outside for you, since you haven't been home for them to let you in for the night. Oh, I wish you could talk, Monique. You could tell them I'm down here. And maybe, when you go back up tomorrow morning, you could grab some more fruit and bring it back. What do you think?"

Monique had started sniffing and licking again. Down her arm to her hand, then down her leg all the way to her feet. She couldn't feel the foot of her hurt leg. Katy looked down; she'd lost her house shoe. She didn't see it in the leaves close by, and she didn't see Cuddle Bunny either.

Where…? She'd fallen, hadn't she? All the way to the bottom of the ravine. Cuddle Bunny could be anywhere.

Monique quit licking and snuggled up against Katy, warm, her head on her paws, her breathing steady, even.

Sometime later, when Katy woke up in the darkness, the space next to her was cold and the dog was gone.

She didn't want to be here. She felt sick. She turned her head and gagged, but nothing came up.

Where had Monique gone?

She closed her eyes. All around her, crickets chirped.

*I wish I was lying on our back lawn on a beach towel, staring up at the stars through the branches of the trees.*

*I could be in the tippy-top of a rainforest, with monkeys and parrots and orchids.*

*I'm a superhero, on vacation in between saving people, lying on a mossy carpet in a forest somewhere, waiting for my next life-saving mission.*

An owl hooted.

Katy stared up at the trees and saw shreds of twinkling sky. She knew exactly where she was. She had started to walk home from Emily's. She had heard a dog bark. Maybe Monique. She had started down the path in the dark, calling the dog's name.

She tried to shift, and the pain in her leg roared. Oh, she wanted water. And something to eat.

Monique?

She closed her eyes. Earlier—today?—she had looked up above at the hillside of vines and bushes. The ledge had stopped her from falling to the bottom of the ravine—barely. A few inches more and she would have been in the water.

Maybe that wouldn't have been so bad. She could get a drink. It would be nice to get a drink.

Sometime this afternoon, she heard a different sound. "Monique? Here, girl. I'm here!" Monique didn't come.

Then, someone laughed, far down the streambed. Another voice answered.

"Help! I've fallen!" Her voice was a croak. She had no spit.

The boys laughed and called, moving away from her in the woods. Soon, all she heard were bird chirps and chickadee calls.

All afternoon, she'd expected Monique to come back. Sometimes she thought she heard her in the distance, barking, even howling. Monique wanted to help her. But when you're a dog, you have to get a human to listen. Maybe they all thought the dog was only playing.

Monique was smart, she could think of some way to get someone to realize she wasn't playing. She was serious.

Katy turned her head and felt the scratchy dirt against her cheek. Every ounce of hope she had rested with Monique. And just like in the dream, she knew Monique would save her. The dog would do whatever it took.

Katy was sure of it.

Chapter 36

Randy stepped out of the house and closed the door. He stood for a moment in the moonlight, letting the night wash over him. He couldn't believe Lynn had kicked him out.

He jiggled the keys in his pocket, his car keys, his house key, and the key to the Lopez house. What was he going to do? Where was he going to go?

The keys slipped from his hand and fell to the cement patio. As he bent over to pick them up, the answer became obvious. Jim and Gwen were on vacation. They wouldn't care if he slept on their sofa for one night.

That would give Lynn a good scare in the morning. She'd wonder where he'd gone. He could imagine her checking the driveway and seeing the car still there. She'd make some phone calls, but she wouldn't call the Lopez house. Why bother? They were on vacation.

He flicked on the flashlight and hurried across the lush side lawn to their property line. Lopez had a pool, and the pool lights glowed in the light blue water, orbs of light reaching toward the depths in the center. Maybe he'd go for a swim. He knew where the gate key was, and it wouldn't be any big deal to Jim or Gwen if he took a dip.

When was it they were coming home? He thought he remembered they'd be gone two weeks. Water the lawn if it doesn't rain. Water the houseplants on Sunday. Those were his only instructions. He'd take care of the plants tonight, and the lawn tomorrow.

Randy stepped up onto the deck and paused beside one of the deck chairs. He glanced back at his own house.

Lynn's anger shook him. He hadn't wanted her to find out he was attracted to Jennifer, he'd been afraid of it from the beginning. But still, in an odd way, he was relieved. He hated keeping secrets from her. They'd always told each other everything, from the very beginning.

She'd told him about her parents, her dad's infidelity. Lynn was so afraid the same situation could happen in her life. She wanted to trust him completely, and he'd assured her she had every reason to trust him. He would never hurt her. He had even admitted to her he'd been a virgin before they made love for the first time. It hadn't mattered that she wasn't.

But now, she didn't believe nothing had happened between him and Jennifer. And since Lynn knew about Jennifer, nothing would ever happen between them. His stomach churned, and so did his heart. How was it possible to want something and to not want it at the same time?

Lynn's reaction must mean she still loved him. She was jealous. But she was also disappointed. He had let her down, betrayed her trust. How long would it take to build it all back up, to get back to where they'd been before Jennifer walked into his office Friday?

Then there were the kids. Would she tell them what he had almost done—had contemplated doing? He didn't think so. They were too young to be told about infidelity—none of them even knew about sex yet, did they? He hadn't been the one to have that talk with either of the boys, and Lynn had not mentioned telling Katy about the birds and the bees.

He'd forgotten how things had been between Lynn's mom and dad. Regret tied a big knot in his stomach. This thing with Jennifer must have really thrown Lynn for a loop. She'd always had trust issues—how could he have done this to her? Had something pushed them along the path to his infidelity because her father had been unfaithful to her mother? He shook his head. *This is your fault, buddy. No one else's.* The voice in his head sounded a little like his dad's.

To believe otherwise—that his infidelity was predestined—reeked of karma, or destiny, or some type of mystical sentiment he didn't believe in. He was at this point in his life simply because Jennifer was beautiful, she smelled great, and she thought he was still handsome. Most days, he didn't feel handsome. Life had pushed him into the slow lane where there was no excitement, nothing to look forward to. It was in that slow lane where people got fat and lazy and unattractive to everyone, even their spouses.

Randy crossed the deck to the back door of the Lopez house. From here, he could see a lamp on inside. Probably on one of those timers. Supposed to make people think someone was at home. He didn't quite get that. There weren't any other lights on, so that would still be a telltale sign of vacancy to a burglar, wouldn't it?

As he stared into the darkness, he began to make out another light, farther back in the house, probably down the hallway. He peered at the glow. It flickered, then came back on again. Had someone walked in front of the light?

Maybe the Lopez family had come home early. Maybe he shouldn't use the key. Jim or Gwen might think someone was breaking in. Lopez might have a gun. Al Tilton was the only one he knew of on the hilltop who kept one handy—but then he didn't know everything about Jim, did he? They weren't exactly friends. Gwen and Lynn kept up with one another. He rapped on the doorframe. Seconds passed. He rapped again, fully expecting the back porch light to come on and the door to open. It didn't.

The door unlatched when he turned the key. Inside, the house was silent.

"Jim? Gwen? It's Randy. Are you here?"

He pushed the door open and stepped into the dimly lit room. "Jim? Yo, buddy. Anyone here?"

The door swung shut behind him. His heart thudded. He wasn't sure if he really had seen a shadow. Could have been anything. Could have been his eyes, tired at the end of the day. Could have been his imagination. If Jim and Gwen were here, they would have responded, wouldn't they?

He thought for a minute about what to do next. His mind recalled what it could of their floor plan. From this back hallway, the kitchen was on the right, and through there, the living room. His eyes began to adjust to the darkness. Randy stepped down the hallway and into the kitchen.

Air moved fast above him and something slammed into the top of his head. He fell to the floor. The stars that exploded weren't bright enough to clearly show him the face of the man who leaned over him, but it wasn't Jim Lopez.

Blackness descended.

Chapter 37

The jungle stank. Wet, soggy, breathing vegetation, alive with giant insects and bugs that Al didn't want to see. He kept his eyes closed.

He crept with the rest of them through the brush, those on the outside edge with one hand on their rifles, the ones in the middle stooped, ready for action, the others in front at the green wall, hacking into it with machetes.

Al stepped carefully, eased down with his foot to muffle the sound of his step. Six of them, sneaking through the brush, alert to every sound.

Monkeys and birds would be silent on their approach. He hated the silence. It throbbed. It stank. It was pregnant with his fear.

Gunfire! Rapid shots off to their right. They crouched and waited. A sheet of sweat poured down over his face. How long should they wait? An arc of movement in the semi-darkness. A hand signal. Move out. They moved forward again.

Slam!

Al was startled to find he was in the living room, in his chair. Starlight and moonlight streamed in through open curtains.

Slam!

He pushed himself to standing on wobbly legs. He closed his eyes and put all his energy into his ears, listening.

Slam!

The back door.

Someone—or something—crashed against it. Not a knock.

He almost called out "Betsy?" but stopped. Could be that someone wanted to know if anyone was home. Then, they'd break in.

Thought he was a weak old man, did they? He'd show them.

He slunk in the blackness over to the bookcase, reached up to the top shelf, back to the ceramic cougars—pieces from his mother's collection—and felt behind the largest cat for the edges of the cigar box. He slid it to the edge of the shelf, then drew it down against his chest. Slowly, he opened the box and inched his hand under the thin top. He curled his fingers around the familiar stock of the gun. In the dark, he popped out the clip and checked it, made sure he had bullets. Full. He stuck it back in the gun again and stepped flat-footed across the living room into the kitchen and to the back door.

A man had every right to protect his property.

Once at the door, he listened. Nothing. Whoever was on the other side was waiting, like he was.

Scratch!

In a split second, he grabbed the knob, wrenched the door open, and fired a low shot through the bottom screen.

Yelp!

The acrid scent of gunfire filled the room. He flicked on the light and shoved the screen door open, ready to fire again.

Something disappeared into the blackness of the yard. He doubted whoever—or whatever—it was would come back to his house. Something light-colored—an animal?—lay in the grass next to the sidewalk. He stepped outside and picked it up with two fingers by what looked like a leg. The thing was covered with mud and leaves and filth. What was it? He held it at arm's length, unable to see exactly what it was or had been. He blinked, pulled it back into the light of the kitchen. Round button eyes shone.

Ke-rist! It was a stuffed rabbit. Wet. Smelled like rotting leaves. Where did *that* come from? Trash, that's all. People threw away everything these days, or left it behind.

He glanced around the yard to make sure whoever or whatever had tried to get in wasn't still lurking and then he hustled back into the house. He pitched the filthy stuffed animal into the trashcan in the laundry room and continued down the dark hallway to the bedroom.

He'd keep the gun with him, right beside the bed, in case whoever it was tried to get in again. If they did, he'd blast them all the way to hell.

Chapter 38

*Sunday*

Across the sky, pink and purple clouds swirled like a child's chalk marks on a sidewalk. Daylight moved closer through the open drapes of his bedroom. Mick blinked. There had been no phone call from the hospital. That was good. After what had happened yesterday, he'd been so afraid...

He reached over and stroked the pillow on the other side of the bed. Josey should be there, not in the hospital hooked up to machines. Might as well get up. Make some coffee for Matthew. If there was coffee. Jo always made the morning coffee. Could he even run the coffee maker? Did Matthew even drink coffee?

Jo would have known. She should be here. Instead, she was lying there in the hospital bed, quiet and still.

Mick wanted her at home, and if that couldn't be, he wanted to be where she was. Better yet, go back to the day before Friday, before this had happened. Go back in time. To the day before the dog arrived, the day when everything changed. Maybe somehow, if he had been in the room with her instead of in the sunroom, looking out the window for the dog, he could have kept her heart attack from happening.

He got out of bed and stood at the window. In the predawn light, something black and low to the ground zigzagged through the yard. Mick squinted to see better, but couldn't make up his mind if it was that black dog.

Didn't move the same. Nothing speedy about it. And it seemed to be dragging something. Dead cat? Rabbit maybe? Wasn't sure from this distance and in this light.

She hadn't seemed like a dog that would kill wild things for fun, but you never knew that about a dog, did you? They could go feral, and then there were those natural instincts that they were always feeling.

That dog wouldn't have to kill because she was hungry. Surely the Werlings were feeding her. The animal probably got on well with all the people on the Hill; he couldn't be the only person who had been offering her tidbits.

Mick slipped on his house shoes and padded through the house to the patio door, then stepped outside and gave a low whistle.

"Here, girl. Show me what you got!" He scanned the bushes looking for some movement, some sign that the animal—if it had been the dog—was still there. The branches of the oak trees waved and that wind, the one that had been darting here and there around the neighborhood ever since Friday morning, was still blowing in fits.

He eyed each of the houses in the odd-shaped quadrangle. No lights on yet in any of them. Course it wasn't even six o'clock, and the sky was barely beginning to lighten. Al often rose early, unable to sleep, but Mick couldn't see any sign of lights at Al's house. Lord knew what kind of mood the man was in since Betsy had moved out and in with him. Al had to have noticed that his wife was living here, but he hadn't been over to see her, hadn't called. The man was too proud for his own good.

Time was when he would have risked his life to save Al, and vice versa. He wasn't sure if that was still true. The man had turned mean and hateful.

Jo didn't want him in their house after that ranting and raving scene last week. He didn't have a clue what Al had been so upset about. He hadn't taken anything that belonged to Al, and Al hadn't even been willing to tell them what he had lost. If he had really lost anything. Al's mind wasn't what it had been since he got back from the Army.

Eventually, Betsy would have to go home to deal with the man and her marriage. When would that be? Lord willing, maybe Monday? But he was forgetting rehab. It could be weeks and weeks before Jo came home. Maybe Betsy would stay with him, and maybe Matthew would, too.

Mick scanned the yard one more time for the animal. The grass needed mowing, little sprigs stuck up around the bases of the trees and over the sidewalks and the patio. He closed the patio door. How in the world was he going to take care of this place without Jo? Did he even want to?

"Pop?" Matthew appeared in the kitchen doorway, toweling his hair. Again, Mick noticed first how thin he was, and second, the dark circles under his eyes. "I want to go see Mom first thing. Soon as I get dressed."

Mick nodded. "Gonna put some coffee on. Is Betsy up?"

"Haven't seen her. Nice of her to come over to stay with you, Pop, but I think she should go home. Al's a loose cannon. Her being over here while Mom's in the hospital may not be wise. I can take care of things for you."

He knew that Matthew was right. Betsy should go home. Maybe she didn't want to. It troubled him that Al hadn't been over to talk to her, hadn't made a move to talk to anyone for days as far as he knew. Wasn't good for a man in Al's mental state to be so completely alone. Couldn't be.

He moved to the coffee maker. Matthew joined him, reached into the cabinet for the bag of coffee grounds, and filled the canister with water for the brew. Mick slipped away to the bedroom to put on his shoes and socks and let Matthew deal with the coffee.

Fifteen minutes later, after Matthew had downed two cups of strong, black coffee and Mick had shaved and dressed, Matthew picked up Mick's car keys and started toward the garage.

"I stay here this morning," Betsy said as the men passed through the kitchen. "You come home, then I go back to sit with her this afternoon. She need time with her men, I think."

Mick nodded. Betsy motioned them out and closed the door.

"What have they said about the heart attack?" Matthew asked his father as they drove to the hospital. Then, "Did they tell you the extent of the damage?" And, "Does she have a blockage?" Finally, "What about rehab?"

Mick blinked, barely able to hear the questions and totally unable to fathom any answers. His head was muddled. He rubbed at his right eyebrow.

"Maybe the doctor will come in while you're there," Mick said as he got out of the car in the hospital parking lot. "Maybe he can tell you more than I can remember. There was so much happening so fast."

Outside the hospital, Mick walked a few steps ahead of his son down the sidewalk toward the revolving entrance door. The wind whipped at the bill of his golf hat. He pushed it firmly down on his head and forged on. He trusted that Matthew was following close behind. His son was as intent to get to Jo as he was.

"Hold on, Josey, hold on, girl," Mick muttered as he barreled through the lobby, down the hall, and onto the elevator. He held his tongue once they were moving up to the fifth floor, but he kept up the mantra in his head. *Hold on, Josey-Jo, hold on.*

He pushed the entry button on the door to the ICU ward and then went straight to the nurses' station. "Josephine Jordan. Where?"

The nurse pointed. "Right there, Mr. Jordan. She's stable. Nothing new since last night."

Nothing new since last night. Nothing new since her heart stopped again. Nothing new since they revived her with the paddles one more time. She'd been gone five minutes, the doctor had said. Where had she gone?

"Josey," Mick whispered as he stepped up to the bed in the open cubicle. Matthew grabbed the edge of the curtain and pulled it closed around them. "Can you hear me, girl?" He laid his hand on the white blanket where it humped up over her arm. "Look who's here. Our Matthew's home."

She was so still. Her eyes looked sunken, her cheeks hollowed out. His mouth dropped open, and he staggered back. The realization of her frailty struck him like a boxer's blow. This might be it. Today, or tomorrow, she might really leave him behind.

His heart heaved.

"Matthew's here, Jo." He forced the words out of his mouth. Could she hear the fearful quiver in his voice? "And Annie and John are landing soon. Betsy's going to pick them up at the airport at eleven. Marilyn wants to bring Lacey; they're working on getting a flight. They'll all be here soon, Josey, to cheer you up." He rubbed her arm.

The song came to him, silly as it was. He hummed, and then began to sing soft and low, "Mares eat oats and does eat oats and little lambs eat ivy. A kid'll eat ivy, too, wouldn't you?" He hummed another chorus, and sang another chorus and hummed another chorus, his mind full of all the things he wanted to say to her but couldn't put to words. He rubbed her arm, and knew that she knew what he wanted to say anyway. He stood and hummed, and rubbed, and hummed, and rubbed.

Matthew came up behind him and put his arm around him. "Let's talk to the doctor, Pop. Then we'll know more. Give her a little time."

Mick looked at his son and saw the graying skin around his eyes, the hollows in his cheeks. It wasn't just Jo that worried him. His son was not well either. His knees failed at that realization, and had it not been for Matthew, Mick would have slipped to the floor. Instead, his son grabbed onto his arms and hauled him over to the plastic-covered recliner.

"Sit down, Pop. I'll get you some water."

Mick closed his eyes; his own heart pounded in between the beats from the monitor that amplified the sounds of Josey's heart.

The two of them sat, one on each side of the bed, each holding one of Jo's hands. Mick cupped her hand between the two of his, Matthew locked his fingers with hers.

"I'm here, Mom. I want you to know that whatever you need, I'm here for you. And for Pop. Nothing matters but that you come back to us. Wake up, get strong, and come home. We're not gonna let you go." Matthew's voice hit a crack. He cleared his throat. "Sis is coming later today with her kids, and my kids are coming with Marilyn. They all want to see those bright eyes of yours, got it? Don't let them down."

Jo's eyes flew open, startling both Matthew and Mick. She focused them on her son. "She came to help. Like before. Help her." Jo swallowed. She didn't squeeze Matthew's hand, or move her fingers in Mick's, she only stared. And not at him, *through* him. Her lips began to move again, but no words came out.

The men leaned over her, straining to hear but could only make out bits and pieces that sounded like "moon" and "shoe" and maybe "ravine."

Mick shook his head. "Can't hear you, Jo. What are you saying?" He pulled back from the bed and spoke softly to Matthew. "Dreaming. Probably the medicine. Make any sense to you?"

Matthew shook his head. "Was she delirious at all yesterday?"

Mick thought back to the strange thing she had said before her heart stopped and had to be shocked back to beating. "She said something yesterday. Same sort of thing. Reminds me of something…"

Mick's brow creased, and he fought through the clouds of his own memories. Something elusive. It was there, almost there. Then it was lost again.

Unbidden, his mind filled with the image of the black dog, racing across the lawn Friday morning. The dog. What was she running from?

He had sensed something on the wind. What if she had not been running from, but running to get ahead of…?

They were doing all they could for Josey. And she was here in the hospital. What other disaster had the dog foreseen?

Yesterday Josie had mentioned Al. Said something that he was supposed to tell Betsy. He couldn't remember the message. Al was all alone in the house while Betsy stayed with Mick. Al wouldn't get into trouble without her would he? Surely he wouldn't do something stupid.

Maybe Al was having shell shock. Anyone who'd done combat duty was likely to get it. He'd probably had it ever since the war. Whatever was wrong with him, it was getting worse.

"…tell her to practice. Don't let her stop." Jo's voice sounded stronger. Her blue eyes drilled into the ceiling.

Katy. She was talking about the Werling family now. But why was she worried about Katy and her practicing? She loved her piano lessons. She wasn't going to quit. The dog wouldn't be a reason to quit piano, would it? If not the dog, what else? With three kids, there were always possibilities for trouble with them or even with the young parents. Randy worked a lot of long days and late nights. Lynn was alone a lot. Those two boys were a handful. Katy was alone a lot, too, with a wild imagination like most ten-year-olds.

Jo's eyes closed. He glanced at the monitor, but the lines were alternating peaks and flat-bottomed valleys with no sign of stopping that he could see.

"She came to help. Like before," Jo had said earlier. His memory clouds stirred. He saw the black dog dash across the yard again. What was chasing her?

Mick shook his head; he'd recognized her. The animal had been there on the hill thirty years ago when they were building the house. He closed his eyes and dropped his head. But that was impossible, dogs don't live to be thirty years old.

He searched his memory. They were building their house, the very first one in the new neighborhood on the hill, and he was there with the contractor. They were talking about which trees needed to stay and how they could situate the windows of the house best to catch the afternoon sun in winter. Big equipment had been crawling over the lot, pushing new top soil over the sandy forest earth so that they could grow Bermuda grass.

At the edge of the forest, Mick caught sight of an old man standing with a dog. His arms were crossed over his chest, shoulder length white hair blew in the wind. The man watched the machinery, he watched them. After a few minutes, Mick crossed the rugged, gouged earth to talk to the man, avoiding torn tree roots and fallen limbs.

They'd nodded at one another, and Mick had stood beside the man, looking over the pre-construction site debris in silence. Deep wrinkles bracketed the man's mouth and divided his forehead. A sad squint crinkled the skin around the man's dark brown eyes.

"Live around here?" Mick had finally asked.

"Hmmm."

"Gonna be a nice neighborhood. Folks'll like it out here."

"Already do." The Indian's voice was a gravelly grumble.

"You live out here?"

"Hmmm."

The dog moved to sit in front of Mick, and he reached out to touch her fine head, to rub the short, soft black fur that covered her skull.

"Nice dog."

The old man looked up at the sky, and then back over at the house site.

"Something I can help you with?" Mick tried again.

"She brings help for you. And a warning to watch out."

The man had walked away through the trees, but the animal stayed. The dog had sat in front of him, looking up with yellow-brown eyes. He'd never seen eyes like that on a dog before, eyes as clear and deep as a hot springs pool.

Day after day, the dog was there as they worked, sometimes watching from the shade of the trees, other times bathing in the sun, her belly up and her legs splayed open, her tongue falling out one side of her mouth.

The workmen adopted the dog, with one exception. Richie was superstitious. And he avoided the dog. The men ribbed him about it, but Richie didn't have much to say. Mick thought that he must be afraid of dogs, must have been bitten by one once or seen a dog maul somebody. The dog wanted to be friends with Richie more than it wanted to be friends with anyone else on the crew.

Mick's memory sharpened, and he could remember it all like it was yesterday. In his mind, the hospital room faded and the construction site—the site where his house was being built—filled the room.

The wind blew in gusts that day, and they were nearly finished cutting down and hauling away what trees they would remove for the footprint of the house. Richie was on a machine, moving dirt, when the black dog began to bark. She sat and barked so loud that even Richie, on the dozer, stopped to look at her. About that time, one of the trees they had marked for removal and done some preliminary cutting on, snapped in the gusty wind and fell. The tree missed Richie by only a few feet. Seconds later, the dog turned and disappeared into the forest.

Josey's voice jerked him back to the present. "It's not too late to save her. Help Lynn!"

Matthew and Mick looked at Jo's face. Her eyes were closed, but her mouth worked as if her lips were forming words that wouldn't quite be words. Her head thrashed on the pillow, and then she lay still.

Mick's eyes went to the heart monitor, but her heart rhythms were spiking and dropping in lines that crept steadily across the screen.

"What does she mean, Pop?"

"Don't know for sure. I think she might be talking about that black dog. And something that's happened to Lynn Werling."

Chapter 39

Shivers shook Katy from head to toe. Her mouth and throat were stuffed with Mom's makeup balls; the air she needed to breathe could barely squeeze through. So cold. Never felt this cold, not even in the middle of winter when she ran outside without a coat to catch a few snowflakes on her tongue. How could the world be so green when it was this cold?

Her head itched, and she reached up to scratch it. A giant knob had grown above her right eyebrow and stretched half way across her forehead. When she opened her eyes, shreds of pink sky glowed between the dark leaves above. A bird trilled off to her right, and a crow called on her left. Leaves rustled not far from her head.

The steady rustle inched toward her; Katy shivered from cold and dread. Whatever it was, it moved too slow for a squirrel, too heavy for a worm, too steady for a rabbit. A snake? Suddenly, she couldn't get enough air to breathe. She thrashed to one side, then screamed with pain. Eyes wide open, she looked in the direction of the noisy leaves and gasped for breath.

The turtle pulled its head into its domed brown shell, but she could see its eyes, rimmed in red, watching her. Eye to eye, both of them held their breaths. The turtle reached one clawed foot in her direction, paused, then pulled itself forward an inch and jutted its head out of dark neck wrinkles. Katy sobbed and tears dropped onto the ground beneath her.

The turtle plowed on through the undergrowth of grass and fallen leaves, moving past her six inches away.

"Come here. Please?" she whispered. Not that she thought the reptile would do it. Turtles didn't have emotions, didn't care about people—not like Monique did. Katy watched the turtle's slow journey until he was hidden in the tall grass.

Katy clenched her teeth and turned her body slowly, expecting pain with every little movement. Finally, she was on her back again. She sighed. That hadn't hurt too much. Tears trickled down her cheeks. A chill shook her body.

Where was Monique? Where were Mom and Dad? Why hadn't they come?

"Monique?" she called. Her voice cracked, and sounded more like a squeak than a cry for help. Monique had been with her last night, in the dark, when she'd fallen asleep. Why wasn't she here?

Katy twisted to one side. Pain raced up her leg and stars danced like fireflies among the trees. She gagged once, twice, but she hadn't eaten for hours and there was nothing in her stomach to throw up. She gulped and sobbed again. Something crawled onto her arm. When she looked at it, eight long legs and a tiny oval body, she squealed and flicked her arm, sending the daddy longlegs flying into the bushes.

"Monique, please come back!" She sobbed. Her leg hurt. She was starving, and sooo thirsty. Monique WOULD come. Maybe not this second, and maybe not in fifteen minutes, but she would come back.

Katy had seen it in her dream, and she knew it would happen.

The trees began to spin, and Katy closed her eyes. The ground beneath her rose and fell; her leg throbbed. Her arms were frozen sticks.

This couldn't be real. The way the world spun around her, it couldn't be real. It was a dream, right?

She'd had the dream so many times. And it was just like Grandma had told her. Dreams were like vacations, but you didn't have to spend any money or go anywhere. She could hear Grandma's voice in her head, even though she'd gone to heaven years ago. "Someday, you'll even know why that dream was in your head," she'd said. "Someone planted a seed."

Eyes closed, the dog ran through her mind. Katy smiled, lips quivering with cold. She knew why the dog had come to her dreams.

Months ago—last fall?—she'd been sitting on the patio, eating cookies with Miss Jo before her piano lesson.

"Did you see that?" Miss Jo stared into the thick trees in the forested lot next door.

Katy looked into the shadowy depths. "No…"

"Wonder if it's that dog again," Jo whispered.

"What dog?"

"It's black and it's been hanging around."

"Do you think it's hungry?"

"Trouble's coming." Jo's voice stretched out and curved into the air.

Katy's leg throbbed. Her teeth chattered.

"When I was a girl," the stretched voice went on, "my folks had a little farm down the dirt road. Way back." Jo's face loomed on the back of Katy's eyelids.

Spit oozed in Katy's desert-dry mouth. Oatmeal-raisin-chocolate chip cookies. Miss Jo made the best ever.

"That dog would slip between the trees or scoot down the bar ditches in early morning. 'Wonder what's gonna happen?' my dad would say. Before that week was out, there'd be an accident."

Katy heard Miss Jo's voice above her, beside her, all around. But Miss Jo wasn't here, was she?

"That dog would be there, barking, before it happened. If people paid attention, they didn't get hurt. But other times, they shooed the dog away. Then things went bad."

Miss Jo's face got real close when she said the word BAD, so close that Katy thought Jo had to be right there with her, at the bottom of the ravine, in the cold forest. Katy reached for Jo, but her fingers closed on air.

Had Miss Jo really seen the dog that day, or was it the memory alive in her head?

Miss Jo pushed all of the air out of her lungs in a long sigh and whispered, "Something will happen, sooooon. You'll seeeeeeee." The words echoed, bouncing from tree to tree.

Katy nodded to herself. Miss Jo had made her dream about the dog. Cleo and Caesar were never in her dreams. And she loved them both a lot. They slept in her room and kept her company. But she didn't dream about them and the way they loved to cuddle with her in her bed.

Katy's eyes flew open. Sweat popped out on her forehead; her arms and legs were on fire. How could it be so hot? The sun was only halfway up the sky. She moved; sticks and rocks jabbed her back. Pain sliced all the way from her leg to her eyes. She cried out and fell into a memory.

After Easter, they were coming home from visiting Grandpa Werling in Kansas City. Daddy was driving. The car drifted over the white line at the edge of the road and rumbled on the shoulder.

"You're going off the road; we're going to end up in that ditch," Mommy said each time it happened. "Where is your mind? Keep it on the road where it belongs."

Daddy gave her a look.

Katy could tell from the way Mommy held her head really, really still that she was irritated. Thank goodness Ty and Will were both asleep and unable to pick on each other. That would make things much worse.

Katy opened her eyes to the green world. "Monique?" Her voice croaked. She twisted her head from side to side. *I have to be dreaming.*

She wasn't really here. She wasn't lying at the bottom of this ravine. Her leg wasn't broken.

She wanted to wake up. She didn't want to have this dream again, this dream where she was somewhere all alone, hungry and sooo thirsty. In the dream, the dog saved her. She wasn't sure exactly what the dog had done…Dreams are that way, sometimes they don't make sense and things don't happen in order or there are chunks that are missing. But in the dream, she had lived because of the black dog.

Why wasn't the dog in her dream right this second? Why wasn't this dream going like all the others?

A twig snapped somewhere up the hillside. Her

insides were on fire, and there was no way she could ever get cool again. Another twig snapped. She tried to open her eyes, but they were heavy, and so hot, like boiled eggs pulled out of the water.

"Monique?" she mumbled. She hoped it was the dog, and she hoped—oh, how she hoped—the dog had brought her something wet and cold—like an orange, or an apple, or a hunk of watermelon—to eat.

## Chapter 40

Mick tried to relax into the smooth plastic waiting-room chair. He couldn't get comfortable. Thing was, he might not ever be able to get comfortable again, not if Josey-Jo didn't come home.

He wanted to have a positive attitude. He wanted to look at Jo and KNOW that she was going to come home again, that everything would be normal at their house again. The two of them would putter around, taking care of the house and the yard, managing somehow, even though they were getting older. Thing was, though, he could hardly look at Jo's gray face and believe that the positive message could really come true. She looked so weak, and so—he had to think it—*old*, lying there. And he had to acknowledge that when he looked in the mirror he looked just as old. Where had the time gone?

"Pop? You okay?"

He looked at Matthew, stared into his eyes, seeing the little boy he had been. Did he still feel like that little boy deep inside? He couldn't imagine that he did. Married, then divorced, and with the diagnosis of HIV positive hanging over his head. It was hard to imagine what he did feel. And it was hard for Mick to acknowledge that his own prejudice might have contributed to the sadness in his son's eyes and the pallor of his skin. He wished he had been there more for

Matthew when he was growing up, that they had spent more time doing things together—fishing, throwing a ball around, working on cars—and more time talking about whatever Matthew wanted to talk about. Matthew's youth had slipped past.

If he had spent the time with his son, would Matthew's marriage have turned out differently? Would he even have married Marilyn and had kids? Would he have admitted earlier in life that he preferred men to women? Was there anything Mick could have done to have prevented it from happening? Mick admitted to himself that he'd never truly focused his attention on either of his children. He'd been thinking about *his* career, and what *he* wanted from life. It was no wonder that Annie was having troubles with marriage, too.

"Pop?"

A tear eased out and travelled down Mick's cheek. "I'm here, Matty, and that's about all I can say. It's hard to see your mother this way, you know."

"I know. But she's going to get better. Didn't the doctor say that she had a 90% chance of a full recovery? She's going to hang in there, go to rehab, and get better. She's going to go home with you again. We need to talk about that. About the future. As soon as Annie gets here." Matthew slid into the chair next to him. "What did you mean about the dog, Pop? And why is Mom thinking about that black dog and Lynn Werling in the middle of all of this?"

Mick squinted out the window where the morning light was rushing in. "It's easier than thinking about what's really happening. Hospital time. Rehab. Recovery time."

"But it's like she's in a trance whenever she talks

about the dog."

"Superstition. Been a black dog around as long as we've lived on The Hill. The dog doesn't bring trouble, but she seems to know something's going to happen. She showed up the morning Jo had her attack. And she stayed. Makes me think it's not over. And Jo doesn't think it's over either. She thinks that something's happening back in the neighborhood with the Werlings." He looked at Matthew, expecting to see a slight smile in his eyes, a sure sign of disbelief, but it wasn't there. "You believe me?"

"There are things we don't understand in life, Pop. Miracles even." Matthew leaned forward, resting his elbows on his knees. "Maybe the dog is a symbol of that to both of you."

"Maybe." Mick laid his hand on his son's knee. "Miracles can come in a lot of shapes. To me, it's a miracle that you came home, after the things I said." He swallowed and plunged ahead, even though he was visiting a territory he'd never entered with his son before. "I love you, Matty. I never stopped. I'm too damn stubborn. Judgmental. I was wrong." He looked into his son's face. "I'm sorry."

Matthew covered his father's hand with his own. "It's okay, Pop." He cleared his throat and blinked.

Mick saw glistening tears.

"I'm getting better," Matthew continued. "They have new medicines. HIV positive is not a death sentence anymore. I'll see my kids graduate from college, and I hope that you and Mom will, too."

They sat in silence, then Mick straightened and scooted to the edge of the seat cushion. "Guess I could go home. Maybe Jo's right, and there's something we could do to help the Werlings. Maybe we ought to go give it a try."

In the bed, Jo groaned and muttered something that sounded like *Katy.*

Chapter 41

Whose damn dog was barking? Al charged through the living room, eyes half open. His eyeballs were dry and sore; they scraped as they moved in their sockets. He staggered to the back door. It had to be that black dog. The Werlings' other dogs—stupid, fraidy-cat dogs—never came right up to the house. What other dog would it be?

He jerked open the door, and there was the black dog, not three feet from the door, barking like crazy. Al tried to focus. The animal barked and turned, ran a few feet away, stopped, then came back to bark more. What was the matter with it? He rubbed his fingers across his forehead and opened the screen door.

"Shut up! Ain't you never heard of peace and quiet," he yelled.

The animal ran up to him and grabbed hold of his pajama pant leg, then jerked.

"Hey! Let go! What the…"

The dog pulled him a little at a time, moved him down the sidewalk toward the yard. "Let go, you black she-devil!" He tried to kick at the dog with his other foot and ended up off-balance, then sprawled on the sidewalk. "Get out-a-here!"

The dog released his pajamas, but stood only a foot away, panting, head down. Looked tired, the dog did. Or maybe something more than that. Hurt? Al pulled himself to sitting and leaned toward her to take a closer look. The dog turned its head to lick its shoulder, but watched him even then.

Blood seeped from a gash several inches long on her shoulder. When he reached for her, the dog limped a few feet away, then looked back at him. She whined.

He wasn't totally ignorant of dogs. He'd grown up with one. And he'd seen every episode of *Lassie* on his parents' black and white television years ago. "You want me to follow. That's what you want, right?"

The dog barked and started off again, this time limping several yards across the Jordan's lawn before it looked back.

He got to his feet, slow, the world spinning around a little before it steadied. Early morning, gray light, pink clouds. Birds twittered, and somewhere on the far side of the hill, a rooster crowed.

The dog limped back toward him, yipping, sounding out dog words in syllables he couldn't translate, but again, her meaning was clear: "Follow me!"

Al looked down at his house shoes. Not the best thing in the world to go for a walk in, but then, he didn't intend to go far. Just far enough to see what the crazy dog was up to. It was obviously hurt, but that wasn't stopping it. Something was troubling the animal.

He followed her across the Jordan's lawn, all the while peering at the windows of the house. Damn Betsy was probably ogling him from behind one of the blinds. Wondering what he was doing. Thinking he couldn't get along without her.

Well, she was wrong. He'd been doing fine, hadn't he? Course, he hadn't eaten much, but he hadn't been drinking. Booze was all gone. Nothing to drink in the house except tap water. God awful stuff that was. And he hadn't felt like making the drive to the liquor store, either. Heavy bones. But he was moving. Yes-sir-ee, he was following the dog.

The dog picked up the pace, stepping unevenly onto the Lopez's lawn and past the swimming pool toward their driveway. That shoulder wound was slowing her down, and he wondered if it was more than that, if something was wrong with one of her legs. Al shuffled along after her.

At the edge of the driveway, he stopped. *What the hell am I doing following this damn dog?* "Hey!" he shouted. "Ain't going to town with you, hound. Where ya goin'?"

The dog trot-limped down the Lopez driveway and into the street. She started down the hill, then sat and looked back at him.

"I've 'bout reached my limit," he called.

The dog barked and looked down into the green jungle of the ravine next to the road. The animal whined, then her whine turned into a howl. She threw her head back and let loose like she was hearing a siren in the distance. He couldn't make out any siren. What was she hearing?

The dog waited.

"God damn it." He looked down at his fleece-lined house shoes. Bits of dried grass stuck to the sides and toe. They'd need a wash. He supposed he could do it if Betsy didn't come home. But she would.

He stared at the dog. She stared back and whined, then licked at the oozing wound on her shoulder. Al stepped toward her. The animal stood, then, when he had almost reached her, she barked and stepped toward the ravine.

"Not going down there," Al said. Just looking at the green mess of shrubs and vines and leafy trees made his heart pound. A thousand needles sprayed into his brain. He swayed on his feet and clutched his head. No, no, no. *I'm here, on the Hill. I'm not there.*

The dog barked at him again, this time from the edge of the jungle, where the slope began, before it slid on down to the creek at the bottom.

It wasn't the jungle he had known, but it was a jungle all the same. Snakes, spiders, rats, insects, critters unknown. They lived down there. It was the last place around here he was willing to go. He turned his back on the dog and crossed the street, headed up the Lopez driveway.

Damn! In a flash, the dog had a hold of his pants again. Shoot! She was dragging him across the road to the ravine. He stumbled after her, tripping over his own feet as she jerked his pant leg. At the edge of the asphalt road, she stopped and looked up at him, and then stared down into the sloping thicket.

"Quit! Ain't goin' on. You stop. Hear me?" He swatted at the animal. She yelped. When he pulled his hand back, it was smeared with blood. Her blood. His blood? He blinked several times to clear his vision and looked down at the dog. She'd grabbed ahold of his pant leg again, but her tug was easier, weaker, and she whined as she pulled at him.

"What happened to you?" He reached down and this time she waited as he softly touched her shoulder. She let go of his pant leg. The three-inch gash across her right shoulder oozed deep red blood onto fur already matted with dried blood.

Al flinched. Could it have been…? Had he…? "Oh, my. My, my, my." He squatted down and stroked her head. She licked his hand. "I'm sorry, girl. It was you, last night, weren't it?"

The black dog turned away and took a few steps into the green tangle of vines and bushes. She looked back at him and whined.

"Why in heaven do we have to go down there?" he asked the dog.

She yipped and darted into the underbrush. Al trudged in a few steps. The brambles weren't too bad here. No poison ivy that he could see. And there was a sort of a path, like someone—kids most likely—had been trampling through. He followed it a few feet. Green briars caught at his pajamas, and he pushed through sumac and buck brush.

Something buzzed in his head, and he stopped. The green forest around him moved.

*Where am I?*

He scanned the underbrush and reached for his gun.

*No gun belt.*

He took a step, his mind skittering in the green. He stared ahead down the shadowy path.

*Was that…a dog?*

Her tail wagged in a circle, and she whined.

*The ravine.*

The damned dog had forced him into the ravine. He took a few steps toward the animal. She charged down the path, whining. He stepped after her.

When she stopped a little further on and cocked her head, he stopped, too.

*What was that? A voice? Bird most likely. What?*

Words soft and some distance away. Or were those sounds really words? He listened, hard, focusing his mind on the sound.

Someone was calling. That, or his ears were ringing again. He squatted there on the trail, off balance, about to fall over. He put one knee down, and the dog was beside him, whining, licking at his hand.

"Help! Monique, help!"

The words were loud enough this time that he was certain he wasn't hearing things.

Who was Monique? Who was calling? He'd known a Monique once, back in his golden years. Back when he could get about any woman he wanted because they all had wanted him, too. He was handsome. Tall, lean, smart-mouthed. They'd smiled and primped for him.

Except for Betsy. He'd been the one who'd had to work to get her interested. But she'd been worth it. They'd had good years together. He'd been the lucky one the day they met.

BARK!

The animal was beside him, agitated, leaping from side to side, racing down the path and then returning to him. She gave him a long look, then charged away. He stood. She glanced back at him and yipped, and then she was off, headed downhill. Last year's leaves, wet and half-decayed, still coated the ground. He trod carefully, picking up his feet and setting them down in his house shoes. He followed the dog, moving with it down the slope.

"Monique, help! Please help me!" The voice sounded closer. He followed the path and the slim black tail that moved a few yards in front of him through the green underbrush. Beads of sweat collected on his brow.

Chapter 42

Lynn opened her eyes. Her heart pounded. The quiet sea-green walls of the bedroom rose solid around her, unlike the ocean she had been drowning in only moments before in a dream. She stretched slowly, expecting a sharp pain, but her muscles and bones moved smoothly under her skin.

The sun filled the room with bright light. She rolled out of bed, exchanged her short nightgown for a pair of shorts and a T-shirt, slipped her feet into flip-flops, and stepped into the hallway. The house was quiet. Ty's door was open and his bed empty. Will was sound asleep in his bed, his teddy bear clutched tight in his arms. Lynn descended the stairs.

She expected to see Randy asleep on the living room sofa. She hadn't really thought he would leave the house, even though she had asked him to go. Lynn couldn't remember ever feeling so angry. And with good reason. She could still hear the soft words he'd spoken to the girl on the phone, when he didn't know Lynn was listening.

Her face went hot with the memory. How could he! They had a family! He was acting just like her father had.

No, he wasn't, she argued with that voice inside her head. He wasn't like her father. He hadn't done anything, he had just thought about it. Or so he said.

Should she believe him?

Lynn peeked into the den, but the couch was empty. She could barely see the back of Ty's head. He lay on the floor, already watching television. A rumpled sheet and lightweight blanket were wadded up against the arm of the couch.

She had no clue what she would have said to Randy if he'd been sitting there. The hollow feeling inside her had shrunk in size, but it was there all the same. Without much urging, it would swell again and fill her mouth with a cold, metallic feeling, as if a robot had taken over her body.

"Hi," she called to Ty as she turned toward the kitchen. She looked at the empty coffee maker canister, and then pulled out a glass and filled it with water. No use tempting fate. She drank too much coffee. Had that been what had caused the gall bladder to go bad?

"Mommy!" Ty yelled. He ran in from the den to hug her around the hips.

"Hey, you." Lynn kissed the top of his head. "How's that arm?"

Ty frowned and tilted his head, putting on his pitiful face.

"Still hurts, huh? You've got a tough couple of days ahead of you, honey. But we'll get through it."

"Mommy!" Will yelled from the top of the stairs. He took them too fast, legs scurrying, and Lynn closed her eyes, imagining he would slip and then slide all the way down, but he made it to the bottom and then across the living room and into the kitchen, taking short, fast little steps with his still-chubby legs. He grabbed her around the knees.

"Feeling better today?" she asked. Her knees

wobbled. She tousled the boys' hair and pushed them away so she could sit down in one of the ladder-backed chairs at the kitchen table.

Will nodded. "I threw up all over. Daddy had to clean it up." He climbed up into her lap.

"I know. I'm so glad you feel better." She patted his head and pulled him close. Lynn smiled into his hair and thought of Randy, cleaning up the mess. She closed her eyes and smiled even wider.

"Can I go outside to play with Moe? Daddy wouldn't let me yesterday. He said he thought she might be sick," Ty said.

"Why would he think that?"

"He said she was acting crazy. He said she might have rabies or something."

"Really? That would be awful. She's such a pretty dog." Lynn set Will down on his feet and got up to look out the side door window.

"I'll check around outside in a minute. Until then, how about you stay inside. I'll take Cleo and Caesar out to Barney's yard for a break."

Lynn called the two dogs and stepped with them outside onto the back patio. She herded the pair to the goat yard and opened the gate. Barney bleated. He stood, stiff-legged on the top of his doghouse; she tossed him a carrot. Angel hopped out of her hutch next to the goat yard and wiggled her velvety nose, asking for her own carrot. Lynn handed her one, and took a minute to stroke her soft ears and scratch between her pink eyes.

Lynn studied the yard, then checked the surrounding bushes and trees looking to see if the black dog was lying out there in the cool green.

Eventually, she eased onto a chair next to the glass-topped patio table. The warm breeze meant that the temperature would reach ninety today. Too early for that, then she corrected herself. It was nearly June, after all.

God, she hoped that dog didn't have rabies. It would break Katy's heart. She was already so attached to it—like Lynn herself had been attached to Lucy. She glanced around the yard, chewing at her lip. Her foot tapped against the leg of the little café table. If the dog was rabid, and if she charged out of the bushes right this very minute, what would she do? Lynn stood.

Inside the house, the phone rang. She hurried in, one hand on her upper right abdomen, over the area where all of yesterday's pain had been concentrated.

"Hello?"

"Hi, Mrs. Werling. It's Emily. Can I speak to Katy, please? I'm calling from Dad's cell phone."

Lynn's eyes lost their focus; she pressed the phone into her ear. "Emily, where are you?"

"I've got something I have to tell her *now*. We won't be home for hours. Can I speak to Katy? Pull-eeze."

Lynn's heart began to race. "Katy's not with you?" Her fingers clutched the edge of the granite countertop.

"Mrs. Werling, you know she didn't come with us. Can I talk to her, pull—eeze?"

"My God." Lynn closed her eyes. She shoved her fist into her mouth to stifle a cry.

The world blackened on the edges, and tiny stars popped out. Lynn fought the feeling that she might faint. "Emily? Let me speak to your mom or dad. Now."

Lynn's hands shook. Behind her, in the den, the volume of the television increased; the room vibrated.

"Lynn, it's Bill. Emmy is crying, something about Katy. What's happened?" Emily's father's voice came clearly through the phone.

"Bill, Katy's not here," Lynn heard her voice say. "She hasn't been home since you all picked her up for dinner Friday night. What happened? Where is she?"

Silence on the other end of the phone. Then Bill said, "Honestly?"

Lynn's world turned fuzzy. Her fingernails dug into the palm of her hand.

"I saw her leave myself, she started up the hill." Bill spoke in a low, calm voice, but concern bubbled through his words. "I was watching the Friday night fight—I asked her to wait, but she was sure your new dog would come down to meet her. She seemed fine. She should have been home in thirty seconds. My God, Lynn, I—what can we do?"

The blood blanched from Lynn's face. "I'm calling the police."

"We'll be home as soon as we can," Bill said.

Lynn disconnected, then dialed 9-1-1.

"Katy? Baby, where are you?" Lynn called as she rushed outside and looked up and down the driveway. She clutched her stomach, prepared for pain but feeling none, except for the remembered pain from yesterday.

"Katy?" she called again and again.

"Mommy?" Ty was at the back door.

"Go inside. Stay inside. *Do what I say!*" Lynn screamed.

She ran to the edge of the trees, and then up the property line to the Jordan's backyard and to their patio door. She hammered on it.

Betsy pulled the door open. "Lynn? What wrong?"

"Have you seen Katy? Is she here?" Lynn saw the answer in Betsy's blank face before her eyes squinted with concern. "God! She's missing. Please—go over to my house. Stay with the boys, I've got to find Katy."

Lynn raced along the edge of the forested lot on the far side of the Jordan's property. Her look darted among the trees and bushes. Katy had always loved to play in the woods. She was fearless, but not fearless enough that she would stay out alone in the woods for two nights.

Lynn gasped for breath, her heart pounded in her ears.

*Oh, God, Katy was out here alone Friday night while we were at the hospital. Where is she?*

Frantically, she combed the property line, peering between the trees and under the bushes.

*Something happened to her, and we've been going on with our lives without her. Where did she go?*

Lynn's whole body quivered, and ocean waves began to crash inside her head.

*Why didn't I know that something was wrong? What kind of mother am I?*

"Katy!" Her throat closed up, and tears flooded her eyes. How could this be happening? And where was Randy?

The boys had said that the dog was acting crazy. Could it have been because Monique knew something had happened to Katy? Maybe she knew where Katy was. Maybe she'd been trying to take them to her.

*Where is the dog?*

"Monique! Monique, we need you!" Lynn called.

Her voice cracked.

*Oh, God.*

"Randy, where are you? We've got to find Katy!" she shouted into the air. She turned around and around and around.

Lynn's lungs burnt. *This can't be happening.*

*Will I ever see Katy again?*

She loved her children more than life itself. She'd tried to be a good mother. Truly she had.

*Has someone taken her? Oh, my God.*

Her mind raced into horrifying possibilities.

*Who?*

Not Mick Jordan or Jo—they loved Katy like a granddaughter. The Lopezes were on vacation—and that only left Al and Betsy.

Surely not Al? He was a little crazy, but surely not Al!

If not Al, then a stranger?

The burglars that had been working the neighborhood? Her heart pounded even faster.

A stranger had taken her. *Those children are never found.* Fear clamped onto her heart.

"Katy? Where are you? Katy?" Lynn sobbed.

She darted to the edge of the woods and scanned the ground for footprints, for any trace of something that showed her daughter had been there last night.

Nothing.

A crow cawed from a tree. A small plane buzzed up in the sky.

Lynn moved, looked, and called, "Katy!" into the bright morning air.

Chapter 43

"Mr. Mick. I go over there," Betsy said into her cell phone.

"My God." Mick spoke on the other end of the call, on Matthew's phone. "But Katy was going to the lake with that friend from down the street."

"Lynn very upset, looking everywhere. I go to be with the boys." Betsy hung up.

Jo had been right. There was more trouble in the neighborhood. Katy. Missing. How could this have happened? Mick leaned against the wall, then eased down into the waiting room chair.

The Werlings were good parents. They enjoyed those kids, spent time with them. They didn't deserve this. How had it happened? It was crazy.

What could he do to help? Thank God Betsy had stayed home. She'd go over to be with the boys while Lynn searched the neighborhood. Lynn had most likely already called the police.

He handed the phone back to Matthew. "Something's happened with one of the neighbor kids. One of them's gone missing."

Mick punched the ICU entry button and shuffled to Jo's cubicle, Matthew close behind him. He leaned over the bed and patted Jo's hand. "We're going home for a while, Josey-Jo. To help Lynn find Katy. You were right about the dog, you know. And I hope you are right that we're not too late."

Matthew kissed his mother's cheek, then followed his father down the hall to the elevator.

Jo's eyes flashed open. Her mouth worked but made no sound.

## Chapter 44

The Tiltons' back door stood open.

"Katy? Oh, dear God, be here, please!" Lynn dashed into the house.

*Oh, God, please let her be alive and safe. Let my daughter be okay. Let my family be okay.*

A sob slipped from her throat, and she swiped at the tears that snaked down her cheek.

"Al, are you here? It's Lynn—I'm looking for Katy. Have you seen her?"

The quiet house pulsating around her. She dashed down the hallway, opened the bedroom and bathroom doors, looked into each room. Katy wasn't here and neither was Al.

*Where is my daughter?*

Lynn checked the laundry room and then dashed back into the kitchen. Her knee brushed the tall garbage can, toppling it over. The contents spilled out, and among the bottles and used paper towels and packaging, a stuffed rabbit, white velour fur covered with dirt and bits of twigs and leaves, stared up at her with glass hazel eyes.

"No…" Lynn moaned as she reached down to pick up the stuffed animal.

Katy's Cuddle Bunny.

Lynn blinked several times, not believing what she saw.

"What is Katy's Cuddle Bunny doing here, in Al's trash can?" she asked the empty kitchen.

A red screen dropped across her vision as she dashed toward the back door. Al's army pistol lay on the kitchen table. Lynn grabbed it and raced out of the house.

## Chapter 45

The world slowly intruded as Randy woke up. His arm was crimped under his body on the hard wood floor, dead asleep. But that wasn't the worst of it. When he tried to move, it became clear that his arms were tied behind him, his wrists bound. Sweat broke out on his brow. He tried to move his legs, but his ankles were tied together, too. His heart raced; saliva filled his mouth. He gulped and swallowed to keep from choking on the liquid in his panic.

"He's coming around." The deep voice sounded bored.

Randy opened his eyes when the tip of a shoe nudged his head. Light peeked around the edges of the dark drapes at the window. He didn't recognize the curtains or the furniture. Not only did he not know where he was, he couldn't remember how he'd gotten here.

"Why'd you come over here?" the same voice asked. The shoe nudged harder.

Randy turned his head so that the man came into view. Tall and muscled, his pectorals stretched the fabric of the white t-shirt. A tattoo ran up his arm from wrist to neck, swirls of red, blue, and green covering the flesh in a pattern that Randy couldn't make out. The man's light hair was cut short, less than an inch long all over, and did nothing to hide the scar that started at the corner of his mouth and puckered the skin across his cheek to his ear.

"Answer me. Who are you?" the tattooed man asked.

Randy started to speak, but his dry mouth wouldn't allow any words. He cleared his throat. "Could I have a drink?"

The man with the scarred face barked, "Water. Now." Footsteps sounded across the room. Water ran in the kitchen sink. Seconds later, someone—not the scarred man—pulled him upright and held a water glass to his lips.

He swallowed several mouthfuls; his mind worked. He looked around and recognized the Lopez living room. And then he remembered. Lynn had kicked him out. He'd come over here to sleep. He'd come inside the house, and one of these goons had knocked him out. The water was pulled away. He squinted in the dim light to watch the second, smaller man with a shiny bald head stomp back to the kitchen.

"What time is it?" he asked.

"Why'd you come over here?" Scarface demanded again.

"I live next door. We've been watching the house while they're on vacation."

The scarred man smirked. "Not doing a very good job of it, are you? We been here—what?—three days?" He sat down on the sofa, stretched out his legs then slammed his boot heels on the top of the coffee table as he leaned back into the thick sofa cushions. "When are they coming back?"

Randy's mind jumped a thousand different directions. He wanted out of here and he wanted these men out of the Lopez house and away from his neighborhood and his children. "Today. I came over to let in some fresh air."

Scarface threw his head back and laughed. "Fresh air? What a good neighbor you are. So tell me, Mr. Rogers Wannabe, what time will they be back?"

Randy followed the man's look to the mantel clock and saw that it was still early, barely eight o'clock. Lynn wouldn't be missing him yet. And once she did, would she come looking for him? Oh, Lord, what if she and the boys came over here? He swallowed a ball of saliva. "They'll be back early. Back to work tomorrow."

Scarface leaned forward. "We'll get out of here, then."

The smaller man stepped up. "What'll we do with him?"

Scarface scowled. "We could leave him as a welcome home present. Dead or alive? I wonder if they really are coming home today. Hope it's not another week." He smiled, his teeth yellow in the dim morning light.

Randy couldn't remember if Jim Lopez would actually be home tonight. He was more certain that Lynn would come over here to look for him before the end of the day. What kind of shape would they leave him in? Beaten? *Dead*? Randy imagined a goose egg swelling under his scalp where his head ached the most. They had nearly cracked his head in two.

"Something's going on." The bald man stood at the narrow gap between the draperies on the front window. "There's a crazy woman running around." Sunlight shone on his sweaty bald pate as he peered through the narrow opening he'd made in the curtains. "She's coming here."

Scarface stepped over to the window and looked through the opening. The two men watched a few seconds more.

"She's got a gun and she's coming here," Scarface said under his breath.

The bald man stayed at the window. Scarface crossed the room in three long strides and grabbed Randy's arm.

A crazy woman with a gun? Heading for this house? Lynn had been mad at him, but a gun? Pain jarred his teeth as the man jerked him to his feet.

"When I open the door, maybe you should just shoot her!" the smaller man said.

"You stupid ass. The whole neighborhood will know we're in here, then. The cops'll be here before we can grab the stuff and split."

Someone pounded at the door.

"Damn." Scarface glared at Randy. "Open the door, see what she wants. And don't try anything—I'm right behind you."

Randy stumbled as Scarface shoved him toward the door.

The pounding intensified.

"Get outta sight!" Scarface hissed at the second man. He moved behind the door, then nudged Randy. "Open it!"

Randy pulled the door open an inch.

"Randy! My God—Katy's not with Emily!" She shoved the door hard enough to step across the threshold and into the house. "I think Al Tilton—"

A tattooed arm reached around Randy to grab

Lynn's shoulder and jerk her into the house. She crashed against Randy, knocking him to the floor.

The tall man yanked Lynn farther into the room. He released her and she thudded into the wall. The gun skidded across the wood floor.

Scarface kicked the door shut with his foot and rushed across the room, his look focused on the gun.

"Randy? We've got to find Katy!" Lynn stared wild-eyed at her husband.

"Shut up!" Scarface hollered.

"Do as he says, honey, please." Randy pulled himself up from the floor, but the room swirled around him. He gritted his teeth against the pounding in his brain. What was Lynn saying about Katy? Not with Emily?

"Our daughter is lost!" Lynn screamed at the men as she scrambled to her feet.

"Shut the fuck up!" Scarface bellowed. He reached for the gun on the floor.

Lynn tucked her head and charged.

Scarface slammed one fist into her shoulder when she reached him, and she fell hard, to the floor. He pulled his leg back to kick her where she lay.

Randy propelled himself headfirst into the back of the man's knee. The big man's body folded and landed on top of Randy.

The man roared and rolled off Randy as the bald man vaulted across the room.

Lynn scrambled for the gun.

Chapter 46

Matthew pulled the car into the Werlings' driveway. Mick bolted out and hurried toward the house with Matthew close behind. Betsy stood in the front doorway, a boy at each side.

"Any word about Katy? What's happening?" Mick asked.

Betsy shook her head. "Lynn not come back. There. I hear siren. The police are coming."

"What's going on?" Ty asked. "Mommy's yelling for Katy, and Katy's at the lake, she's not even here!"

"Where's Daddy?" Will added.

"Boys, we don't know," Mick said. "Let's all go inside. Your mom will come tell us what's going on, soon."

"We could watch TV," Ty suggested.

"Or maybe, you find favorite book and we read together," Betsy said. She pulled the boys farther into the house, away from the front door and the windows.

"Ooh, Ty, tell Mr. Mick, Matthew, and me what happen to your arm," Betsy said.

The boy launched into a long story about what had happened to his arm at Friday night's soccer game, and Will added bits and pieces about going to the emergency room. Betsy nodded as they spoke, but Mick saw that her look was not focused on the boys. It flitted back and forth to the window.

And Mick only half-heard Ty's story himself. Katy was missing. He wanted to know when it had happened, and how. The boys were easily distracted from the crisis outside, but he wasn't.

Mick glanced at Matthew. He was also lost in thought. Unimaginable things seemed to happen to kids these days. Was that what Matthew was thinking about, his own divorce, his own children?

Something unimaginable had happened right in Mick's own neighborhood. The black dog had tried to warn them.

A siren screamed up the Werlings' driveway. A glint of light reflected into the house as the police arrived.

"It's about time," Mick said. He glanced at the two boys, who stood at the edge of the living room carpet, eyes on the front door, and then moved to watch out the front window.

Two policemen jumped from their patrol car and ran for the Werlings' house. As Betsy opened the glass storm door, the unmistakable report of a gun sounded nearby.

"What's going on?" a muscular policeman in the blue uniform of the Tulsa Police Department asked as he reached the front door.

"Little girl's missing. Her mother's searching for her," Mick said as he joined Betsy at the front door. "But I don't think she had a gun…"

"Wait here," the other policeman said.

The two policemen hurried away, their hands cupped around their gun holsters. One of them spoke into a radio unit hooked onto his shoulder.

"Was that a gunshot?" Betsy asked. Ty and Will

crowded close behind her, pushing into Mick's legs as they stood in the doorway.

"Did somebody get shot?" Ty asked.

"Where's Mommy? Where's Daddy?" Will's voice quivered.

The boys stared up at Mick.

"Don't know, boys, but I think we can be more help staying put than going out there getting in the way. The police will take care of it. That's their job. We'll wait here for them. They'll come back and answer all of our questions." He nudged the boys back into the house and closed the front door. "So, tell me more about that soccer game, Ty. Did your team win?"

Mick led the boys back to the den, once again talking about Friday night's game. Will peered out the picture window at the expanse of back yard that the four hilltop houses shared.

"Has anyone seen Moe?" Will's face held a pout when he turned back to them.

Chapter 47

Lynn's whole body shook. She took deep cleansing yoga breaths and did her best to hold her arm steady, keeping the gun focused on the men. The bald one held his arm and cursed. Blood oozed from beneath his hand. Scarface scowled, and looked ready to pounce.

"I'll shoot you if you move. Don't think I won't." Lynn glared at the two thieves.

Randy crawled away from the reach of the two strangers, his arms still tied behind his back and his ankles still roped together. He used the wall to help him stand, and then shuffled his way to Lynn. Unshaven, his hair stuck up from his head at odd angles, and his glasses were crooked on his face.

A pang of something touched her heart as she looked at her disheveled husband.

"Katy's missing, Randy." She chewed at her lip, but kept the muzzle of the gun pointed at the men. "Do you think she's here? Do you think they have her?"

Randy shook his head. "I've been here all night. I haven't heard anyone but these two. And they didn't talk as if anyone else was here."

Scarface shifted his weight, preparing to charge.

"Don't move," Lynn stated. "I will shoot you."

Someone pounded on the front door.

"Police! We're coming in!"

The front door frame splintered and the door

crashed open. Two policemen rushed inside.

"Freeze! Put the gun down, slowly, and drop to your knees," one of them ordered, his gun pointed at Lynn.

"I'm the one who called you." Lynn lowered the gun. "My little girl is missing. Please, we've got to find her."

"On the ground. Now."

Lynn dropped to her knees and laid the gun on the floor in front of her. She lifted both hands into the air.

Scarface sprang from the room. One of the policemen leaped after him, slammed him into the wall and then shoved him down to the ground. The second burglar sank onto his knees, his hands raised. "Don't shoot me again. Okay?"

As he cuffed the bald burglar, the second officer glanced at Lynn, who had moved over to Randy and was working at the knots that tied his hands. "On the ground! You! Now!"

"I called 9-1-1," Lynn said in a shaky voice. "I was trying to find my husband to tell him about Katy." Her heart galloped, as it had since Emily's phone call. "I don't know these men. Please help me find my little girl. Katy's been all alone for two nights!"

"Where'd you get the gun?" the officer asked. Outside, another siren screamed up the driveway.

"It's my neighbor's gun. I went to his house looking for Katy. I picked it up there, before I came here looking for my husband."

"This your husband?" The policeman gestured at Randy with his pistol. She nodded.

Randy rubbed at the red marks on his wrists. "I don't know who these men are, either. I came over to check on my neighbor's house last night—they've been on vacation. These guys ambushed me, knocked me out. I woke up only minutes before Lynn—my wife—ran over here to find me."

Three more policemen swarmed into the house. They slapped handcuffs on the scar-faced thief and cut the ropes from Randy's ankles.

Randy moved over to Lynn and folded his arms around her in a one-sided hug.

"I don't know where she is, Randy." Lynn swallowed the sob that threatened to erupt from deep within her. "Emily called to talk to Katy." She cleared the tears from her throat.

"You're telling me she didn't go to the lake with them?"

"She's been here, or somewhere, for the whole weekend."

"She walked away from Emily's?"

"Yes. Friday night she walked home. But somewhere between here and Em's, something happened." The sob broke open in her throat. "I think Al Tilton had something to do with it."

Randy's face paled. "Al?"

Lynn pulled away from Randy and wrapped her arms around herself. "I found Katy's Cuddle Bunny in his trash can. We've got to find her."

"Can you all step outside with us please?" one of the policemen asked as another powerful engine roared up outside.

Lynn snatched up Cuddle Bunny from the floor where she had dropped it and hurried out of the house. She stared at the black police SUV. A K-9 unit decal was plastered on the side doors. *This can't be happening.*

One of the officers touched Lynn's shoulder. "The team's all here; we'll finish with these guys. Go talk to the K-9 unit. They'll get the search under way."

Lynn straightened her shoulders and let Randy take her hand.

On the driveway, Lynn repeated the story again to the new team of detectives. "We thought she was with her friend and her family for the weekend. We had no idea she never left town."

Randy squeezed her hand.

From the corner of her eye, she saw Betsy step out of their house and move toward them, her eyes wide and full of concern. She placed one hand on Lynn's arm.

"Mrs. Werling, do you have something that belonged to your daughter? We'll use it to start a search of the neighborhood," the woman detective said. "The SAR unit includes a scent hound."

Lynn held out Cuddle Bunny. The stuffed animal looked more like a dirty rug than the beloved rabbit her daughter slept with. Her fingers curled around the dirty, matted fur one last time before she handed it to the policewoman. "Her stuffed bunny. I found it at Al's." Tears tumbled down her face.

Randy's brow furrowed. "What was it doing there?"

Betsy stiffened. "I never see this there." Her head shook back and forth, whipping her long black hair across her face. "Al loves Katy. He not do anything."

The policewoman shot Betsy a curious look. "What?"

"He loves her. My husband would not hurt her."

Betsy looked from face to face, registering their responses. Her own face fell. "Not like that," she moaned.

"Where?" the policewoman asked.

Lynn pointed across the yard toward the Tiltons' house.

"We'll start there." With one hand signal, several of the team members struck out for the Tiltons' house. One of them led a black and tan German shepherd dog on a short metal leash. The animal sniffed the old stuffed rabbit, barked, and then pulled on the lead.

The detective instructed the other officers. "Three search parties. Comb the neighborhood. Johnson, give us ten minutes, then get an Amber Alert issued with Tilton's vehicle information."

She turned to Betsy. "Can you give me the make, model, and license number of your husband's vehicle?"

Stiffly, Betsy turned toward her home. She stopped and pointed, shaking her head. "His car is in the driveway, and mine is in the garage. He not home?" she asked Lynn.

"Not when I was there." Lynn's head swam.

The detective focused on Lynn. "Mrs. Werling, do you have a recent photograph of Katy?" To Lynn, the detective's voice sounded as if she was talking through a thick fog.

Randy pulled out his billfold and handed the woman a wallet-sized picture of Katy.

*This can't be happening. Where is my daughter?*

The detective was giving instructions to the search team. "Talk with all the neighbors. Check to see if they've seen anything odd or noticed any strangers in the area over the past week."

"What about those two guys? What if they took Katy? Did you check the upstairs bedrooms?" Randy asked.

"An officer is going through the house right now."

Lynn thought of the black dog. Monique had been barking all day yesterday, the boys had said. Randy thought the dog was rabid. She felt very sure it had been trying to get their attention. "We've had a stray black dog in the neighborhood," Lynn said. She scanned the yards for any sign of the black dog. "I haven't seen her yet today."

"The dog's sick, honey. Best that it's not here when Katy comes home."

Lynn looked at Randy and shook her head. "I don't think she's sick." Her heart grasped his words and held on. *He believes Katy will come home. God, please let him be right.*

The detective scribbled on her pad with a stubby pencil. "Anything else we should know about this dog?"

Lynn chewed at her lip and scanned the lawns one more time. "It is well-behaved, house-trained, and all the kids want to keep it. They've named it Monique."

"Why are we talking about that dog? We need to find Katy." Randy swiped his hand across his eyes. "The dog didn't take Katy. My daughter's stuffed animal was at Tilton's house. You need to find Al."

Randy's voice had an edge to it. He sounded as scared as she felt. Lynn's shoulders shook. *Why would Al take Katy?*

The search party divided into groups and hurried away to search.

"That s.o.b.," Randy growled. "If he hurt Katy, I'll

kill him." Randy clenched his hand into a fist as the search party crossed the yard toward Al Tilton's house.

"Is there anyone else's home nearby that your daughter might have gone Friday night instead of coming home?" The detective asked.

"Katy would never have gone anywhere without letting me know. She always made sure I knew where she was and what she was doing. Always." Lynn covered her mouth and swallowed the sob in her throat.

*Except for Friday night.*

"Emily's house was only a hundred yards down the street," Randy explained. "She should have been home in one minute, less time than the phone call would have taken. Something happened along the way."

"I'll get a team to search the road as soon as a group comes back. Meanwhile, let's go inside." The detective put one hand firmly on Lynn's arm.

Lynn stumbled as she turned and when she reached for Randy, he was gone.

The police dog barked far across the lawn. Inside the Werling house, Caesar and Cleo yipped.

And somewhere, not too far away, another dog barked and barked again.

Lynn recognized that bark.

She pulled away from the policewoman and ran.

Chapter 48

Damn, the leaves were slippery. He should have put on a different pair of shoes, but then, he hadn't been awake and the dog…Well, the dog had dragged him out of the house.

Where was the animal taking him? There was no doubt that it wanted him to follow. The animal wouldn't take five steps without turning to make sure he was close behind.

*Jeez. Hard to see in this mottled morning light.* Birds squawked at him, and critters scampered away in the leaves. A fly buzzed around his head, and a mosquito hummed in his ear.

Al swallowed hard. He jerked and stopped when a squirrel chattered from a branch above him. His body shook.

The dog barked. She ran back to him, planted herself on the path, and yipped. He held one hand out and she licked it.

*That's right, I'm here at home. This isn't the jungle.*

He swallowed hard again, and touched the dog's smooth, black head with his fingertips.

*I shot this dog last night. Could have killed her. Would have, if the light had been better.* He was a marksman. Hadn't he saved their whole patrol by taking out those snipers with only two shots? They'd given him a medal for it.

*The medal. Where was it? Somebody took it!*

And not just that one—it and all the others he'd received for giving twenty years of his life to the service. Why would anyone want them? Didn't mean anything to anybody else. But without them, he was a nobody. Just a scared old soldier, sliding in the leaves in his house shoes on some crazy trek after a dog.

The dog whined and backed a few steps down the path.

She whirled and thrashed into the woods. She knew where she was going and she wanted him to go, too. He didn't want to go, but what choice did he have? He looked around at the thick undergrowth and the trees, their limbs entwining like a net all round him.

Al's breath caught. He listened for the voice he'd heard a while ago. Monique? Who was Monique? There was no Monique in their neighborhood.

The dog crashed through the underbrush on down the path. Squirrels jabbered. There was no voice. His crazy mind. He didn't really hear half of what he thought he heard these days.

Part of him didn't want to admit that some of those sounds he heard weren't real, but sometimes he knew it was true. A swarm of gnats encircled his head, buzzing, getting in his eyes and his ears. He swatted them away and pushed on down the trail, feeling rocks beneath the soft soles of his house shoes.

"Slow down there, mutt!" Al called.

*Why am I following the dog in the first place?*

Fool's errand this was, if he'd ever been on one. He stopped again to get his breath.

Bark! The dog ran through the brush and back to

him. She snapped at his pant leg.

"Okay, okay. I'm coming." He began to move again.

Woof! Woof! Woof!

The dog scampered on, still headed down, farther into the ravine where Nickel Creek cut through the boulders.

Al slipped on a large flat rock; he grabbed at a thin oak tree. He righted himself.

Rocks jutted from the uneven ground. Leftover leaves from years and years of leaf fall had packed thick—and slick—on the ground.

*Where'd that path go?* The more he thought about it, the more he remembered that path, he'd even walked it a couple of times in winter when there were no leaves on the trees, and no ticks or chiggers or mosquitoes to bother him. Nothing to remind him of jungle.

He'd probably taken that walk on one of those warm winter days when the world seemed right and a person could get out and really feel a part of the forest. The kids made that path, probably those boys he sometimes heard hollering in the woods.

The path in front of him was visible only because the leaves had been broken into bits by footfall and the undergrowth of bushes had been trampled aside.

The black dog barked again, more shrill, more insistent. She waited for him on the path ahead, about ten yards farther.

"I'm coming!" Al hollered.

The animal turned and trotted ahead. Then the dog stopped and sat. She turned and looked at him. Her whining sounded like crying.

He came up to her and saw why she had stopped.

The path dropped into nothingness.

He'd have gone over the edge himself if the dog hadn't stopped in the middle of the path to block the way.

Spring rains had eroded the soil, causing a pair of boulders to tumble toward the creek and sheer the path away. The dog stepped off the path and eased her way down the steep hillside. She stopped and looked up at him.

"Where we going now? Damn animal," he muttered.

Then, he heard something. The voice again?

"Monique!" someone called softly.

So weak. He couldn't even be sure it was real. A fairy voice.

"Help."

The dog stopped and looked back at him; she whined louder, and the whine turned into a howl. Someone was in trouble. The old soldier rallied. *Help was on the way!*

"I'm right behind you," he called. Carefully, he stepped off the path behind the dog and picked his way down, toward the bottom of the ravine.

The dog forged ahead, then turned to bark at him.

"Okay, okay. I'm coming. Slow it down, would you?"

The critter was wearing him out. All weekend he'd been feeling the heavy weight of his body, and moving through the brush, it felt even heavier than before.

He put his right foot out to take one more step, but when he set it down on the wet ground, it slid out from under him. Next thing he knew, he was on his rear end slipping through the slick leaves like they were a playground slide, straight through the brush. He grabbed at a thick grape vine and stopped his skid down the slope.

But his mind kept tumbling. The world turned upside down, and his brain roared. He lay still, trying to make the world level again.

"Help me!"

The small voice surprised him, and he shook his head to straighten out his brain. His eyes were out of focus. He closed them, then opened them again.

"Help! Please, Mr. Tilton. I'm down here, right below you."

He turned his head. A little girl, dark-haired, lay a few feet farther down the slope, inches from where the ground fell straight down to the rocky creek bed.

"Hey," he said. He blinked, trying to steady the world that circled around him. The girl was above him, then below him, then beside him. Which way should he go to reach her?

Bark! The dog tugged at him again, this time grabbing his sleeve. She tugged and tugged, and he crawled over one bush then another and then finally, there was the girl.

She looked up at him from where she lay at the very edge of another drop off. Her eyes were swollen and dilated, her face puffy. The girl's leg bent in a painful direction, and she was missing a shoe. He blinked again. She was wearing pajamas like he was, but hers were even more covered with dirt and bits of leaves. Below them, water gurgled, unreachable. Her lips were cracked and gray.

The girl was familiar. He concentrated. He'd seen her before, and often. Looking at her brought Betsy to mind. He knew her because of Betsy. When his mind pulled up an image of Betsy and Jo at their flowerbed with this little girl helping them, he knew who she was.

Katy…wasn't it?

Chapter 49

Lynn's breath came in gasps. Adrenaline pumped through her arteries, filling her with a need, pushing aside the fatigue of yesterday and leaving no room for the pain in her abdomen. She raced across the expanse of yard, then down the drive into the street and on down the hill toward Emily's house.

Monique had barked. Where was she? Lynn slowed to a jog and tilted her head, listening. Someone was mowing their yard. The sound buzzed through the air so that she stopped and closed her eyes to concentrate. Not far away, a little child shrieked with joy, and an older voice laughed deeply. The sounds slashed into her heart.

There. Barking. In the ravine.

Lynn darted to the side of the road. There was a path somewhere, used by the kids as they cut through the neighborhoods. In summer the underbrush, bushes, and vines made the pathway hard to find. This year, the path was already nearly grown over, and it wasn't even officially summer yet. A strip of open soil was evident between two bushes. She stepped off the asphalt road.

The thick undergrowth, mostly sumac and buck brush, scratched her legs as she followed the path. A blackberry vine caught the skin of her legs and grabbed at her arms, but she pushed on, ignoring the pricks as she moved deeper into the cool of the shadowy ravine.

The dog barked again, closer this time. Something was moving through the ravine. What if it was Monique—and what if Monique had rabies like Randy had said? Lynn stopped.

The crashing came closer and then the black dog burst from bushes onto the faint path and limped straight to her.

Woof! Her tail wagged in a circle, and her tongue hung long from the left side of her mouth.

There was no spittle dripping off her tongue or coating the opening of her mouth, and the dog's shoulder was red and bloody. The dog danced awkward circles around her, and then, as suddenly as she had burst out of the underbrush, she ran back down the faded path and deeper into the ravine.

Lynn started after the dog. She had only moved a few yards farther when she could hear—and see—someone moving in the half-darkness, struggling up through the undergrowth.

She strained to see the figure in the dappled sunlight. It was a man, slumped over. She heard his wheezing breath yards away. He staggered up the path carrying something heavy.

Chapter 50

Randy followed the policemen to the Tiltons' house. "Sir, please stay back. Let the dog do his job."

He stopped on the patio beside the metal café table and waited, his head throbbing.

*Damn him. Why did he take Katy? What had he done to her?*

He wanted to be there when the police found Al. He was personally going to take care of Al if he'd hurt Katy. The bastard didn't deserve to live.

Randy's heart thudded in his stomach. The throbbing pain in his head where the burglars had clobbered him was nothing compared to the ache and fear in his heart. What if they lost Katy? What if they never saw her again? What if it had all happened, somehow, because he had been so caught up in Jennifer?

He rubbed at his head and closed his eyes. He'd do anything if he could go back to Friday night. When had she gotten lost? Had it been while they were at the hospital? Had Katy been unable to get into the house? Or had he somehow not heard her when she came home because his mind was on one hot chick from his Civil War class? He groaned.

The policemen were in Al's house, intent on their search. They'd forgotten all about him. And he couldn't wait here any longer, doing nothing. It was his daughter

who was missing. And if Al Tilton was responsible...
*I'll kill him. I will. If he harmed her in any way—*

The back door opened and a German shepherd,
straining at his lead, led the group out of the house. The
dog's nose went to the ground, and the animal sniffed
his way around the patio.

"She hasn't been in the house recently, Mr.
Werling. The dog didn't find any scent to follow."

Randy frowned. "But Lynn said she found the
stuffed animal inside."

"Maybe so, but your daughter hasn't been in
there."

Randy's mind worked. Al had to have gotten
Cuddle Bunny from Katy. He knew where she was.
He'd hidden her someplace.

His heart pounded and pounded louder and louder
in his ears. What could he do? The sun shone on his
face, but the breeze dried his sweat as soon as it popped
out on his upper lip and forehead.

He had to find Al.

He had to find Katy.

He turned in a circle, and then—not knowing what
else to do—he ran home.

Randy threw the back door open. Betsy, Mick, Ty
and Will looked up at him from the den.

"Daddy!" The boys raced across the room and
grabbed at him.

"What are the policemen doing out there?" Ty
asked as Randy pushed into the house. Will wrapped
his arms around his legs so that Randy had to drag him
along as he moved into the kitchen.

"We have to stay calm," Randy said, knowing that
he couldn't do what he was asking of them. He

squeezed his eyes closed. How could he be calm when his little girl was out there somewhere? Who knew what had happened to her, what Al Tilton might have done?

He opened his eyes and looked at Betsy.

"Lynn found Katy's Cuddle Bunny in your house. Where's Al?" he asked in an icy voice.

Betsy's eyes widened, and her arms folded across her stomach. "I not know, Randy. I been helping Mr. Mick since Miss Jo had her heart attack. Since Friday night." Betsy blinked, and reached one hand toward him. "You think that Al..." She shook her head quickly. "No."

Randy blinked and looked at Mick and then Matthew. "Heart attack? Is Jo okay?" His mind considered this news as he watched his elderly neighbor. More than one bad thing had happened on their hill Friday night.

Mick shrugged. "She will be, we hope."

Randy took a step closer to Betsy, frowning. "I think Al's taken her somewhere. Where would he go, Betsy?" He closed his hand into a fist and squeezed until his fingernails cut into his palm. He couldn't stand thinking Katy was somewhere, either hurt, or being hurt, and prevented from coming home.

*Where had Al taken her? What if she was never found?*

"Wait a minute, Randy," Mick said. "I know Al can seem a little hard sometimes, but he loves Katy. We all do. He wouldn't ever..."

"Daddy?" Will asked.

Randy patted Will's head and gave Ty's shoulder a squeeze. "Boys, you stay here with Betsy and Mick."

"Where's Katy, Daddy?" Ty asked. "Where're you going?"

Randy unclasped Will's fingers from their grip on his leg and squatted down in front of the two boys.

"We're not sure where your sister is," Randy said.

"She went to the lake with Em, Dad. 'Member?" Will said in a small voice.

"They'll be home today. You know that, Daddy, and so does Mommy," Ty added. He rested his hand on Randy's shoulder. "Where's Mommy?"

Randy blinked. He glanced around the room. Where was Lynn? He'd last seen her outside. She was probably searching alongside the other policemen.

"Katy didn't go to the lake." Randy kept his voice low. "Katy didn't go with Emily. The police are here to try to find her. They think she might have gotten lost. Maybe in the woods close by."

"Katy got lost?" Will asked.

"Maybe," Randy answered.

"She didn't get lost. Katy goes places on purpose." Ty hunched forward, and then turned around to look out the window at the scene in the front yard. "I bet when you find her, she knew where she was all the time."

The muscles in Randy's shoulders bunched even as he tried to smile at Ty. "I'm sure you're right, son." Katy probably knew exactly where she was. *But where was that?*

*Oh, God, let us find her and let her be all right.*

Randy stood. "I need to know what's happening." He pushed the hair off his forehead.

"Do what you feel you have to do," Mick said. "Things happen, like my Jo having her heart attack, and there's nothing in the world you can do about it except hope that it turns out for the best. Life will go on, but it won't ever be the same."

Randy looked at Mick and then at Matthew. "I'm sorry about Jo. I didn't know. I hope she recovers and can come home soon." His voice cracked.

*Never be the same.* It already wasn't the same. It hadn't been the same since Friday, not since that meeting in his office. And he couldn't go back. He couldn't make it right, couldn't make it not have happened.

Mick laid his hand softly on Randy's upper back and gave him a pat.

"Dad?" Matthew called from the front hallway. "There's a dog outside. That black one. Won't quit barking. Come take a look."

"Monique!" the boys shouted. "Come on!" the boys tugged at Randy and Mick's hands and pulled them to the front door.

Outside, the black dog stood on the driveway, barking and barking. She limped a few steps down the driveway and then turned back to look at them and bark again.

"She's hurt, Dad!" Ty yelled. He dropped Randy's hand, shoved open the door, and ran toward the dog.

"I don't speak dog language, but if you ask me, she's trying to tell us something," Mick said.

"Ty! Wait," Randy called just before he dashed after his son.

Chapter 51

Lynn hurried down the path, trying not to lose her footing in the thin flip-flops she was wearing. Earthy green smells rose from the forest floor and birds fluttered in the trees. She peered at the figure as he came closer.

It was Al Tilton.

Her heart somersaulted in her chest.

*What—or who—is he carrying?! Katy? Oh, God. What did he do to her?*

"Katy!" She sped up, mindless of the slick leaves beneath her feet. She slipped, fell. Her heart leaped into her throat and then dove into her stomach.

*Damn him! Damn crazy Al!* She had to stop him, had to save—

"Mommy?"

Katy spoke as Lynn scrambled to her feet.

"Mommy!" Her daughter's head was turned toward her now, not buried in Mr. Tilton's chest.

"My God, Katy." As Lynn rushed the last few feet down the path to meet the pair, she saw the branch that had been tied with strips of striped cloth around Katy's leg. Al Tilton's torso was bare, his chest scratched and bleeding. Sweat and dirt coated his face, his arms. His fierce eyes focused on her.

"Katy's broken her leg. Don't ask me how she got down here. Seems like you'd be the one who ought to know where she was and how she got there. Not me."

The three of them met on the path, and Lynn pushed the sticky, filthy hair off her daughter's pale face. Red welts dotted her skin.

Katy reached for her mother, but Tilton clutched the girl tightly.

"I got you, girl. You're too heavy for your mom. Let me get you up to the road. Then we'll get you to the hospital."

"Monique brought Mr. Tilton," Katy whispered in a hoarse voice. She licked at her dry, cracked lips with a swollen tongue. "Like she brought you."

Lynn cupped her daughter's face in her hands and blinked away tears. Her lips quivered. Katy's splotched face puckered, and she began to cry.

"Mommy, my leg hurts," she moaned in a hoarse whisper. "I'm so hungry…And I need a drink."

## Chapter 52

Mick, Will, and Matthew rushed outside onto the porch as Ty and Randy ran toward the dog. Monique barked and kept on barking as she turned and hobbled toward the road again, mostly on three legs.

"Moe!" Ty called. "Come back!"

Randy put his hands on Ty's shoulders and turned him toward the house.

"I'm betting she knows where Katy is. She knows what's happened," Mick said.

Randy grimly herded Ty to the group and then turned back toward the dog. *And so do I. Tilton's behind this.*

Randy felt the shape of the revolver under his shirt, the one he'd picked up from the floor of his neighbor's house and tucked into his belt. Lynn had laid it down like the policeman had asked, but they hadn't retrieved it. He'd grabbed it impulsively, not knowing why at the time. Now, he did.

"Mick, Betsy, take the boys back to the house. I'll follow the dog."

"Probably best," Mick said. "Boys, come here. Let your dad do what he needs to do. We'll know what's happened soon enough." Mick put his hand on Ty's shoulder and steered him toward the house.

Betsy slipped an arm around Will as Randy turned away from his home.

Below him, on the street, Monique disappeared into the trees at the edge of the ravine, still barking. Randy hurried down the driveway and across the road.

He stepped off the asphalt and moved along the dense jumble of trees, looking for a way through the bushes and vines. Two robins darted out, squawking in alarm. He peered between the trunks of the trees. Leaves stirred and he could make out someone moving in the shadows, coming toward him near the edge of the wood.

Monique dashed out, barking as she turned in circles. She danced on three legs back toward the woods, then limped forward to him.

Randy pulled the revolver from the waistband of his shorts and flicked off the safety.

A gray-haired man emerged from the green forest. Randy's heart pounded in his throat. Tilton was half-naked. Mud and leaves stuck to his thin pajama pants. He carried a girl in his arms. Katy.

Randy hurried closer, heart hammering in his head, adrenaline rushing. "Tilton! You s.o.b. What have you done?"

He tried to aim the gun, but his hands shook. Katy was in the man's arms; he couldn't risk hurting his daughter. "Stop! Put her down!"

Someone stepped out from behind Tilton. "Randy? What are you doing?"

Randy blinked at his wife. "Al's got Katy!"

"He found her. He saved her. Put the gun down."

Randy's breath let out in a whoosh, and the gun dropped. His thumb twitched on the trigger; the gun blasted.

Al, with Katy in his arms, crumpled to the ground.

Chapter 53

Randy sprinted down the road to his daughter.

"Daddy! Help Mr. Tilton. Oh…" Her raspy voice fell away.

Randy pulled Katy up and into his arms, away from where Al Tilton lay. Her matted hair was filthy with dirt, twigs and leaves. "Katy, baby, are you all right?"

"I hurt my leg," her voice croaked.

Lynn squatted next to Al on the ground. "Al?"

The black dog stood a few feet away, her tongue hanging from the right side of her jaw, her head drooping, her eyes half-closed. Randy peered at the bloody wound on her shoulder. The animal was hurt. She'd been trying to tell them about Katy, and he had thought she was rabid. His heart felt squeezed.

Tilton raised up on his elbows, then dropped down. "My legs gave out on me. I'm all right."

"You weren't shot?" Lynn looked for signs of a gunshot wound or spurting blood. Al's torso was covered with bloody scratches from the briars and bushes of the ravine.

"Old bones. That's all this is." Al closed his eyes.

Lynn straightened and reached for her daughter. Katy's head rested against her father's chest.

"Monique found me," Katy whispered. "She kept me warm."

"Shhh. It's all right, Katy. Don't try to talk." Lynn's fingertips stroked Katy's face. Randy counted eleven insect welts and five long scratches.

"She brought fruit. And dog biscuits."

"Shhh. Be quiet now. You're safe." Randy clutched his daughter close and swayed, stroking the back of her head.

"Can I have a drink of water, Daddy?"

Randy saw his daughter's filthy pajamas and her bloody leg, which had been tied to a branch with torn fabric strips. His throat tightened and tears filled his eyes. "Sure, honey. Let's get you home."

His look met Lynn's. Relief was evident on her face, but her exhaustion was plain as well. He turned up the street and started toward home.

"Owwww. Something's wrong with my leg," Katy groaned. "Go slow."

Randy adjusted her weight to be sure that her splinted leg was fully supported. He climbed the hill as evenly as he could.

"Mr. Tilton tried to fix my leg, but it really hurts," Katy whispered.

A trio of police officers appeared where the road crested; they jogged down to meet the Werlings.

"I need to get Katy to the house," Randy said. "Somebody, please call an ambulance." He glanced back at Al. "Make that two. Mr. Tilton is hurt."

Five minutes later, inside his house, Randy rushed to the kitchen. Tears streamed down his cheeks.

*She's going to be all right. A broken leg, but she's alive, and...whole.*

He bent over the sink and sobbed, huge giant sobs that pulled the breath out of him and left him so weak he held tight onto the edge of the countertop to keep himself from falling to the tile floor.

If he had had his mind on his daughter, and had not been thinking about—He wouldn't say her name. His focus should have been on his family every second. He should have talked to Em's father on Friday night. He should have talked to him again Saturday before Em's family left for the lake. He should have made sure that Katy was feeling all right and found out for sure what their time frame was. But because Katy had gone with them so many times, he hadn't even bothered to make a single phone call to confirm the plans with Bill or Jillian. How could he have been so lax?

If only he had checked, Katy wouldn't have gone through this ordeal. They would have known instantly that she was not where she was supposed to be. Most likely, he would have gone down the road to meet her and none of this would have ever happened.

What had he been thinking? His face burned with shame, and his throat felt raw. Lust had kept him from being a good father. He choked back another sob.

*Water.* Katy needed water. He cleared his throat, wiped his eyes, and ran his hands through his hair. She was okay, and she needed water. He filled a glass with cold filtered water from the refrigerator and carried it into the living room.

Lynn sat next to Katy on the sofa. Mick and his son, Matthew, hovered nearby. Ty and Will huddled on the floor at her feet, with Caesar and Chloe in their arms. Monique lay on the floor beside the sofa, licking her shoulder repeatedly.

"You're going to be okay, baby. You're safe." Randy handed her the water glass.

"I was safe down there, I really was," Katy said after a long swallow of water. "Monique was with me a lot. She kept me warm. I was hungry, and she brought fruit. And dog biscuits. Today, she brought Mr. Tilton."

Monique looked up at Katy.

Randy remembered how crazy the dog had seemed yesterday. He closed his eyes and shook his head. Why had he not seen how distressed she was? Not rabid.

"I told you she was smart," Katy said in her almost-normal voice.

Monique sat up and rested her head on the sofa cushion next to Katy. His daughter stroked the dog's head. Randy eased down beside Lynn on the sofa.

"I told her to get help, and she did," Katy said. She smiled. "That's my Monique."

Randy reached out and touched Katy's hair. "Yes," he whispered.

Katy looked at him. "I'm sorry, Daddy."

"Oh, baby, what do you have to be sorry about?"

"I'm sorry I didn't tell you I was coming home. But I couldn't spend the night away from Monique." She sipped the water.

"It's okay, honey. You don't have to tell us everything this second," Lynn said. "The ambulance should be here any minute."

Katy cleared her throat. "When I was coming home, I heard Monique barking. In the ravine. The stars were so bright, I could see okay. I went down that path but then, I guess I fell." She closed her eyes and sank back into the sofa cushions.

"Don't talk, honey. Rest," Randy said.

Katy took another long sip of water. "Monique was right next to me." The animal perked up her ears. Her black tail thumped the carpet. Katy stroked the dog's head.

She struggled to sit up again, and said, "I called for help, but no one came. Except Monique. She went to get help, didn't she, Dad? You must have been busy, so she brought Mr. Tilton instead. Right?" She held the glass to her lips and drained the rest of the water.

Randy's throat was so tight he could only nod. He hated himself.

"You were so brave, Katy. I don't think I would have been that brave," Lynn said.

"With Monique there, I was never scared. I always hoped." Katy tried to smile, but grimaced instead; sweat popped out on her forehead. She leaned against her mother, then lifted one limp hand to rub her splotchy, dirty face.

"Yes, baby, and she brought your Cuddle Bunny back here, too." A sob broke from Lynn's throat.

Randy slipped one arm around his wife's shoulders and scooted close. With his other hand, he smoothed Katy's hair away from her face and then whispered, "I'm so sorry this happened."

Katy stroked the dog's head again, and Monique stretched her neck and leaned in to lick Katy's face. "Whenever it got dark, she was there, lying right next to me, keeping me warm. What a good dog!" She kissed the animal's muzzle. "She's our dog, isn't she, Daddy?"

"Shhhh. Baby, don't talk anymore," Randy said. "Save your strength. I hear a siren. The ambulance is here. We'll talk more about everything later."

"Is Mr. Tilton okay?" Katy asked.

"He's with Betsy outside, waiting on the ambulance," Randy said. "I'm sure he'll be fine."

*No thanks to me. The gun had discharged, and Al dropped to the ground. What if I really did hit him?*

Chapter 54

"You need go to hospital, Al. You know that." Betsy's voice was stern. "Don't move. Please." She sat, hunched on the grass, close to the police cruiser, which had been parked on the side of the road between the ravine and the blacktop. A policeman hovered nearby, one hand on his radio. "You're bleeding." She ran one hand over Al's spiky gray hair.

"Yeah, yeah, yeah. You'd like that, me in the hospital, wouldn't you? Right where you want me, so you can see everything I do and feed me like I was a baby!" Al squirmed as he tried to get comfortable, but his legs were useless.

Betsy tried to smile. "It okay, Al. I take care of you."

"Legs give out, that's all. Quit yer mothering." Al's eyes locked on Betsy's face.

"Yes, husband." Betsy leaned over and kissed him.

Al closed his eyes. His heart was calm, not banging around in his chest. And the world wasn't spinning. He couldn't feel a thing in his legs, though, and his lower back hurt like someone had kicked him.

Two ambulances roared up the hill; the wailing sirens stopped and one of the vehicles parked next to where Al lay. The other rolled on up the Werlings' driveway. EMTs piled out, unloaded a gurney, and moved quickly to him.

Betsy stepped back and let the EMTs lean over him, checking his vital signs. Al closed his eyes; the world spun. Their words sifted over him as they called out blood pressure, heart rate, and oxygen levels. Then, he thought he heard the words "gunshot" and "ricochet." His eyes popped open. No gunshot. *I'm here, not in the jungle.* No one fired a gun, did they? But if not, why did he remember a popping sound, just as he and Katy made it to the road?

The EMTs positioned themselves around Al and then moved him onto the gurney.

"You going with me?" he asked Betsy.

"Yes."

Al sighed. He reached out his pointer finger and touched the end of her nose.

The EMTs rolled him the few feet to the ambulance.

Mick and Matthew appeared at Betsy's side.

"When you're ready to come home, we'll come get you, Al," Mick said.

Al grunted. "Sure thing. You be ready in a couple hours. Ain't staying there overnight. No way in hell that'll happen."

Mick patted Betsy's arm and stepped back as the EMTs opened the ambulance doors.

Betsy climbed up into the ambulance after they'd shifted Al's gurney inside. "I check on Miss Jo while Al get settled," she said to Mick. "How was she this morning?"

*Jo, in the hospital?* First he'd heard of it. That's why his wife had been spending so much time at Mick's house.

"They'll move her to the rehab unit mid-week,"

Matthew said. "She'll be home in another couple of weeks."

Betsy settled in beside him and patted his hand. In the distance, a door slammed. He figured that meant the other ambulance had picked up Katy.

"Scary thing for little Katy, two nights alone down there in the ravine," Al muttered. "She must have been terrified."

"The amazing thing is that black dog," Mick said, peering into the vehicle and shaking his head. "She tried to get help. I heard her barking, but didn't do anything about it. Guess she finally badgered you into following her. Don't know how in the world she managed that. She's some smart dog."

"Wouldn't take no for an answer." Al closed his eyes and remembered how the dog jerked his pant leg and pulled him toward the ravine. "You get her to the vet today, okay? She's got a serious gouge on her shoulder that needs tending."

"Sure thing, Al," Mick said. "We'll get it taken care of. Probably hurt herself running in and out of the ravine all weekend."

Al shut his eyes. "Could be."

He didn't think so, though.

Chapter 55

Mick's wristwatch read 4:30 p.m. He stepped up to Jo's bedside. "I'm going home, Josey. I'll be back in the morning. You okay?"

"A little tired, Mickey. All the company today. I'll be in a new place tomorrow. Don't come in here looking for me and get all bothered."

He smiled and patted her arm where it lay under the white hospital blanket.

"They'll move my things, so don't worry. Just go home with Matthew and Annie and have a good visit. I'll catch up in a day or two, after I've had some good sleep."

A pretty pink color was beginning to bloom again in her cheeks, and specks of light were evident in her eyes although they were not exactly twinkling, yet. His own heart, which hadn't beat evenly for days, pounded away at a regular rhythm.

He hummed a little of the "Mares Eat Oats" song, and she smiled. "Love you, Josey-Jo. See you in the morning."

"I love you, Mickey."

Mick let the door swing shut behind him. Down the hall, his daughter Annie, her husband John, and Matthew waited by the elevator. Matthew's daughter Lacey, and Marilyn, his ex-wife, stood with them. The five of them were talking, laughing even. They were all back home together, finally. Even Marilyn was smiling at Matthew, and standing close to him with her hands on Lacey's shoulders.

His granddaughter glanced down the hall at him, then waved. "See you at home, Grandpa!" she called.

He didn't know how long any of them would stay. But it didn't matter. They were here now. He and Jo could stay in their house a little while longer with some adjustments, if the kids helped them work through it.

The group broke up, and Matthew came toward him; a smile lingered on his face.

"Ready?" Matthew asked.

He nodded. "Remember we're picking up the dog on our way home."

"Sure thing. They've had more than enough time to clean and patch up her wound," Matthew said. He pushed the elevator button.

"At first inspection, the doc said it looked like a bullet grazed her." Mick shook his head. "Like someone took a shot at the dog."

Matthew didn't respond. Mick kept his eyes on the elevator doors as they opened.

*Didn't have to wonder too long about that one.* The dog had been frantic to get someone's attention. In his state of mind, Al had probably taken action to shut her up. The good thing was, he'd paid attention to the animal eventually, and found Katy.

"So you'll keep Monique with you for a few days, Dad?"

"Yes. Until Katy comes home. You don't mind, do you?" Mick had every intention of feeding the dog lots of biscuits to let her know he was glad to have her in the neighborhood.

"Of course not."

They reached the first floor. Mick stepped out of the elevator and paused. "One more stop to make, okay?"

Matthew followed him down the hall toward the Emergency Room.

"Betsy?"

Big dark eyes full of tears looked up at him. "Mr. Mick! How is Miss Jo?" Betsy straightened in the blue plastic chair which she had shoved up beside Al's bed in one of the ER cubicles.

Al raised his head. "Mick, you son of a gun, that you?"

"Jo's doing better. They're thinking to move her out of the ICU tomorrow. How are you?" He gestured at Al.

"Legs give out. Most work they've done in a long while, going down into that ravine and then climbing out again. Tests won't tell 'em anything new. I'm an old soldier, never be anything else. And my bones are giving out." He cleared his throat and tried to reposition himself in the bed, but his legs remained straight. "Betsy wants me to stay here and have a bunch of tests. Make sure everything's okay. Guess she's not ready for me to die after all. One night—that's all I'll stay."

Mick nodded, eying the deep scratches on Al's hands and arms. "And you should. No denying we're not what we used to be." Mick glanced over at Betsy and saw worry and sadness in her eyes. She blinked at him, and tipped her head toward the door.

Al ran one hand over his spikey gray hair and stared up at the ceiling.

"Best be on my way, then. I'll come by tomorrow,

in the morning. If you'll be here." Mick stepped through the door.

"You check before you come. I may be home by then." Al's voice followed him, like Betsy, out into the hallway.

Betsy bowed her head.

Mick waited for her to speak.

"I no tell Al, yet," she said softly. "The bullet... The doctor say...No operate...Stay there." Betsy blinked away tears.

"What? Operate why?"

She shook her head. "Bullet in spine. His legs...paralyzed."

Mick stepped back and pushed against the wall. "He got shot? Today?"

Betsy nodded, silently. "Randy had Al's gun. He think that Al..."

"My God." Mick felt blindsided. "But they can operate later, can't they?"

Again, Betsy shook her head. "Too much danger. My Al...he no walk again."

Mick's head spun, then his knees unlocked, and he slipped down the wall to the floor. Betsy crouched beside him, her arms wrapped around her knees, and cried.

Chapter 56

Lynn sat on the edge of the chair in the waiting room, tapping her feet on the floor. What was taking so long? Katy had been in surgery for over an hour. How much longer would this take?

Randy paced back and forth across the waiting room, running one hand through his hair, the other stuffed into the pocket of his shorts.

Thank God they had found her. And thank God it was only a broken leg. It could have been so much worse, she told herself. She could be one of those mothers out there who lost a child in an instant, and never saw them again. Never knew if they were dead or alive. Never knew what the child had been through.

But Lynn knew. The reality of what Katy had endured was so much better than what it could have been. Given other options, she wouldn't have wanted Katy's leg—or any bone—broken. But she was whole, she hadn't been damaged. She would recover from this, and might even, eventually, forget.

Lynn was quite sure she would never forget the weekend. Her heart would never heal from the two-pronged pain she had experienced, her missing daughter and her husband's infatuation. Even if, as he claimed, he had not acted on his desire for the student—Jennifer, did he say her name was?—he had wanted to. Was there much difference between wanting and doing? Ah, she knew there was. But the truth was, she didn't want to forgive him, yet. She wanted him to suffer, to feel pain like hers. She wanted him to fear that his entire future was in doubt, to fear that he and he alone had caused the earthquake cracking the foundation of their home. She wanted him to know the consequences of his desire.

"Lynn? Are you all right? Your face is chalk white. Are you in pain?" Randy's hand touched her shoulder.

She looked up at him, feeling the fury building inside her. Fury mixed with pain, mixed with incredulity. How could she have been so stupid?

She shrugged out from under his hand and turned away.

"Mr. and Mrs. Werling?"

The young doctor, still in his operating room scrubs, stood in the doorway of the waiting room. "We've finished the operation. She's in recovery, and should be back up in her room within the hour. We've pinned the bone together and will eventually put on a cast. We'd like to keep her for a couple of nights. More of a precaution. She was severely dehydrated, and we want to be sure the infection at the wound site is under control and there aren't any other issues caused by her exposure. She had a good thirty-six hours out there on her own."

Lynn nodded. "Poor baby. I'll stay here with her."

The doctor nodded. "I'll check on her again before I leave the hospital for the day. See you then." His thick-soled shoes moved silently away from them down the hall.

"You think it's wise for you to stay here, Lynn? What about the boys?"

"They're with the Bauers, and they'll be fine there. Unless you want to take them home. I'm staying here with Katy. She won't be alone tonight." She hoped he got the purpose of the look she shot at him. The topic was not negotiable.

"Lynn, you and the kids are the most important things in the world to me," Randy said. "I'll do whatever it takes to make things right with you again. My family means everything. I'll stay here with you. Otherwise, I'll pick up the boys and take them home. They'll sleep much better in their own beds." His look was glued to her face.

She nodded but continued to look past him, not at him. "Go get the boys then, and take them home. I'll handle things here."

Chapter 57

Mick stared out the window as Matthew drove the car up Mick's driveway and maneuvered it past two vehicles, parked one behind the other, on the far side of the drive.

"Home, Pop. Looks like the girls are both here." Matthew reached over and touched him on the knee. In the back seat, the black dog whined.

"Sure we are." He made no move to get out of the car.

"You going to get out?" Matthew asked.

No doubt his son wondered what was going on in his brain. He hadn't been able to talk about Al. Didn't want to let the word pass his lips. It was bad enough to hear it in his own head. *Paralyzed.*

The injustice of it hurt Mick's heart. The man had been in the service. He'd been awarded medals for valor. He'd saved people in the war. He'd saved Katy. And now, he'd taken a bullet from his own gun and gotten paralyzed. It was tragic.

"Pop?"

Mick waved his hand at Matthew and grabbed the door handle. "Yeah. I'm moving. Slowly, but I am moving."

Once he was standing on his own two feet, he reached for the back door handle and opened the door so the dog could jump out. She wasted no time leaping to the ground, but then, as Mick turned to go into the house, the dog stopped and stood, waiting for something.

Her tail wagged in a circle. Mick returned to her, bent over, and scratched her behind the ears. "You can stay here with me tonight. But probably just for tonight. Katy will most likely be home tomorrow and I know she's going to want to spend every minute she can with you. That's one special little lady, you know, and you're one special dog. You know that, right?"

Matthew grabbed his elbow and turned him back toward the house. The backdoor was open, and they could hear the sound of voices through the screen door. Mick shuffled toward the house.

The dog followed at his heels, whining.

Marilyn had fixed ham sandwiches, and the five of them ate on the patio table, the black dog lying nearby.

"What do you think about Mom, Matthew?" Annie asked. "She seemed a little confused to me and so awfully pale."

Mick looked at his daughter. He didn't agree, but he didn't say so. Jo had seemed better today. Her face had more color to it. If Annie thought Jo looked bad today, she should have seen her yesterday, in between and during all of her "episodes."

"She was so glad to see you all. It meant so much to her. She'll get her strength back up after your visit today," Mick said.

"Hope so, Pop. It's such a shock to see her in the hospital. She's always been so active, so busy at something. Seems like she'd be the last person to have a heart attack." Annie shooed away a fly, and then chomped into a potato chip.

"When we saw you at Christmas, she seemed okay." Lacey squirmed on the bench, then scooted over to get a better look at the dog, lying there on the cement close to Mick's chair. She scooted the toe of her shoe along the animal's spine. The dog's tail wagged once. "Brave doggie. How long will she have to wear that bandage?"

"Just a few days. I have some ointment I have to rub on it, to make sure it doesn't get infected. And she's got some pills she has to take. Another five or six days and she should be good as new."

"And your neighbor friend, Katy? Have you talked to her parents, Pop?" Annie asked.

"Not yet. I expect they've been at the hospital. Katy will have to get that leg set. They may have to give her some medicine for a little while to bring the swelling down before they can put on a cast."

"So, you're in charge of the dog until she comes home?" his former daughter-in-law asked.

"Not necessarily. I expect those boys will be knocking on the door to get her as soon as they get home. Katy's not the only one attached to that dog."

Marilyn swatted at Lacey's leg. "Leave the dog alone. She may not feel much like being messed with. Would you, if you'd just been shot in the shoulder?"

"Shot!" Annie exclaimed. "Who shot her?"

"I'd make a wild guess, but then I'd be speaking out of turn. No way to prove it, anyway." Mick chewed the last bit of his sandwich and sat back in the rocking deck chair.

"Why did they shoot her? She's such a good dog." Lacey pulled back her foot but leaned over and stretched down to stroke the top of the animal's head.

"Hard to say. She's been barking a lot," Mick acknowledged. "If you ask me, she was trying to get one of us to follow her down to the ravine, where Katy fell. Took a while, but she finally managed to get Al to do it."

"Thank goodness. But I'm confused. If he's the one who brought her out of the ravine—the one who saved her—why did Randy Werling shoot him?" Annie asked.

"An accident, according to Randy," Matthew said. "He had cocked the gun, and his finger twitched on the trigger as he was dropping it to his side. The bullet hit something and ricocheted; it hit Al in the lower back."

"Tough break for Al. Will he be all right?" Marilyn watched Lacey pet the black dog.

Mick held his tongue. He wasn't going to say anything. The paralysis wasn't certain yet, was it? He'd hold on to hope for his fellow soldier.

An hour later, Annie and Marilyn had set themselves up in the bedrooms, Lacey and Marilyn in one, Annie in the second, and Mick in his usual room. They made up the sofa in the living room for Matthew.

Lacey and her mother disappeared into their room, leaving Mick with his two children.

"Been a long time since we've been here together, like this, just us," Mick said.

Matthew nodded, looking at his hands.

Annie glanced from one man to the other. "I'm really glad we're all speaking again. I'm especially glad you've made up with Matthew, Pop. I know it was hard on Mom when you were mad, or whatever it was you were."

"I wasn't mad," Mick said slowly. How could he

explain it to them? He tried to get it straight in his mind first, before he gave voice to the words. Sometimes a person gets so caught up in the way they think things ought to be, when it isn't really so. It's more that things have always been a certain way, and a person can't see them ever being any different. Was that it? Could he say those words without getting the whole miserable discussion on homosexuality going again?

"Took me some time to get used to it. I never stopped loving Matthew. I could never stop loving either of you, no matter what you did."

"But he didn't do anything, really. It's the way he is." Annie reached over and grabbed Matthew's hand.

Mick didn't want to talk about this again. Couldn't they see how hard it was for him? Couldn't they understand that for his generation to accept something like this—his son's homosexuality—was nigh on impossible? He thought he'd gotten over it, but the more they wanted to talk about it, the more he squirmed in his seat. He held up one hand.

"Let it be, Annie. We've mended our bridge. I love you, both. If you don't mind, I'm tired. I think maybe tonight I can finally sleep. It helps to have family around." Mick stood.

As he trudged from the room, he felt their eyes drill into his back. He was determined not to falter, not to stop, but to keep going. The black dog pulled herself up from her place by the kitchen doorway and limped after him.

Once inside his room with the door closed, he sank down onto the bed, hands shaking. Tears fell freely down his face. The dog settled on her haunches in front of him, her head resting on his knee. He bent over as far as he could and buried his face in the ruff of her neck.

\*\*\*\*

Mick stirred in his sleep. Something was wrong. Outside his bedroom, the hallway lights were on. Someone was sobbing. He pulled on his robe and moved into the hall, touching the walls to keep his balance and blinking as his brain tried to wake up.

In the living room, Annie stood in a huddle with Marilyn and Lacey, her hands covering her face. Matthew stood slightly apart, head down.

"Annie? Matthew?"

Matthew stepped quickly to his father and put his hand on Mick's shoulder.

Mick's body sagged. Matthew eased him down into a chair.

"She's gone," Matthew whispered.

Annie sobbed and threw herself across the room to Mick's feet.

Mick stared out into the room, seeing nothing. "But she told me she'd see me tomorrow. Everything...seemed...better."

Marilyn and Lacey crossed the room to Matthew, and the three of them locked into a hug.

The black dog, her body warm—hot, almost—leaned against Mick's leg. He stroked her smooth head, rubbed her ears. She grunted softly and looked up at him with her yellow-brown eyes.

He stared down at her, remembering that other time, knowing him and Jo had not been mistaken. The dog had come here, knowing.

He closed his eyes and let the tears roll down his face. Annie lifted herself to her knees in front of him and wrapped her arms around him. The pressure of the dog against his leg let up. He kept his eyes closed.

Later, when the five of them finally lifted their grief-filled faces to look at one another, Mick saw the dog had returned to her place by the door, her nose pressed to the crack where the night air tried to get in.

Chapter 58

Lynn looked at her husband over the rim of her water glass. "This changed me. Changed us."

Across the room, young people moved through the cafeteria line in the student union's dining area. The tables closest to them were empty.

A line of concern deepened between his eyes. "Lynn—"

She held up her hand and pushed on. "With Will in school, I think it's time I look for a job, or start a business. I need to be someone other than Mommy."

Randy blew out his breath. "Okay. Just tell me that we can stay together, that you still want our family whole. I want that more than I've ever wanted anything."

She took a long drink of water. "It's important to me, too. But you need to know that I've done a lot of thinking. This gallbladder flare up scared me. And you hardly noticed."

"I know." Randy shook his head back and forth and drummed his fingers on the table. "I don't have an excuse. I'm ashamed."

"I haven't been happy for a while."

Randy looked at her. "I didn't know. Have I been that preoccupied with myself?"

"You really want an answer?"

"Ouch. I just got it. I'm sorry."

"My surgery is set for Thursday. Outpatient. But I need your help with the kids. And I need you to take me to the hospital and then home afterwards. Can you?"

"Of course. And whatever you need me to do before the surgery, honey. I'll do it. I need you to forgive me. Will you?"

She fingered the glass again. "I'm working on it." She glanced at her watch. "I've got to get home. Betsy's with the boys, and she'll want to know how my appointment went this morning. Thanks for taking time to meet me at the doctor's office."

"I mean what I'm saying, Lynn. You are the most important thing. I wanted to be there. I want to be with you everywhere, whatever is going on."

A pretty blonde dressed in khaki shorts and a sleeveless white shell stopped beside them. "Hi, Professor. Um, you know we've got that test tomorrow, and I was wondering if maybe you couldn't wait 'til Thursday to give it to us. I haven't really gotten it all down, yet, and I haven't found a good study partner." She batted her eyes at him.

Lynn looked at the girl closely, saw her heavy makeup, and smelled her heady perfume. She looked at Randy.

He glanced at the girl, and then looked back at Lynn and smiled. "Sorry, Jennifer," he said. "The test's been scheduled from Day One of the intersession, and you've had plenty of time to study. I know I said I'd help you last weekend, but we had a family crisis that came first. Oh, and I'd like you to meet my wife, Lynn."

"Oh, hi." The girl shifted her weight and chewed on her bottom lip. "Well, okay, then. Can you recommend a study partner?" She dropped her chin and her eyes widened as she looked at Randy.

Lynn almost laughed out loud. She knew that men fell for this, and in that instant knew Randy wasn't the first teacher in her life that sweet little Jennifer had tried this on. Poor Randy had fallen for it. He was as starved for something different in his life as she was. She glanced at Randy to check his reaction to Jennifer again, but he was looking and smiling at her, not Jennifer.

"There are some postings on the bulletin board in the student union. And there's an online help service. You should have started looking a little earlier." He took a long sip from his coffee cup.

Chapter 59

"See, Mom. I'm fine on my crutches, really! Can't I please go outside to throw the ball with Monique a little while?" Why was her mother still being so protective? It had been a whole week since she got lost. And Monique would be out there with her. It wasn't even like she would be alone!

"Only if I go out, too. Then, I have to get back inside to work on my resume. I'd like to get some job interviews set up for next week."

"You can watch us from the window, can't you, Mommy? I want you to see how good Monique is at catching the ball." Katy looked out the window. "And look, everybody's outside anyway. Mr. Tilton's out there in his wheelchair with Betsy over at Mr. Mick's patio. It's not like I'll be alone."

Her mother got up from the table carefully.

"I'll miss Mrs. Jordan and taking piano lessons. It's so sad," Katy said, her eyes lingering on the adults in the yard behind theirs. "I know Mr. Jordan is sad, too." She looked at her mother again. "Is your scar healing okay?" Her mother didn't lift up her shirt to show her the tiny bright red scar from her operation. Instead, she held out her arms so Katy could rush into them. "I love you, Mommy. And I love Daddy, too, and Caesar and Cleo and Angel and Barney. Some days I even love Will, but it's hardest to love Ty. He's too weird. And he's not really any good at soccer. Most of all, I think, except for you and Daddy, I love Monique the most." She pushed away from her mom and ran for the back door.

"Come on, Monique. Let's go outside."

The black dog yipped and leaped up on her hind legs, dancing her way to the back door.

**A word about the author…**

A life-long writer, Mary Coley was born and raised in Oklahoma. She lives in Tulsa with her husband and rescue dog, Trixie. Coley has been employed as a park planner, a naturalist, a journalist, a public relations director, education director, and communications officer. Currently, she writes full time. Find her on Facebook at Mary Coley Author, and on Pinterest.

http://marycoley.com